Oasis Center Library
317 East Call Street
Tallahassee, Florida 32301

Never too Late for Love

Irene Gilliam

NEVER TOO LATE FOR LOVE

Copyright©2012 by Irene Gilliam

All rights reserved.

ISBN-10: 1480257354
ISBN-13: 978-1480257351

This book is a work of fiction. The names, characters, incidents and places are the products of the author's imagination or used fictitiously and are not to be construed as real. While the author was inspired in part by actual events, none of the characters in the book is based on an actual person. Any resemblance to persons living or dead is entirely coincidental and unintentional.

For my lovely daughter, Mickey, and my wonderful grandchildren, Kristopher and Kennedy

Hold on to your dreams, for dreams really do come true!

Acknowledgements

Writing has always been my greatest passion, and the words 'thank you' are never enough to express the deep gratitude for all of the love and support I've received over the years.

First, I have to thank my wonderful family – those who are still with me: my sister and very best friend, Mildred; my brothers, Alpha ('Mega) and Simond; and those who are still with me in spirit: my parents, Annie & Ike Gilliam, Jr., and my sisters, Louise (Vicky) and Estelle. You have always believed in me! I love you!

I've been writing most of my life, and over the years my 'fan club' has grown to include my daughter, Mickey, nieces Carla and Michelle, nephews Gerald, Al, Andre, and Simon, son-in-law, Kenny, all of my brothers/sisters-in-law, and extended family and friends. You're wonderful!

And last but certainly not least, I wouldn't have reached publication if not for those faithful and honest individuals who took their valuable time to read my entire manuscript or the prologue or a chapter or to correct my formatting mistakes and who also encouraged me to do more than just write a novel; they pushed me to publication. A special 'thank you' to Ann Lee, Angelia Rivers, Adrienne Michelle Alexander, Paulette Rosier, Larina 'Mickey' Cornileus, Carla Alexander Clark, and Gina Henderson. You're the greatest!

Prologue

White Oaks Plantation
*Leon County, FL – **1855***

"I want her out of my house. Now!"
Beaufort Collins sighed deeply. He had gotten tired of this constant nagging. "Madame, be careful how you speak in me. This is my house in which I let you live!"
"Beau, how dare….. " He cut her off with a look. "Ma'am, I'm trying to get dressed. Please stop your constant whining and leave me in peace."
"I won't stand for it, you hear?" Camilla Harpson Colllins shouted. "Her and her children in my house! Why, everybody's laughing at me behind my back and ….."
Beaufort raised his eyebrows and his wife, Camilla, stopped in mid-sentence. Anger always made his eyebrows rise and for Beaufort, who was rarely angry, this meant trouble for whoever was around.
He sighed and shook his head. "Camilla, I was honest with you before we married. Nothing has changed." Beaufort went back to straightening his tie.
Camilla's pale face turned even whiter.
"Nothing has changed?!! I'm your wife now. She's a slave! I want her out! I want her out now!"

"My dear, you knew what you were getting into when you married me." Beaufort turned slowly and faced his wife. "Be careful what you ask for. I just might give it to you." He calmly put on his jacket and left the room.

A week later, Camilla could see land being cleared across from White Oaks, and it seemed as though every slave and freedman on the plantation was over there working. 'What in the world could be going on?' she wondered as she sat on the porch. It was hard to see because so many trees stood in the way. She and Beau had not spoken in over a week, and she was nervous. And she hadn't seen Sadie Mae or her children all day. She was terrified. Something was very wrong.

"When I see her black hide, I'll......." But she knew that there was nothing she could do to Sadie Mae; Beau would not allow it.

No, Beaufort wouldn't let anything happen to his precious Sadie Mae. Camilla's own sorry father had protected Sadie, only his reason wasn't because he cared anything for her. He'd just wanted to sleep with her.

Oh, yes, Camilla remembered Sadie Mae. She had been a young slave on the Harpson's tobacco plantation. Before Beaufort's father had bought her. And Camilla clearly remembered the first time Beau and his father had come to their plantation. She remembered how furious her father, Jessup Harpson, had been that day. He'd had to sale thirty of his slaves to Beaufort Sr., and he was not happy! He had gotten sloppy drunk! And getting drunk meant trouble for Camilla.

"That son of a bitch!" he'd railed as he'd tossed another drink down. "Stole my best slave!" Like he'd let Sadie Mae do any hard work. No, he'd wanted to keep her soft so that when he laid with her, well....

"That little sniveling son of his. I saw how he looked at Sadie. My Sadie! Wanted her to tend to his mother!"

Think I'm a fool! And took her before I could bed her! Bastards! But they'll pay! They'll pay!"

He'd stopped ranting long enough to run his gaze up and down Camilla's body. His blurry eye stopped at her breasts. And he just kept staring until she put up her hands to cover herself. He licked his lips and laughed.

"Can't hide from me, girl. Get to your room! And you know what I expect when I get there. Your sorry ass mama ain't here to do her wifely duties. Sorry bitch! But she left me you, and I've trained you well, haven't I?! Get up there now! And I don't want none of your whining this time. Or I'll take my whip to you!"

"PaPa, please, not again!" Camilla begged. Jessup slapped her into the wall.

"Get up those stairs now!" As Camilla started to flee, Jessup reached out and grabbed her close. "Hell, girl. I got something new for you to learn. You'll like it. Do it good and maybe there's a new dress for you. Now go get ready!"

Those hateful memories! Camilla shuddered as she sat in the heat of the afternoon. She had been a fool to challenge Beau. She owed him her life. He had saved her. He'd come to her rescue when no one else would. That day long ago had been her salvation. As she rocked in the swing, Camilla's mind slipped again to the past.

She'd seen Beau come into the house. It had been some years since he had been to the Jessup plantation. The last time had been when his father had purchased those slaves. But her father had been expecting him. He'd made her clean the library and sent her upstairs an hour ago. These days he didn't let anyone see her. She was his shame, he said. He was too ashamed of her to let good people see what she'd become. His shame?! He'd shamed her!

She was terrified of her father and knew she'd be punished if he caught her, but she was curious about this visit.

It had to be important for Beau Collins to speak to her father, so she'd crept down the stairs, knowing that her father wouldn't keep his voice down. He hated Beaufort Collins, and she wanted to know what was going on.

"So, you want my little girl, Collins? She won't come cheap!"

"She's not a slave, Harpson. You can't sell her. I'm asking for her hand in marriage."

Jessup spit on the floor just in front of Beaufort's boot. "Hell no! No! Hell, she's all I got left! Who the hell gonna cook and clean around here? She gets to go and live in that big house of yours, and I'm left here with nothing?! Hell no! Now get out!"

"I have the notes on your property, Harpson. Bought them from the bank. Since you like business, this is all about business. Let me speak with your daughter. If we come to an agreement, the notes are yours, free and clear."

"And if she don't agree?"

"Pray that she does. Now, if you don't mind, call her down."

"I'll just go up and get her. Want her to be presentable and all, you know," *he said with a smirk.*

Camilla could hear her father step toward the library door. She started to run up the stairs when she heard Beau's voice.

"No, call her down. Then leave us alone."

"What's the hell wrong with you, man? You can't tell me what to do in my own home."

"Remember the notes, Harpson. If you want them, call her down now."

"Camilla, bring your ……. Come down here for a minute," *her father bellowed. Camilla could hear the anger in his voice. Please, God, she prayed. Don't let Beau leave me here. And she kept praying as she entered the library.*

4

Beau stood at the window with his back to the room. Jessup Harpson gave his daughter a threatening look and stomped out of the door. Once the door shut, Beau turned to her. Her breath caught in her throat. He had grown into a handsome young man. He was tall, over six feet, muscular and tanned as if he worked outside a lot. He wore his jet black hair long, and it looked so clean and alive. His hair, his face, his hands! All clean. Camilla felt dirty.

He couldn't know about her. If he did, he wouldn't be here. He certainly wouldn't want her once he knew her terrible shame. He had to be the only person in the county not to know what happened in this house, and that was probably because he didn't go out in society. His mother had died, and his father was very ill. And his life was no secret. Everyone knew about him and Sadie Mae. But Camilla was desperate; this was her last chance to escape the hell she was living.

"We have to talk," Beaufort said as he walked to where she stood. "You probably should take a sit."

Camilla knew she looked terrible. Her long blonde hair was limp and lifeless. She didn't eat much; there really wasn't much to eat in the house, and she'd lost too much weight. Her dresses were baggy on her thin frame. Jessup always promised to buy her something new if she…… well, if she did what he asked, but he never did.

Camilla shook her head. "No, I'll stand, thank you. What is it?"

"I've come to ask you to be my wife, Camilla, but there are some things you have to agree to before that can happen."

"Why do you want to marry me? You're wealthy. You can choose from any of the families in town. Why me?"

He looked her straight in the eyes. "I really do not want to get married. I had not planned to do so. But my father heard what's been happening to you, and he, and I, feel that marriage is the only way to get you out of this house."

Camilla felt a shame so intense that she felt numb. "Oh, my God!"

"Are you with child, Camilla?"

"No! No!" she could barely speak. She shook her head. "One of our former slaves brings herbs to me to protect me from that. Thank God. But if you know, why would you want to marry me? I'm ruined!"

"It's the only way to get you out of this house. I could use the notes on the property to force him to let you leave, but where would you go? What would you do? Marriage is the only solution for you. For your respectability. But you have to understand what you're accepting. As I've told you, I never planned to get married. My parents understood and accepted that. You probably know why, but I'll tell you anyway. You need to hear it from me. I love Sadie Mae."

"But she's a slave!"

"She's the woman I love. She's the only woman I'll ever love. We have children together. I won't give her up."

"If I say yes, will she continue to live in the house? In White Oaks?"

"Yes. It's her home. Camilla, you don't have to accept this. I can force your father to free you. To let you leave. You have a choice. Choose what is best for you. If you'd rather try a life on your own, I will provide funds for you to travel to any place you choose so that you can get started in a new life."

"And if I choose marriage, I'll be mistress of White Oaks?"

Beau turned back to the window. He stood there for so long, Camilla was afraid he had changed his mind. She'd die if he took back his offer. She wouldn't go on living the shameful hell she was living.

"Sadie Mae and I have discussed this situation. You would take your place as mistress of White Oaks, but you would not be Sadie's mistress. In this, Sadie and I disagree. For whatever reasons, she still believes that she is a slave and should act like one if or when you become mistress. I have reasons why I haven't legally freed her yet, but I am the master of my house, and Sadie and her children will answer only to me. You'll show her respect. She wanted to leave, but I will not let her go. She is my life. My heart! This is the situation you'll be agreeing to."

"And children?"

Beau actually shuddered. "I'll not cheat you of a child. But Camilla, do not confuse anything we may share as a commitment of my affections. I'm sorry if I sound so blunt, but this is the best arrangement I can honestly offer you. I can't allow you misunderstand the situation at White Oaks."

Camilla could hear her father stumbling down the stairs.

"I understand, Beaufort. And I accept."

She'd moved to White Oaks that day, and three days later, she and Beaufort Collins were married. By then she'd come to the realization that she wanted to be married to Beau. He was a kind, generous, and forgiving man. He was seldom angry and never vindictive. He was the total opposite of her father. And she was in love with him.

Camilla wiped the sweat from her face. She should not have made any demands about Sadie Mae. After all, they had all lived this way since she and Beau had gotten married. Sadie had continued to manage the house as any house slave would do. She didn't make decisions about the house without consulting Camilla. Camilla had nothing to complain about, except that Sadie had Beau's love, and she did not.

Camilla now had two children although Beau had told her that there would be no more. He'd had to get drunk just to *get those two. But she hadn't cared. He'd touched her, even if it was just to push up her gown and take her as quickly as possible. As soon as he was through, he'd left. She wanted that touch again. Lately she'd thought if she could just get rid of Sadie Mae and her children, maybe Beau would touch her again, maybe even learn to love her.*

Memories. They kept haunting her. But she couldn't lose Beau. She missed his presence in the house. Something was definitely wrong. Beau was always around when Sadie Mae was in the house. Maybe, Camilla thought, if she sat on the porch long enough, she'd see him when he came home. Another hour passed as she sat on the porch in the hot Florida sun and listened to the fall of trees and the constant hammering. The house was quiet. Perhaps too quiet.

"Sadie," she called. She was hot, so damned hot! "Sadie, bring me some cold lemonade!"

She waited and waited. Sadie never came with the lemonade. Sadie Mae was finally gone.

3 months later

The hammering and cutting seemed to go on day and night. But finally Camilla knew what was happening. Beaufort was building another house – bigger and grander than White Oaks. She smiled with joy! Even though she and Beaufort had barely spoken since their argument three months ago -- really she had hardly seen him since that time – a new house meant a new beginning for her and her marriage. A new beginning without Sadie Mae. No one would tell her what he had done with Sadie and her children, but Camilla didn't care. They were gone, and Beau was building her a new house.

She had tried to ask the house slaves about Sadie Mae, but they pretended that they didn't know anything. "Do they think I'm a fool?" thought Camilla. "Slaves know

8

everything, everything about all of us." But no one would say a word. Sadie Mae. How she'd come to hate that name! The woman who had Beau's heart! Well, she wouldn't think about that now. Everything would change when they moved to the new house. And maybe then she would get some better help. The wenches that replaced Sadie Mae were so lazy. They couldn't cook, clean, or wash. They simply knew nothing about running a house like Sadie Mae did. But Sadie Mae was gone. That was enough.

5 months later

The trees that had lined the road were finally coming down; now Camilla could see what they had hidden for so many months. What a magnificent house! Hugh live oaks lined the walks and drive. The house was much closer to the road and the drive was not as impressive as White Oaks, but, oh, the house itself was grand. It made White Oaks look small. Camilla's heart raced as she stood at the end of the drive and gazed across the road to that house - her new home. It had to be. There was no other reason for Beaufort to build another house unless he wanted to begin anew without the memories that White Oaks held for them both.

She was so happy! Tonight, she thought. Beaufort would come to her, would tell her how sorry he was for all of her hurt and pain, and then she would tell the slaves to start packing for their move. Would there be new furniture or would they take the furniture from White Oaks? Even with that, the new house was huge, some new furniture would still be needed. "Beau will talk to me tonight," she thought. "He'll tell me about our new home and our new beginning." She just knew it. Camilla felt like hugging herself. Oh, what a glorious day! A new home and a new life with Beau. And no Sadie Mae.

Camilla had a huge dinner fixed, all of Beau's favorites. She changed her dress at least three times and made

9

sure that her hair was fixed in the same style she'd worn it the day they were married. Beau was coming home tonight. She could feel it in her bones. He was coming home to her and not to Sadie Mae. Everything had to be perfect!

The dinner table was set, the children in bed. Camilla waited and waited. The candles burned low and Camilla still waited. Finally, the front door opened. Beau paused at the dining room door, looked at Camilla, and went to his room. "At least there's no Sadie Mae," she thought as she laid her head on the table. "At least he came home."

Finally, Camilla went to her room, but she could not rest. She was scared and confused. Beaufort had built a new house for them, but he hadn't even spoken to her when he came home. And it was the first time she had seen him in weeks if not months. But he had come home, and there was the new house. So she didn't have anything to worry about. Did she? Too exhausted to think, she finally fell asleep.

Early the next morning Camilla awoke to loud voices and banging, and she could hear Beau giving orders. She quickly put on her wrapper and rushed into the hall. There she saw Beaufort surrounded by trunks and servants moving up and down the stairs.

"Beaufort," she cried. "What's going on?"

Beaufort turned and looked at his wife of four years. Camilla started toward him but stopped when she the look in his eyes, part sadness – part pity.

"I'm leaving, Camilla."

"Leaving? Where are you going? On a business trip?" She held her breath. She wouldn't believe that he was leaving -- her.

"I'm moving to Peaceful Sands."

"Peaceful Sands? Where's Peaceful Sands?" she whispered, afraid to know.

10

Beau looked down for a moment, then sighed. "I'm so sorry, Camilla. I thought you understood before you accepted me. I realize now that I should never have married. It wasn't fair to you, but you said you understood. Haven't you looked across the road? I'm moving across the road to Peaceful Sands -- with Sadie Mae."

Camilla fainted. When she came to, Jacob Beaufort Collins was gone.

1

The Present
Two Plantations, Fl
Feb. 2012

Sixty-year-old Cammy Jackson just *couldn't* shake her sense of dread! Something was going to happen, and she was sure she wasn't going to like it! She'd had terrible dreams all through the night! Caleb, Kimberly, and Frank! All chasing her, screaming, "Secrets! Secrets! Secrets! Tell us your secrets!" until she'd awaken exhausted with tears rolling down her face. She hadn't had *that* nightmare in years! God, what did it mean? And why *now*?

Maybe she'd read too much about Sadie Mae and Camilla these last few days! Yea, maybe that was it. After all, it was a tradition that one of the Collins would tell the story of Two Plantations to the third grade class at the elementary school, and she was always happy to do it. So she'd been reading the history of her family for her presentation. That had to be the reason for the nightmares. Too much Sadie Mae and Camilla!

Normally, the two women didn't give her nightmares; in fact, she couldn't ever remember having a nightmare about either of them. But there could be no other reason. Could there?

She gave her head a little shake. Cammy was extremely proud of her ancestry, and she really loved all of their family traditions, especially reading about her family to the children of the town. Traditions! They were a part of her; she'd been raised with them, and she really enjoyed them. In fact, she had unofficially become the family historian because she, more than anyone else in the family, was determined to keep those traditions alive. However, she wondered sometimes if maybe her family hadn't carried some traditions a bit too far. Like, for instance, the way her family had passed down the same names from one generation to another. Actually, it wasn't even a lot of names. Really, when she thought about, and she'd thought about it quite often lately, there were only two names that her family couldn't seem to let go. *Beaufort and Sadie!* Those two brave ancestors who had started the African-American lineage of the Collins family.

And she *was* proud of her heritage, her bloodlines. Yes, she was! She just really wondered again, for the millionth time, why her grandmother had thought it necessary to keep the tradition going with *her* name. After all, Cammy's older brother was named William Collins Smith and her older sister was named Jasmine Abigail Smith. Surely, one of them could have been a Beaufort or a Sadie. But no, her mom had allowed Grandmother to name her, the baby girl, and Grandmother, with all of her wisdom, had named her Sadie Camilla. Wow! Not only was she named after the first Sadie Mae (and her grandmother who was also a Sadie), but she had also been given Beaufort's wife name, Camilla.

So she, lucky her, was named after the man's wife *and* his slave mistress. Talk about a huge weight around a person's neck! Thank God her mom had decided to call her Cammy. And she didn't really hate her name! Not really! After all, if it hadn't been for the love between Sadie Mae and Beaufort, there would be a very different story for her to tell. But still! To be named after both of them!

When she'd asked why she'd been chosen to carry both names, Grandmother had laughed. "You probably won't understand this right now, but the Collins men didn't produce very many boys. Because most were girls, the Collins' name didn't go very far, at least on our side of the family. So we try to keep their memory and their amazing contributions to us alive through the passing on of their names. We can never forget the foundation that they gave us. You'll see one day. Those two names of yours will bring the two families together. Just you wait and see. They're proud names, and you wear them well."

So far, there had been no joining of Beaufort Collins' two families. They only met in court. It wasn't exactly what Grandmother had meant, and to be honest, Cammy had finally accepted that that was probably the only way they'd ever be together. In a courtroom!

Now, that she was an adult, Cammy understood about the importance of a family's name. After her divorce, she would have gone back to her maiden name, Smith, if she hadn't had her two children. For them, she'd kept her ex-husband's last name, giving them that sense of a complete family.

And Cammy *did* love her heritage. That's why she was here today, in the library of Two Plantations Elementary, sharing the love story of the first Beaufort and Sadie Mae.

The story of Two Plantations was a favorite for everyone in town and, she was so glad that many years ago, some talented writer in her family had finally written it down in a version that could be shared with the children. For years Cammy's mother, Abigail Smith, and Cammy's grandmother had read this same story to the children of Two Plantations. Both were gone now, and Cammy had taken their place. She hoped that she was as good a storyteller as her mother and grandmother had been.

Muffled giggles brought Cammy back to the present. She shook her head again, smiled to the little children sitting on the floor around her, and looked down at the page in the book where she had been reading before her thoughts had drifted. The library quieted as she found her place and continued to read softly from the book in her lap.

"Jacob Beaufort Collins II knew that he was a kind, decent master," read Cammy in a soft, hushed voice. "He had sympathy for his slaves and really treated them as if they were freedmen. Do you remember what a freedman was?"

"Yes!" screamed the room of third graders.

"Sarah, can you tell the class what we've learned about a freedman?"

Sarah stood up and looked at the other students. "A freedman was a black man who had his freedom; he wasn't anyone's property. He was not a slave. Is that right, Ms. Cammy?"

"That's right!" replied Cammy. Sarah beamed as she sat down.

Cammy began to read again. "He knew that he would free all of his slaves. He just wanted to wait awhile so that no one else could claim them and make them slaves again. But Beaufort had another problem. He was in love, and he was being forced to make a choice. Would he choose what was right for the times in the South in which he lived, or would he follow his heart and choose love? He *had* to decide. But Beaufort already knew that life had no meaning if a person did not have love. To love and to be loved was the most important thing in the world. So what would he do?"

Cammy closed the book that she had been reading to the third grade class. Reading the children the story of the origin of Two Plantations was always a part of the school's Black History Month celebration. Since there was only one elementary school in Two Plantations, all of the children, black and white, went there. Segregation had never really existed in the town, and the school had provided the academic foundation to all of the residents of Two Plantations for over a century.

"Please don't stop. Please, Ms. Cammy," cried Monty Reed. Monty was a shy little white boy with a spiky carrot top haircut and deep green eyes, and Cammy was surprised that he had taken his thumb out of his mouth long enough to say anything. His request was echoed by several of the other students. Cammy smiled and then chuckled softly as Monty stuck his thumb back in his mouth.

"I'll finish next week as promised. Now, when you go home, ask your parents if they know what the town was named before it was called Two Plantations."

"Was it Peaceful Sands? My dad said the town should be called Peaceful Sands," said Michelle Preston whose dad owned the only grocery store in town. "Why?"

"Yea, my mama says there ought to be a statue of Beaufort Collins and his wife, Sadie Mae, in the center of town. Why don't we have one, Mrs. Jackson?" inquired chubby little Belinda Rollins. She loved the story of Two Plantations and had dressed in a cute little African outfit for the occasion; her pretty brown face, bright sparkling brown eyes, and long black braids hanging down her back made her look like a precious African princess.

Cammy smiled as she beckoned to their teacher. "We'll discuss all of that next week, too. Now it's time to give you back to Mrs. McCray. It's been great! I had a great time with you. Remember to behave in class, and I'll see you next week."

She waved to the students as they left the library, some quietly but most whispering to each other. Others giggled their way out of the doors. "Oh, to be young again," she thought as she sat for a moment thinking back to the days when she, her sister, Jasmine, and her brother William had listened to her mother and grandmother tell the story of Two Plantations, and they had never tired of hearing it either.

She also sat for another reason. She'd been bothered with arthritis in her left knee for the last two years, and the pain had gotten progressively worse. She did not want the children see her limping away 'like an old lady'. Frank, her son and the doctor in the family, had told her about a shot that would help her. One shot a week for three weeks that could reduce arthritis pain for at least six months. The only problem was that Cammy hated shots!

But the pain had finally made the decision for her, and she had just finished her third shot yesterday. So far so good!

It wasn't as if Sadie Camilla 'Cammy' Jackson was vain. At sixty, she was still a very striking lady. She had inherited the pecan tan skin, long wavy black hair, and beautiful big, bow legs that appeared every so often in the descendants of Sadie Mae Collins, and she had managed to keep her hour glass figure - 36-24-36 - even though she had added a few unwanted pounds to it causing the measurements to increase just a bit. Back in the day, in her youth, the boys used to call her *'stacked'*, curvaceous.

She still was. Her body was still firm, her oval shaped face still held that youthful look, her thick eyebrows were naturally arched, and her even white teeth were all hers. Her coffee colored eyes sparkled, especially when she smiled. Her jet black hair had begun to show a few gray strands, but that didn't bother her. She was proud of the fact that, having had two children, she still looked and felt good. It was just that damned arthritis that caused her limp, her pain and her some embarrassment. Thank goodness for modern medicine.

Cammy stood slowly, shifted her weight on her knees and feet, and paused. Wow! No pain yet! She straightened to her full five feet seven inches, walked around the table where she had been sitting for the last thirty minutes, and headed toward the door.

"See you next week," she called to Paul Landry, the school librarian and then stepped out into the warm Florida sunshine. The early morning frost had disappeared, and Two Plantations seemed to sparkle on this mild winter's day. Soft white clouds floated through the beautiful blue sky. Cammy smiled as she plucked one of the wild red roses that graced the landscape of the school. Located in southwest Leon County about twenty miles from Florida's capital city, Tallahassee, Two Plantations was ablaze with color.

Early February in North Florida was like springtime this year. The smell of pine was in the air, the warm weather had tricked the azaleas and camellias into opening their pink, purple, and white blossoms, pollen was falling from the moss covered live oak trees, and the crape myrtle trees that lined both sides of the main street of Two Plantations, now State Road 373, were alive with color.

Hills and flatlands could be found throughout Leon County, and Two Plantations was no exception. White Oaks and Peaceful Sands plantations had been built near the top of the highest hill on the Collins property and were located directly across from each other. About a half mile pass the two plantations at the very top of the hill stood a beautiful white church that was situated right in the middle of the road, its tall steeple sparkled like a beacon in the Florida sun.

The town of Two Plantations had been built about five miles down from the two plantation houses where the gentle slope of the hill leveled off. Now homes and farms dotted the country side, and tall slender pines and majestic, moss covered live oaks stood tall and proud and decorated the landscape which included several lakes, some small and some large. It was a small, rural community, and over the years, new residents had built new homes on small plots of land, and new businesses had been built behind the downtown section of the town. The county had paved SR373 many years ago, and now Moss Road, which dissected the main street, and all of the other side streets had finally been paved.

The three "down town" blocks were lined with rows of store fronts. All the storefronts were alike; they all had rosy brick and stone facades and were two stories tall with big glass windows in front that looked out on the road. Each block housed six stores; there were three stores joined together, then an alley, then three more stores.

"Hi, Ms. Cammy. Pretty rose you have there."

She hadn't noticed Melissa Cork, manager of Jackson's Five & Dime Store, standing in the open doorway.

"Good morning, Melissa. Yes, I just love roses. Beautiful morning, isn't it?"

"Goodness yes! This is one of the reasons why I love living here. You can't get this perfection anywhere that I've ever been." Melissa waved her arms. "Just look at all this! I just love it! And the town made a wise decision when they added these benches. Tourists shop, sit, rest, and shop some more! I know you've been sitting all morning with the kids, but sit with me for a minute. You stay so busy we seldom get a chance to talk anymore."

As they sat together on the wooden bench in front of the store, Cammy couldn't help but smile.

"My schedule *has* been a little hectic lately. But things are slowing down a little. And this weather's fabulous! We'd be crazy not to get out and about! We seldom have such a long spell of spring like weather so early in February, but when we do, wonderful things begin to happen."

"For real?" asked Melissa. "Like what?"

Cammy laughed. "Well, it won't affect you because you already have your Jake, but if you're single in *our* family, great things can happen when spring comes early."

"Now I'm really curious! Is this one of those Collins traditions that you and your family are so famous for?"

"Sort of. This probably sounds a little silly, but we kind of have a family song."

"You're kidding! Is that right up there with your coat of arms and your family motto?" Melissa teased.

Cammy laughed. "No coat of arms, but we do have a family motto, smarty! But the song *has* been passed down from the very first Sadie Mae. Our family calls it her love song! It's said that she sang this song to Beaufort's mother every day as she was tending to her, and her voice was so lovely and soothing that both Beaufort and his mother fell in love with her. Sally Collins gave Sadie Mae the love for a daughter that Sally could never have and for Beaufort, well, he fell in love with a woman that he should *not* have loved and could *never* marry. My grandmother taught the song to me. It's really a silly little song, but we love it! Want to hear it?"

21

"You mean with everything else you can do you sing too? You are amazing! Go ahead. Let me hear it."

Cammy made a big performance of clearing her throat. Then she began to sing softly.

*"When spring comes early
True love you're bound to find.
When flowers bloom early
True love is close behind.*

*Don't look beneath the bushes,
You won't find it there;
When spring comes early
True love is in the air!"*

Cammy's soft and melodious voice drifted through the silent street, and a couple walking along the sidewalk stopped to listen. When she was finished, they clapped along with Melissa. Cammy, in turn, stood and made an overly dramatic bow to her audience.

"How sweet," exclaimed Melissa. "You have such a beautiful voice, Ms. Cammy! And you're single! Be careful! Your true love just might be waiting around the corner!"

Cammy winked at her. "Wrong! My true love is right down the street! Unfortunately, it's one of Babee's cinnamon roll!"

They both laughed at that!

"You know, people talk about your lifelong friendship with Mrs. Babee all most as much as they talk about Beaufort and Sadie Mae. That's something that this town has given me – a chance to form friendships with other women. We've moved so much that I've never been able to form any kind of lasting bond with another woman. Now, that's changed. I've gotten really close to Heather, Mrs. Babee's daughter; we get along really good. I know she may not stay around, but I think we've made the kind of friendship that will last even if she does go back to Texas."

"You've been good for Heather. In fact, you've been good for this town. Melissa, I know I probably say this too much, but I'm so glad that you and Jake settled here. The whole town is. But *I* don't know what I would have done with the store if you and your husband hadn't liked it here."

Melissa and her husband, Jake, had settled in Two Plantations about five years ago. Cammy knew that Jake had served time in jail for selling drugs back in their home town. Once he'd been released, he'd had a hard time finding work. By the time they'd come to Two Plantations, they'd moved at least a dozen times. Now Jake was working with Sinclair Construction, and Melissa ran the dime store for Cammy.

"You are awesome, Ms. Cammy, and if you're as entertaining at the school like you just were here, no wonder the children are so excited whenever you come to visit with them. Your reading to them is all Colleen could talk about. Even though she has heard the story of Two Plantations before, she said your reading it to the third graders was a treat that the whole class looked forward to. I also suspect that there are some sweet treats at the end of the day if they behaved?"

Cammy laughed. "You bet! And they deserve it; they have been a great audience all week. I feel sorry for all of you parents! A third grader filled with Babee's sweet cakes! Wild!"

"Try mixing that with crawling twins!"

"How you manage that and manage this store I'll never know. By the way, what do you think about Mrs. Dodd's idea of opening up a daycare here? We've never had one before. Everyone was either a stay-at-home mom, had an elderly grandmother or aunt or cousin, or had someone to babysit during the day at our homes. Mrs. Dodd's daughter, Patricia, takes care of your two, right?"

"Yes, and I don't know how I would make it without her. But I like the idea of a daycare. As you already know, Mrs. Dodd manages a very successful daycare in Tallahassee, and Patricia's taking online courses in early childhood development from the community college there. The two of them together would be awesome for the town. Your idea of a questionnaire was a good one. That'll give Mrs. Dodd an idea of just how much one is needed here. I, for one, am for it."

"Great! Once she has all of the data together, she can present it to the Foundation for some funding."

"And you're the Foundation! You must be so proud of your ancestry. Not many people believe in giving back like your family!"

"Well, I think the new way of saying it these days is paying it forward. Either way, it's what we're supposed to do, help wherever we can. And the town really has to thank the very first Beaufort Collins for his insight. After all, he was the one who was smart enough to buy thousands of acres of land here in southwest Leon County shortly before Florida became a state. You know the story, so don't let me bore you to death."

"Yea, I've heard it a couple of times, but that's the part that I couldn't quite explain to Colleen. And I sure like it when you tell the story; you're such a great storyteller, Ms. Cammy. I often try to picture them, you know, Beaufort and Sadie Mae. What made them so generous and kind? I mean, back then the South had to be a rather terrible place to live."

"Well, not for whites. And the Collins was a very wealthy white family from upper New York. Beaufort, Sr. was a deeply religious man, was highly educated, and had many successful business ventures in the north. Luckily for us, he was smart enough to leave them there; he wasn't sure about the stability of the south, but he needed to move his family during the fall and winter months because his wife, Sally Collins, had developed a weakness in the lungs, and the cold weather was terrible for her.

After White Oaks was built, Beaufort, Sr., his wife Sally, and their twelve year old son, Beau, Jr. traveled to Florida. You can see why they stayed; this place is beautiful. They soon fell in love with the slow pace of life, but it was difficult for them to embrace the institution of slavery. However, living so close to the state's capital city, Tallahassee, Beaufort Sr. wanted his wife and son accepted into the local society , so he compromised – he hired freedmen and struggling white sharecroppers, and he bought several slaves from Jessup Harpson, a local tobacco producer who was experiencing some financial troubles. Sadie Mae was one of those slaves. Thus the real drama began; Beaufort, Jr. and the slave, Sadie Mae, became lovers. It happened all the time back then you know.

The plantation owners sleeping with the slaves. But how many masters left their wives for a slave? Anyway, you know the rest."

"Sure, but that was so many years ago. Over a hundred! And your family *still* give back. You still help people and give them a chance to get a new start in life. Look at me and Jake. He was actually talking about leaving me and Colleen. He felt like he was dead weight for us, dragging us down. And then we came here. Look at us now!"

"Things always fall into place if we let it. The store needed a manager at the time your family arrived in town, and Danny Sinclair needed some extra workers."

"That was certainly our blessing. Well, guess I'd better go in and restock. Had four buses from a middle school pass through here this morning! Even though 373 was the longer route, the teachers said the students insisted on coming through Two Plantations so they could stop. I've been that busy! And I bet Ms. Babee is out of everything, too. You know it's hard to pass her place without stopping and buying. I'm sure you're headed there to meet your true love!"

"Parked my car there so I could get in some exercise. And, yes, maybe get one of her cinnamon rolls as a reward. Have a great day and tell Jake I said hello."

"I will, Ms. Cammy. Tell Ms. Babee I'll see her later!"

2

Thank God there was a breeze, Cammy thought as she continued down the sidewalk. Those extra pounds really made a difference in the warm Florida sunshine. She really was going to have to make an extra effort to lose some weight. After today, of course.

She thought about what Melissa had said. She loved reading to the children, and she was glad that there was a children's version of the story of Beaufort and Sadie Mae. The adult version was a little too confusing for children. Shoot! Sometimes it was confusing for her. Both a love story and a tragedy, it had taken two families and pitted them against each other, the whites Collins against the black Collins, and it had made one family rich and another bitter. How do you explain all of that to children? Sometimes even Cammy couldn't understand it, and she'd read Beaufort's journals over and over again! Brain drain! Probably what caused her awful dreams!

As she strolled along, Cammy continued to replay the story of Beaufort and Sadie Mae over in her mind. It *was* a rather crazy love story. After all, Beaufort Collins, II *had* fallen in love with a slave. He hadn't been the master of the plantation then; he'd just been a young boy whose mother was ill, and he and the slave girl, Sadie Mae, had spent long hours together tending to her.

Sadie Mae had lived in the house with him and his parents, and he'd fathered five children by her. And what she'd told Melissa was no more that what had had been recorded in history books. That behavior *wasn't* so strange for those times. Many masters *had* fathered children on their slaves, but Cammy had never heard of one that actually left his family to live with one.

Of Sadie Mae's five children, only three lived to become adults. The oldest, Beaufort, died at the age of thirteen. The next oldest was Pearlie, then Mary who died in infancy, then Jacob, and finally Mae Belle.

Beaufort and his father had taught Sadie Mae to read, to write, and to do math, and she had insisted that her children were taught those skills, too. For *their* children to survive in the South, both she and Beaufort knew that they would need an education. That's why they'd built the first little school and why education had become so important to the generations that had followed Sadie Mae. And all of them, to the present generation, owed their successes to their ancestors' deeply rooted belief in a quality education.

The little schoolhouse in Two Plantations was only the beginning. By 1887, a school in Tallahassee made it possible for black students to get a college degree. Now, the walls in the library at Peaceful Sands were covered with diplomas dating as far back as 1892 when Beaufort and Sadie Mae's great-grandchildren graduated from what was then called the State Normal College for Colored Students to the diplomas from the early 1900s when the school's name was changed to Florida Agriculture and Mechanical College. Since 1955, when the school was made a university, several diplomas carrying the proud name of Florida Agriculture and Mechanical University had been added. Cammy had been so proud to hang Frank and Kim's FAMU diplomas next to hers, and there was plenty of room for more.

The vibration of her cell phone interrupted Cammy's thoughts. She looked at the caller ID and smiled.

"Well, if it isn't my big sis! I thought you'd be calling. How's it going, Jazzy?" Only Grandmother had called her Jasmine.

"It's all good! You left the school yet?" Jazzy didn't wait for Cammy to answer. "I miss them so much, Cammy. You know, Mama and Grandmother. This time of year was always so special for them! I should have come home. We could have done this together like they did so many times."

Cammy stopped walking. "Wanna talk?"

Jazzy sighed. "Just for a minute. I don't know what's wrong with me, but I guess I just need a reminder of home, of Mama and Grandmother, of our history. Got time?"

"All the time in the world! Since we've added these benches along the sidewalks, I can just sit and talk and enjoy this great day. Is the weather as pretty there?"

Cammy's sister Jazzy lived in New Orleans with her husband, David.

"A little cloudy but warm." Then in a soft voice, Jazzy whispered, "Cammy, remember the year Mama and Grandmother did the skit about education and how important it was to Sadie Mae and Beaufort?"

"How could I forget? It was entitled 'Children Must Be Educated'. We had to play Beaufort and Sadie Mae's children, Grandmother played Sadie Mae, and she convinced Mr. Moby to play Beaufort. Grandfather didn't like that too much until Grandmother reminded him that if the play was to be believable, the man who played Beaufort had to be white. Mama was the teacher."

They were both quiet for a moment, caught up in their memories.

"It took them forever to figure out how to explain why the first school was built in Two Plantations and why Camilla's children didn't go there," Cammy said. "Grandmother wrote that little play so that it *implied* that Camilla's children were too shy to leave White Oaks, and that's why Beaufort had paid the teacher extra to stop there to give them their lessons."

Jazzy laughed. "Grandmother was a very smart woman, and both she and Mama were so wise. I do miss them. They certainly taught us how to be strong, independent women. But I am always glad and thankful that Beaufort and his father were smart businessmen. Where would we be if Beaufort's father hadn't left his business ventures in the north? Because of him, Sadie Mae and Beaufort were able to provide financial stability for their children and grandchildren and eventually for us."

"Sis," said Cammy. "I totally agree with you! I mean Beaufort even made provisions for Camilla's offspring. And after the way they'd treated him! But as of yet, none of them have ever satisfied the terms of his will, so that money is just sitting there, growing, waiting on someone to want to settle at White Oaks. Whoever does is in for a big surprise! But all they know how to do is sue! If that last one, Ethan, had just thought about it, all he had to do was to *live* at White Oaks to get his inheritance, or at least he and his sister would be very wealthy people by now. And maybe he wouldn't have kept us in court for so long!"

"Ethan! He was too greedy! He wanted his and ours!" Jazzy laughed. "What a jerk! Thank God we belong to Sadie Mae's side of the family." She paused, and when she spoke again, Cammy could hear the uncertainty in her voice. "We've done well haven't we, Cammy? Me, you, and Smitty? They'd be proud of us, Mama and Grandmother. Wouldn't they?"

"Jazzy, we couldn't have done better. Look at all we've accomplished with our lives! All of the charities you work with and all of your community service! Look at Smitty! He keeps funding projects and grants for the inner city schools of Memphis! And look at Two Plantations and Peaceful Sands! Of course they'd be proud of us. We've kept their deepest values alive! And we should be proud! We have what some would call a 'rich history'!"

"That's true. And our good deeds do come back to us! We are also what some would call *rich*!" Jazzy laughed again. "Okay! Thanks! I needed that! And next year I'm coming home for African-American History month! You've been a great custodian for Two Plantations since Mama died, but I could do more. Thanks, Sis. I feel better now! Let's change the subject for a minute. Look! I've met this really nice widower who I would love for you to meet. When are you coming for a visit?"

Cammy groaned. "Jazzy, don't start. Stop trying to fix me up with someone. I'm great just as I am!"

"Please girl! You're still pining after all these years! You've got to let go of….."

"Stop! Don't take me *there*! For years I walked around afraid. It seems as if I've spent every moment waiting for the past to catch up with me! I felt like my head was in a guillotine and any minute the blade was going to drop, but that's long past. *He's* in the past! I'm actually very happy, Jazzy. I really am! And before you say anything else, just give me a break. I just don't want to talk about *him*! So, let's just end this touching conversation by saying that when I'm ready to start dating, I will. Who knows? It might be sooner than you think."

"*That's* what I'm talking about! And I want to be the *first* to know! I'm glad I called! Thanks! Love you, girl!"

"Love you more! Talk to you later, Jazzy."

As Cammy ended the call, she wondered if she should have told Jazzy about the nightmares. No! Jazzy was too ready to bring up Caleb's name anyway. And Cammy really was happy! Well, maybe really content was a better choice of words, but if she'd said *that* to Jazzy, there would have been another lengthy conversation. Jazzy would never be satisfied with content. She wouldn't be satisfied with anything less that bubbling over and running down happiness for her little sister!

And it seemed, at least in her family, that happiness for little sisters in the Collins' family meant home and hearth! Years ago, Mae Belle, Sadie and Beaufort's youngest daughter, had not followed *her* older brother and sister to the North; neither of them had wanted to live in the South. Instead, Mae Belle had stayed at Peaceful Sands with her parents even after she'd married. She'd loved her home as much as her parents did, and her devotion was rewarded. Peaceful Sands and all of the land owned by Beaufort at that time were willed to Mae Belle and her descendents.

Peaceful Sands had then passed to Cammy's grandmother, then to Cammy's mother, Abigail, and now to Cammy. Neither Jazzy nor Smitty had wanted to live in Two Plantations, but Cammy did. So Cammy had followed in her mother's footsteps.

But whether his children had moved to the North or reminded in the South, Beaufort had taught them all how to survive and prosper. Now, Sadie Mae's branch of the Collins' family was some of the wealthiest and influential African-American families in the country. And although their initial wealth had been passed down from one generation to the next, they all had professions and they all gave back to the communities in which they lived.

All thanks to Beaufort Collins, the man whose love blessed one woman and destroyed another! After his father died, Beaufort, Jr. became the master of White Oaks, and like his father, he was a kind and fair master to his slaves. But he wasn't happy there after his marriage to Camilla Harpson. She'd become resentful, particularly about Sadie Mae. Camilla had done what Beaufort had not counted on; she'd fallen in love with him! He'd had to choose between White Oaks and Sadie Mae, so he'd built Peaceful Sands.

Life had to have been hard for him once he left his white wife. White families shunned him, and Camilla taught *her* children to hate him. All he had was Sadie Mae, *their* children, and his wealth! Camilla shook her head. That's why he and Sadie Mae built the town of Two Plantations – to help others *and* to end their own isolation. But why he'd built Peaceful Sands directly across the road from White Oaks and Camilla, his wife, no one could ever explain. It was the one thing that Beau had never talked about to anyone.

 What a story! Beaufort became the master of two plantations built directly across from each other! In one lived his wife; in the other, he lived with his black mistress. Sadie Mae's descendants called it a wonderful sacrifice for true love, a white master and his slave mistress living together for everyone to see. The Harpson family called it an insult to their family and all of the white families in the area.

 But Cammy was proud of her ancestors. Without their love for each other, their sense of business, and their belief in helping others, this town would not have survived. Goodness! Beaufort was ninety-two years old when he'd started the Cottages at the Lake at Peaceful Sands.

 Originally old slave quarters, most had simply fallen down or been torn down over the years, but several remained situated throughout the woods surrounding Serenity Lake. Long before Sadie Mae died, she'd decided that she wanted the slave shacks rebuilt into different size cottages so that when their children and other family members and friends came to visit, there was enough room for everyone to stay.

Back then it was hard for black folks to find a room in a motel or even a room in a boarding house.

One day, Beaufort offered the use of a cottage to an old white man who appeared to be on hard times. As it turned out, the man was, in fact, a wealthy rancher looking for a quiet, secluded place to 'get away' for a few days. During his stay, he and Beaufort became friends, and it was the rancher's idea to make the cottages a retreat for the wealthy. He knew several people who'd pay dearly for the peace and seclusion that Peaceful Sands offered. The cottages were now quite profitable, a President had even stayed in one, and they helped to fund Rachel's Haven, a refuge for abused women also located on Peaceful Sands property, and helped to pay for many of the improvements needed in the town of Two Plantations.

The main road through Two Plantations, SR373, was never really a busy roadway, but it brought its fair share of tourists to the town. The kids on the field trip were a good example. Most of the people who traveled 373 were usually trying to avoid the traffic of the busier highways. They weren't in a rush to get to their next destination, so this quaint town called to them to stop. Most did.

Cammy loved everything about this town. The scenery was magnificent, and the town itself was like a page out of a history book; it was like stepping back to another era. The stores had been built in the late 1860s and early 70s, renovated in the 1930s, and again in the late 50s, so as travelers passed through they were taken back in time and that was just how the residents liked it. Once they heard the story of Two Plantations, of Beaufort, Camilla, and Sadie Mae, many travelers wanted to spend at least one night in town, but if they had already passed through Tallahassee, most didn't want go back twenty miles just to get a room, and there was no inn or hotel in town. But the storefronts always sent out an invitation to all who passed through, and business was good.

These 19th century buildings now housed a grocery store, an antique shop, a hardware store, a 'dime' store, and several other businesses started by people, families and individuals, who had come to Two Plantations looking for something, and stayed because they had finally found it –a home.

Now, a new police station had recently been completed, and three years ago a new courthouse had been built on Moss Road. Further down Moss Road was a new housing development that was being built by Sinclair Construction, and there was already a waiting list for homes. Yes, the town was growing, but everyone, including the new residents, was determined to keep its small town charm.

Cammy's eyes wandered down the street where she saw Ms. Moby leaving Preston's Grocery Store. She waved to Mr. Preston as he put groceries in the back of Ms. Moby's golf cart. Even though golf carts were not allowed on the main road, everyone, including Chief Roscoe turned a blind eye when it came to Ms. Moby who had to be closer to one hundred than to ninety and was the oldest resident of the town. No more than five feet tall, she was a force to be reckoned with. She was a direct descendent of a white sharecropper who had worked on both White Oaks and Peaceful Sands before the Civil War. After the war, he and his family had stayed on to work for Beaufort and Sadie Mae. Ms. Moby was proud that her ancestors had worked for a white man of such character like Beaufort Collins, and she never let anyone forget it.

"Hell, I ain't color blind," she'd once said in a speech she'd given as the Women in History Month honoree. "I love color, and we need every shade to beautify this wonderful world we live in. Black and white and shades in between. We're all special because we're different, and we're better people for it." She was a sassy old white lady with a colorful vocabulary.

Nobody messed with Ms. Moby and her golf cart. That golf cart gave her a sense of independence. It hadn't presented a problem yet since she still had a brilliant mind and great eye sight. Plus, who had the nerve to try to take it away from her? Cammy watched as Ms. Moby backed out and threw her hand up to Mr. Preston. As she passed close to Cammy, she slowed down.

"Gal, every day you're looking more and more like your grandmother did at your age," Ms. Moby said.

Cammy laughed. "If I can look as good as Grandmother at any age, I'm more than blessed, and I hope that wasn't a crack about my age, Ms. Moby."

"Hell, girl, you're just getting old like the rest of us," she cackled. "At least you're pretty while you're doing it. Hear Smitty's finally come home."

"Yea! He calls it retirement, but if you know he's home, you know that he's planning to open one of his cafés here."

"Great idea! The town's growing, and a good place to eat will be a great addition. I ate at one of his

37

cafés in Memphis once. Great food! Bet he ain't staying with you in that big old house is he?"

"You know him too well! Says he needs his privacy. He's in one of the cottages until he really decides what he's going to do. He says he's staying, but you know Smitty."

William Collins Smith, known to everyone as Smitty, was the oldest of the three Smith children and the only boy. He had moved to Memphis right after graduation from college. Although he'd earned a degree in education, he'd never worked as a teacher. Instead, he'd gotten a job as a cook in a restaurant. He'd eventually bought that restaurant, renamed it Smitty's Café, and now it was world famous. Whenever people went to Memphis, they always wanted to eat at one of Smitty's cafés.

"Oh, he's staying all right. It'll lighten your load some, and it's about time. You've carried this town all by yourself since your mama died. Not that that brother and sister wouldn't have helped you if you'd asked. But you need a life now. You're not getting any younger, and the children are grown. You need to start courtin' again. Well, gal, I can't sit here talking. I gotta go. I'm missing my daytime stories. See ya!" she yelled as she rolled to the intersection of Moss Road, turned right, and sped out of sight.

Cammy waved and laughed. She really loved this little town. The air seemed fresher and cleaner here. The soil was richer. The people kinder. This town was her heritage, her home. She had Collins' blood running through her, and for now she was the custodian of Peaceful Sands and of Two Plantations and its residents, and it was a responsibility and commitment that she was proud to keep.

38

Yes, this was home, and Cammy was glad that she still lived here. Close enough to Tallahassee to enjoy musical and theatrical performances, movies, shopping, college football and other sporting events, and far enough away to enjoy the peace and contentment that only a small town like Two Plantations could provide.

She'd told Jazzy the truth. She *was* content with her life, but lately, something was missing for Cammy. Oh, she was always busy. Managing the Cottages and Rachel's Haven kept her on her toes. She'd secretly hoped that one of her children, either Frank or Kimberly, would take some interest in her work at Peaceful Sands, but they'd decided on their own careers and neither included managing Peaceful Sands.

And if it had not been for Peaceful Sands and its enterprises, Cammy knew that she probably wouldn't have survived for so many years. She'd needed something, anything to keep her going and to keep her dreadful secret from destroying her. But it couldn't now, could it? No! No way! So why was she worrying? After all of these years, that was a secret that she really would take to the grave with her!

She just needed to get on with her life! That's what these feeling were all about! For the first time in years, Cammy was feeling lonely. She needed a real social life, and she didn't have one! With her children grown, she now had time to take a really good look at her life. And what she saw she didn't like. These years should be some of the best years of her life, and she was spending them alone. Maybe she *should* consider dating again. It'd been years since she'd had a real date. Babee and Jazzy would be *so* glad! They couldn't stop yapping about it. And even her children had begun to chime in.

"You ought to at least go to dinner with someone, Mom," Kimberly had suggested just a couple of weeks ago.

Imagine Kim giving her advice on dating. And Kim had even gotten to Frank.

"Mom, when's the last time you went on a date?" he'd asked.

"Since when have you become interested in my love life, young man?" she'd replied the last time he brought up the subject. "Have you forgotten that I'm sixty? I'm too old to start dating now."

Frank had simply smiled and kissed her on her cheek. "You're certainly not old, and no one is ever too old for true love."

As she walked along lost in her thoughts, Cammy realized that she'd started humming *that song*! Jeez! It'd been a long time since she'd even thought of it! *'I've Been Loving' You Too Long"* had been her song for years! Her 'true love' song! And she'd had her chance at true love and had messed it up royally. *Caleb Wellington!* She'd spent too much of her life thinking about him! Loving him! Had she really loved him for so long that she couldn't stop? And Lord, she had loved him! *Was* loving him a habit that she *couldn't* break or was it one that she didn't *want* to break? *Please!* It was just a song, and now so much time had passed her by without her even realizing it. Now, she wanted a life, some companionship. Maybe it *wasn't* too late for her.

Caleb Wellington! Why had Jazzy even mentioned him? Caleb and her secret! Her nightmares couldn't have anything to do with Caleb!

No way! Cammy had only seen him from a distance twice since he'd left twenty-six years ago. But she'd never forgotten him or stopped loving him. She only wished she could! The song *had* to be wrong! It *wasn't* too late to stop loving him; it was time!

3

    The Delta flight was scheduled to arrive on time. It had been a good flight so far. Caleb Wellington turned from the window and looked around the first class cabin. It was full today. He glanced over at the little red head who had flirted with him all through the flight from D.C. until he'd faked sleep. He wasn't annoyed or bothered about the flirting; in fact, he was used to that kind of attention from women of all ages and races. At sixty-four, he wasn't a bad looking man. He had that *'damn, you're good lookin'* swagger about him. He always had. Hell, most people thought he was Puerto Rican with his curly black hair which had grayed in the temples, his slightly flared nose, and his buttery light brown complexion. All of this gave him a rather sexy, sort of Spanish, European, and African mix, and when his hazel eyes were added, well, yea, he was something to look at.

    His six foot two frame was as straight and lean as it was when he was thirty-five. Being a former police officer and now a retired federal marshal had helped to keep him in great shape. He was all muscle, and his tall, athletic body fitted nicely in his snug shirt and jeans. Caleb wasn't conceited; maybe a little arrogant, but looks didn't lie, and he was pleased that he had aged so well. Folks said he was the splitting image of his dad. Well, he was glad that he just *looked* like him.

His dad and mom had married young and had eight children together. But his father had messed around with too many women, and there were several outside children that didn't carry the Wellington name. Caleb had loved women, too, but he'd made damned sure that he wouldn't have children scattered all over town. He made sure he wouldn't be like his father. He'd always been careful; he'd only let down his guard once. But thank God nothing had come of that.

Caleb turned to the window. He had made this flight many times over the years. Not in first class in the beginning; that started happening after he became a marshal. No, before that it was coach, and even before that it was that long fifteen hour drive from D.C. to Tallahassee. Tallahassee, the capital city of Florida. Home! And Caleb was going home for good. Most of the time he was happy to be moving back. He'd never planned to leave in the first place. But twenty-six years ago he had bolted. Had run or rather driven so fast he couldn't really remember any of the trip. All he could remember was the pain, the betrayal, the need to just get away as fast as possible, and he did. All because of Cam!

He'd had a good job before he'd left. As an officer with the Tallahassee Police Department, Caleb had been a good cop. He should have been because he would *never* forget how close he had come to being on the *other* side -- instead of putting people in jail, he could have been *in* jail. A little incident that had started out as a teenage prank, knocking over mail boxes, had brought him so close to going to jail that it had scared him to death.

He'd always had that *'thuggish'*, bad boy image and had done some silly things. But he knew when to draw the line. Jail was *not* where a 'player' belonged, and he had thought himself a real player in his youth. That incident had shown him that it was time for a change, so he'd gone to community college, gotten accepted to the police academy, and landed a job with the police department while he got his bachelor's degree from Florida State. And he had been a damned good police officer. So good that when he'd had to leave, when he'd 'hauled ass' out of town, he had no problem getting a job with the D.C. police. And he'd run like the devil was chasing him, leaving behind everything except the memories. He'd never been able to leave those behind.

The pilot announced the arrival to Hartsfield-Jackson Atlanta International Airport. Caleb turned to the little red head. "So, you're home."

She smiled her little sexy smile. "Yes," she replied. "You sure you don't want to stay over for a while? My folks don't expect me home until tomorrow. I came a day early to surprise them."

He smiled and shook his head. "Sorry, darlin'. I have a little one like you waiting for me in Tallahassee. Can't disappoint her."

"Lucky lady! Oh, well. Maybe there'll be a next time. Safe flight." She pecked Caleb on the cheek as she made her way into the aisle and strutted away. He shook his head again. She didn't know that the little one waiting for him was his twenty-year-old daughter, Candice. And he couldn't wait to see her.

He eased his long frame out of his seat and waited as several business men rushed through the door.

Caleb waited for the elderly woman who had sat across from him to rise.

"Let me get your bag for you," he offered and began to reach into the overhead compartment above her.

"Don't bother. Let the cute little male flight attendant get it for me. You go on ahead of me, good looking," she purred. "I saw you when you got on the plane. I want to get a good look at your butt as you walk away. It'll give me something to dream about!" She watched Caleb closely as he hesitated. "Oh, believe me. I insist. Don't deny an old lady." She smiled and winked at him. He smiled, winked, and eased into the aisle. As he walked away, he could have sworn that he heard a whistle.

Atlanta's airport was huge, and today, Caleb wouldn't have minded a long walk to his connecting flight to Tallahassee. It would have given him some time to walk off the nerves that he had begun to feel the closer he got to the end of the trip. But no such luck today. His flight was in the next terminal, and he had arrived in plenty of time. While he waited for his plane to depart, Caleb decided to walk, to stretch his legs. He needed to clear his head, get his thoughts together. Get control. Let go of the memories *before* he started his new job.

He couldn't understand it. He had had a great marriage, he had a beautiful daughter, and he had had a rewarding career. So why couldn't he get one woman out of his mind? Oh, for the longest, he had pushed her back, way back. Margaret, his wife, had been a great wife and companion for him, and he missed her. The heart attack had been so sudden, so unexpected and had left him a single dad with a seven year old daughter.

Maggie *had* been a good wife to him. The best! He'd met her about six months after his arrival in D.C. She was a waitress at the deli where he'd eat some days; he was the new guy in town and home sick.

"Are you ever going to try something different?" she'd inquired one day.

They'd always shared a little conversation, about his job, about her job. He'd even asked her out right after they'd met. But she'd turned him down.

"What do you suggest, baby?"

"Oh, I don't know. Something with a little spice to it to take your mind off your troubles."

"I don't have troubles," he'd snapped.

She'd flinched as if she'd been struck.

"Look, I'm sorry. Didn't mean to be rude." He *was* sorry. It just had been one of those days that he was really missing home – and everyone he'd left. He'd almost made a phone call to Two Plantations. Shit! He'd actually made the call, but he'd hung up before anyone could answer. Maybe she was right. He did have troubles. His trouble was he couldn't forget who he had left behind.

"Look, I didn't mean to snap. Tell you what. It *is* time I tried something different. When's your next evening off?"

She looked startled. "Oh, you weren't that rude!"

Caleb laughed. In fact, it was the first time he'd really laughed since he'd left home.

"Hey! I'm asking you out for a date – for the second time. If you turn me down again, I'll have to take it personally and start eating someplace else."

She smiled, and Caleb noticed not for the first time that she had a really pretty smile. "Well, we can't have that. The boss wouldn't like it. And I wouldn't either. You leave some pretty good tips. Actually, I'm off tomorrow evening."

"Good! Write your address on the back of my card. I'll pick you up around seven, okay? By the way Maggie, I'm Caleb. Caleb Wellington in case you've forgotten."

"No, believe me, I couldn't forget." She wrote the information down. "A detective, huh? Big shot! Good! See you at seven."

That was the beginning. In no time at all, they were spending all of their free time together. They were really alike in some ways, but they did have one very important thing in common. They were both recovering from a bad relationship. Maggie had been in an abusive relationship. A bad relationship that *she* hadn't ended. She guessed that her boyfriend just got tired of beating on her and left. Caleb couldn't really understand why a man would hit a woman, but he knew how close to the edge pain and disappointment could push someone.

Caleb liked Maggie. She was safe, comfortable, open, and honest. The intimacy was nice. There was none of that out of control passion that he had shared with Cam. No mind blowing explosions. No near death experience, and Caleb liked it that way. All of that was in the past, and he knew by then that Maggie was his future.

By the end of the year, Caleb and Maggie had gotten married. His family had all come to D.C. for the wedding. After all, once he'd passed his thirty-fifth birthday, they'd all assumed that he loved women too much to settle down with one. But after they had met Maggie, they understood.

He and Maggie had been married for six years when they'd had Candice. They'd thought that they wouldn't be able to have children and had actually begun talking about adopting. Then the miracle! She was pregnant! Caleb remembered how he'd cried when Candice was born. They'd been such a happy family!

Then, suddenly Maggie was gone. Only seven years after Candice was born. Massive heart attack!

Caleb had felt lost. And punished! He had truly loved Maggie, but he had always felt that he had in some way cheated her because he hadn't given her all of him, all of his love. He'd never physically cheated on her. No, not with his body! He really did care for her, and there wasn't anyone else that he'd had any desire for. But that wasn't actually true. He'd never stopped wanting Cam. He'd given Maggie his heart. It just wasn't *all* of his heart. A little cheating witch had robbed him of the ability to love completely, to trust completely. But how could he accuse Cam of cheating with her own husband?

And each time he thought about how much of his heart he had given to someone else's wife, how stupid he'd been, the anger and pain was as fresh as if it had happened yesterday. Hell, he'd even bought an engagement ring for another man's wife. Thank God, he hadn't given it to her and that he'd been smart enough to throw the ring away.

Still, he'd never forgotten her, never gotten over her. He'd tried. When he'd had Maggie with him, it was easier. But after Maggie had died, Cam had come back to his dreams. He could feel the touch of her. The scent of her haunted him. And he couldn't seem to get rid of her. He'd had other women after Maggie's death, but none could wipe away the memory of Cam. Caleb knew he had to do something with these feelings. But what? If twenty-six years hadn't erased her from his mind, his body, what would?

Caleb sat in first class on the short flight to Tallahassee. Everyone must be traveling today, he thought. This plane was also full. He was restless now, anxious. He'd made the right decision, right? He took a deep breath. Then another. He had to get over this and soon. He had accepted the job. He was now the new police chief of Two Plantations.

He knew *she* still lived there. He'd checked up on her; knew she had never remarried and from what he could tell, didn't date much. She'd stopped working some years ago, and now spent her time running the local enterprises that were owned by Peaceful Sands. He hadn't been able to find out much about either enterprise. That was surprising since he had contacts at the highest levels of all of the major federal investigative services, but he figured neither company could be very big if they were headquartered in Two Plantations.

He hadn't been able to resist checking up on her; he knew he'd have to see Cam on a regular basis once he moved to Two Plantations. He had to get control of himself, a control he never was able to

49

have when he was around her. But he was a different man now. He could do this.

The short forty-five minute flight from Atlanta to Tallahassee seemed to be over before it had time to begin. This time, Caleb was one of the first to rush from the plane.

"Daddy! Daddy! Over here!" Caleb saw his daughter waving her hand, and she was surrounded by Wellingtons. So many! Most of them calling, "Sug! Sugar! Welcome home!"

Sug! Yea, he knew he was home.

He hugged his daughter and laughingly asked, "How many Wellingtons do they allow in this place at one time?"

4

    Her thoughts still on Ms. Moby, Two Plantations, and Caleb, Cammy almost passed the bakery and her car.
    "So, you coming in or what?" asked Babee Sinclair as she stood in the door of her shop. The smell of freshly baked doughnuts, cupcakes, pastries, and her legendary cinnamon rolls floated out of the door.
    Back in the day, Babee would have been called a 'broad'. She was about five feet eleven with flawless white skin and long blonde hair that she now colored to hide the gray. Her eyes were a sparkling baby blue, and when she smiled, well, all of the men around her were left speechless. Like Cammy, she had picked up more than a few pounds sampling her own cooking, but her height hid it well. Her husband, Danny, her high school sweetheart, didn't mind at all since he loved sampling her baking, too.
    "Oh, yes, I'm coming in. God, it smells great in here," Cammy said as she leaned on the counter. "Remember high school? When we first met?"
    "How could I forget? What's brought this on?"

"Just thinking about something Melissa said. Oh, by the way, she said to tell you that she'd see you later."

"She always stops by on her way home to pick up something for dessert for her family. I like that girl, but I wish she'd stop calling me Ms. Babee. It makes me sound so old."

"You are old."

"You're older than I am, *Ms.* Cammy! Now! How you like that?"

"And to believe that I actually thought you were once truly shy!"

Babee was silent for a moment. "I'm not sure if I was shy or embarrassed. Have you forgotten that I was homeless? I was so ashamed!"

"You bet I remember *all* of that time. How could I forget? I was only a sophomore in high school when the county decided to close the one all black public high school. A few of us black kids chose to go to the oldest predominantly white high school where about eight black students had gone a couple of years before. Those were some difficult days for us. You remember that most of the white students and most of the white teachers didn't want us there."

Those days were hell! Even though a few black teachers had been transferred to the school, they were outnumbered just like the black students. The turbulent 60s!

"*'Do your people proud,'* Grandmother had instructed me." Cammy laughed. "She was something else! *'You've got Collins blood in you. You're smart and talented. Don't let anybody tell you differently. And be safe!'* "

"Your grandmother was amazing! Nothing seemed to faze her!"

"You're right about that! Safe! *Really? Be safe?* Every day of those two years was like preparing to enter a war zone. There were fights in the hallways, on the stairs, and even in the classrooms. It didn't matter who started the fights, the black students were always the ones who were suspended and sometimes even expelled. The black boys caught it more that the black girls, and a lot of boys didn't finish high school during those years. Do you remember the day when most of the black students were suspended for two days for walking out of an assembly in protest?"

"I thought you all were so brave! And you were out front, leading the crowd! All *I* wanted to do in those days was to stay as invisible as possible, so no one would know my family's predicament."

Cammy couldn't imagine what life must have been like for Babee during that time. Oh, she'd talked about it some later on, but Cammy knew there was still a part of her friend that Babee kept close to her heart, a place that she didn't share with anyone.

"You know, I wasn't scared the first day of classes, but I sure was nervous." Cammy continued to reminisce. "I knew what to expect – they had coached us well at our old high school – but, I knew that what we'd been told to expect was mild compared to what the reality could or would be. Thank you so much for befriending me that day. Remember?"

****

Going to an integrated high school in the South in 1967 was hell for a black girl. The first day was could have been horrific. And it would have been if it hadn't been for Babee.

"Hi. I'm Babee Musgrove, and I'm the shyest person in the room." She seemed more nervous that Cammy which helped to ease some of the tension that Cammy felt.

"I'm Sadie Camilla Smith, but everybody calls me Cammy. Nice to meet you. And if you are the shyest, I'm in trouble." Cammy laughed. Babee had broken the ice, and soon, all of the other students in the class had scrambled to be introduced to her.

She'd thought for sure that she'd comfortable in her classes. After all, she was from Two Plantations, and race had never been an issue there. But this wasn't Two Plantations, and she and the other black students weren't welcomed.

However, the journalism class was different. Even though she was the only black in the class, the students and the instructor seemed pretty liberal, so it was easy for was Cammy and Babee, who only saw each other in the journalism class, to become good friends. Because the class was so casual, it was easy for them to talk to each other as they worked on news stories for the school paper. And they talked about everything! About Two Plantations, about hopes and dream, and about boys and boys and more boys! They'd laughed and giggled together the entire class period. Ebony and Ivory! That's what the staff called them; they'd become that close.

Every two weeks, the staff had to stay after school to 'paste up' the paper. Most of the kids drove or lived near each other. Of course, Cammy lived in

Two Plantations, so someone would pick her up. Many of the residents of Two Plantations worked in Tallahassee and were only too happy to bring Mrs. Abigail's daughter home.

"Hey, Babee. Let me give you a ride home," Tom Bettings always offered. He'd had a big crush on Babee. But Babee never accepted a ride from anyone. She always walked, even when it was dark. Everyone figured that she lived near the high school. And because Babee really was shy back then, nobody really bothered her when she declined a ride.

However, that all changed on April 4, 1968, the day that Martin Luther King, Jr. was assassinated in Memphis, Tennessee. It was a 'paste up' day. Everyone was busy with paste and strips of news stories when the phone rang in the office where Ms. Mathis, who'd sponsored the school newspaper and yearbook for the last twenty years, was working.

"What?!! My God! My God!" was all the students heard, and then Ms. Mathis came to the door. She was deathly pale. Everybody stopped. "My God," she whispered as tears rolled down her face. "Dr. King has been killed!" No one moved; it seemed as if no one could breathe.

Ms. Mathis looked around. "Everyone call home, starting with Sadie." Ms. Mathis always used the students' names that were on the official class roster. She looked at Cammy, came to her, and hugged her. "Call your parents, honey. I don't want you going home with anyone else."

Cammy looked through her tears and saw that everyone, girls and boys, had tears in their eyes. She was stunned and shocked.

"Go ahead, Sadie, so the other students can use the phone. I'll wait here with you until your parents come."

Grandmother answered the phone on the second ring. "Your mama and daddy are on their way now, child," she said softly. Cammy could tell that she had been crying. "You just sit tight until they get there. Those children up at FAMU ain't taking this too well, and there's no telling what else might be happening in the town. You just sit tight. Your folks left as soon as they heard the news." As Cammy hung up, she could hear her grandmother crying.

As students called parents and left to go home, they could hear sirens and, at times, shouts from passing cars. Three of the boys stayed with Ms. Mathis, Cammy and Babee. Babee said that her family didn't have a phone. She'd wanted to walk, but Ms. Mathis wouldn't let her. No way. It was too dangerous.

They didn't have to wait long for Cammy's parents to get there; they must have been speeding. As Cammy collected her books, Babee whispered to her, "Let me ride with you. Please. I can't let Ms. Mathis take me home. Please, let me."

"Ms. Mathis, my parents will take Babee home. Is that okay?"

"Yes, that would be great. We'll all walk out together and be sure everybody gets off safely. Sadie, you have my number don't you? Call me when you get home. I just want to be sure that you and your family are all right."

They walked down the two flights of stairs. Everyone was quiet, caught up in their own thoughts.

56

Cammy's parents were parked right in front of the doors.

"Good evening," said Ms. Mathis as Cammy's dad, Abraham, got out to open the door for Cammy and Babee. "I'm Ms. Mathis. I'm really glad to finally meet you. I'm just sorry it has to be on a day like this. Sadie said it was okay for Babee to ride with you? It won't cause you any trouble?"

Ms. Mathis was worried about what would happen if someone saw a white girl riding with a black family, especially that night.

Abraham gave a crooked little smile as he shook her hand. "It won't be a problem. I know how to take care of my women folk, ma'am." He waited until everybody got in their cars before he got back under the steering wheel.

"It's a sad night tonight, girls," he sighed as he pulled away from the school. There was absolute silence in the car as police cars and fire trucks sailed through the streets. The country would never be the same.

"So, where do you live, young lady?" Abraham asked as they left the school.

Babee had been very quiet, everyone in the car was quiet, but when Abraham asked that question, Babee whimpered and turned deathly pale.

Everyone turned at once to look at her.

"What's wrong, child?" Abigail whispered softly. "We aren't going to do anything except take you home."

"Could you just drop me off at the corner?" It sounded as if Babee was crying. "I don't live far. I'll be okay."

"I'm sorry, child, but I can't do that. It's just too dangerous. It's bad on any day for a girl to be walking by herself, but tonight? No. If you're concerned about your parents' reaction to black folks bringing you home, well, don't worry about that. It won't hurt our feelings none. We gonna get you home safely tonight. Now, where do you live again?" Abraham slowed to almost a crawl and waited.

****

Babee shook her head as if to clear it and looked across the table at Cammy. "I loved my mom and dad. But to be homeless as a high school student back then was …….. well, it was awful. But they did their best, and I knew it then, and I haven't forgotten it now. When they told me about everything that had happened to them that night when Dr. King died, I vowed I'd never be ashamed of my family again."

Babee fell silent again, remembering, memories swirling through her mind.

Mr. and Mrs. Musgrove had been worried that night. They'd parked about two blocks from the high school in the Winn Dixie parking lot where they always waited for Babee. It was late, later than usual, and they didn't know if they should move closer to the school or just wait. They didn't want to miss her; this is where she would come. But it was a dangerous night, and they were scared. Really scared! They had no idea where they would stay tonight.

They had already had to move from the rear of several stores. The manager at this Winn Dixie knew that they had been parking in the rear of his building at night, but he hadn't said much. He did bring food out to their Volkswagen minibus from time to time. Ben Musgrove hated charity, didn't want any man's pity. But his family was more important that his pride. He'd take what he could get. Where *was* Babee?

Ben had lost his last full time job over a year ago. Since he'd been unable to pay the rent on their apartment, he had moved his wife and four children into their '66 minibus and moved to Tallahassee hoping to find work in a larger city. So far he'd only been able to get a day or two a week of day labor. If the weather was bad, he didn't get that.

He was handy with his hands and had rigged up the bus so they could have some lights and use a little hot plate without killing the battery. Liz, his wife, had made curtains for all of the windows, and they had installed a rod and curtains on the inside so the girls could have some sense of privacy. The younger children, Ben, Jr., Mary Beth, and Josephine, had to participate in P.E. everyone day. That way, they got a chance to take a shower. It was harder for Babee now that she was in high school, but she never complained.

Even though steady work was hard to find, Ben didn't stop trying. Every day Liz dropped him off at the corner of Tennessee and Macomb Streets before she took the children to school. In fact, she dropped both him and Babee off. Babee wanted to walk to school, and it wasn't that far. Liz stayed with the van in case it had to be moved. They couldn't lose the van. For the time being, it was their home.

They always waited for Babee in the parking lot. That way they just looked like an ordinary family who picked up their child from school and went home. They had pulled around from the back of the grocery store to the front parking lot when they heard the news on the radio. Martin Luther King, Jr. had been killed. They had both wept. Before times had gotten bad, before the children, Ben and Liz had proudly participated in civil rights marches. They had lost some their so-called friends for sure, but they knew that it was the right thing to do. Now those 'friends' were glad to see them fall so low. *That's what happened*, they had snickered as they'd turned their backs, *when good white people mixed with the wrong kind.*

Now the Musgroves were nervous. They could hear the sirens and could see the red lights flashing as police cars and fire trucks passed by. In the last thirty minutes cars filled with young white boys had started parking in the lot. Ben could see that they were drinking beer and maybe more. A couple of times someone had banged on the side of the van.

"We know somebody's in there. Come on out, you black asses!" Then they threw beer cans at the windows, but the windows didn't break. Ben wanted to show his face; show them that they were white, not black. But the boys were drinking and looking for trouble. Being white tonight might not matter.   Ben wanted to move the van, but he couldn't let Babee walk into a group of young, drunk boys. No telling what would happen to her.

Suddenly the minivan began to rock from side to side.

"Come out of there! You low life son of a bitches! Come out! Hell, we'll burn you out!"

The children began to cry!

60

"Get away from my van," Ben yelled. "Get away before I start shooting!"

"We ain't scared of you! Shit! Shoot!" Then shots rang out. Ben and Liz fell to the floor and covered the children who were now crying hysterically.

Then as quickly as it had begun, the van stopped rocking, and all they could hear were the slamming of doors and the squealing of tires. Then silence.

A minute later there was a knock on the door. "Open up in there. This is the police!"

They could see lights flashing, and Ben peeped out of the curtains. Sure enough, there were two black and whites parked in front of the van.

Ben opened the door to the passenger side and stepped down into the parking lot. As he began to talk to the police, Abraham Smith pulled up!

"Papa! Papa! What's happened?" cried Babee as she jumped from the car even before it had stopped completely.

The side door of the van opened, and Liz Musgrove leaped down and grabbed her daughter. "Oh, baby," she cried as she hugged Babee tightly. "Oh, baby!"

Cammy and Abigail could see the inside of the van from their car. They exchanged glances. Abraham had gotten out of the car; he looked back at Abigail with a questioning look on his face. She gave a slight nod and turned back to Cammy.

"Everything is going to be all right, Cammy. Don't worry about your friend. We'll help make it all right."

"Lord!" the officer mumbled. "What's a colored man doing with a white girl tonight? What more trouble do we need right now?"

"We're not trying to cause trouble for anyone, officer. If you're really looking for an answer to that first question, my family and I were giving her a ride home from school."

"Well, I'm sure they'll thank you for that, but that's another problem. Hell, they ain't got no home, and they can't stay here. Already been trouble. And we ain't got time to protect them. Shit, this is one hell of a night! Do you know how dangerous it is for a colored man to be out tonight?"

"Yes sir, and me and my family are on our way home now. Just wanted to make sure the child got home safely. I'm Abraham Smith from out at Two Plantations."

"Oh, man, I'm sorry, Mr. Smith. I've heard a lot about your family. My wife, Dally, is from Two Plantations. It's a great little town. You'll be safer there than here in Tallahassee tonight."

"What about the family here? Where will they go?"

"Don't know, sir. They can't stay here, and it's too dangerous for them to park anywhere else and stay in that van. It just ain't safe. And they got children, too. You got any ideas?"

Ben Musgrove and the second officer had walked up to the two men.

"Be best if they came with us. You're right. Two Plantations is the safest place to be right now. Chief Roscoe and his deputy are the best there is. What do you think?" Abraham looked at Ben.

"Well, I don't know......."

"Think about the children, Ben," whispered Liz. "This van isn't safe tonight."

Abraham reached out his hand. "I'm Abraham Smith, and that's my wife, Abigail and my daughter, Cammy, in the car. You're welcome to follow us home. You and your family will be safe."

Ben shook his hand, relief washing over him. "Thank you, sir. Thanks for bringing our daughter to us. God bless you. I've heard a lot about your daughter already. I'll load up my family, and we'll follow you to this place where ever it is."

The officers hurried to their cars. "You won't be sorry," said the first officer to Ben. "Like I said, wife's from Two Plantations. You can't go wrong there." As he got in his patrol car he turned to Abraham.

"Sorry about your loss tonight, sir. Travel safely and good luck to you." The patrol cars sped away.

Ben Musgrove and his family traveled to Two Plantations that night. A week later Ben had a full-time job at the hardware store, and his family was living in the apartment above the store.

Babee sighed as her thoughts finally came back to the present. "No, I should be thanking you and your family. Not only did your parents bring us to safety that night, they gave my family a new start. We'll never forget it. And, of course, I met my Danny! I can't imagine life without him!"

5

Babee's face turned a bright red. "Jezz! Did someone turn up the heat?!" Fanning herself, she laughed. "Whew! Just thinking about my man gets me….."

"Hot? Girl, cool off! Babee, are you blushing? It isn't that hot in here. But something smells so good! Are you baking again? Why, it's just after eleven o'clock!"

"Yap," replied Babee. "A real busy morning with the field trip kids and everything, and I'm not complaining. But I am glad to have a few minutes to myself; these days the shop is rarely empty. Have a seat and keep me company for a little while. I've just put my last batch in the oven."

"I forgot about the field trip kids; Melissa mentioned them. Must have cleaned her out."

"Me, too. That's why I'm baking again. The day is not half way over, and the lunch hour and afternoons are always busy now."

"Just hand me one of those cinnamon rolls and a cup of coffee, and you won't be able to get rid of me," laughed Cammy.

She left the counter and took a seat at her favorite table – right in front of the bakery's triple sized window. The lettering on the window was high enough for the bright Florida sun to shine through, and Cammy had a perfect view of the main street and the row of shops across the street. Even though every shop seemed to be identical in structure, they each had their own unique personality, and watching the customers and owners was a relaxing way to spend a few minutes.

Cammy leaned back and smiled. Yes, Beaufort and Sadie Mae had done well. In order for the town to grow, Beau and Sadie had personally provided financial backing for people who wanted to settle and start businesses in Two Plantations, and many of those businesses had been passed down from one generation to another, in the same storefronts on the same little road. They'd given jobs to any free man, black or white, who wanted a new start. And when those people knew that they wanted to settle in Two Plantations, Beaufort and Sadie Mae sold them land, a piece of property that they could call their own. People came. Many found contentment and a new start in life and stayed, and some moved on.

Cammy was so happy that Babee and her family had come and stayed. Eventually, Babee's father had gotten a great job in Denver and had moved his family there, but Babee had married a local boy, Danny Sinclair, and now she had her bakery.

Letting her eyes roam over the cute little bakery, Cammy was filled with pride for her friend. Babee had always loved baking. As a stay at home mom, she had baked constantly for her family and friends and really anyone who cared to try her baked goods. As her children got older, she finally started selling some of her goods because people simply refused to take them for free.

After the children were grown, her husband, Danny, decided to take things in his own hands and make her dream come true. He bought the shop, presented it to her on their 25th wedding anniversary, and the rest was history. Now it was unusual to find it empty. Locals, people from Tallahassee, and strangers passing through all loved Babee's sweets. She'd even started baking for the health conscious, and business was booming. She'd had to buy a van to make deliveries because her orders for wedding cakes and other special occasion cakes had tripled.

"I just love it here," Cammy said as she took a bite of her roll. The bakery now had six comfortable stools at the stainless steel counter. Behind the counter was a large glass window that allowed customers to view the sparkling clean state-of-the-art kitchen where Babee did her magic. She believed that people ate more and bought more when they knew that the food came from a really, really clean kitchen. There were eight square wooden tables in the shop, each with four very comfortable chairs. Each table was covered with a checkered table cloth, some blue, some red, some yellow, and some green. In the center of each was a bowl of fresh flowers

Everything at Babee's was freshly baked each morning; the leftovers from the day before were given to the school for snacks and birthday treats for the children. She was open six days a week, Monday through Saturday, from seven a.m. to six p.m. However, after six, her shop became the meeting place for several of the local women who loved spending time together. There was always a group playing bid whist and bridge on Thursday nights. Others would be knitting or crocheting. It had become a time for the women of the town to enjoy themselves and share a little gossip. Chief Roscoe's wife always picked up Ms. Moby, and Ms. Moby always had some gossip. Cammy always looked forward to Thursday nights.

"How's the roll?" Babee asked as she sat down with her own roll and coffee.

"Who're you kidding?! You know it's great! Yummy! Fantastic! Why in the world do you continue to ask? You know you're the best baker in the state, probably the country!"

"Well, it never hurts to hear it from your best friend," Babee said with a wink and then a sigh. "And since Heather has come home with the kids, well, I need something to recharge me."

Cammy knew that Babee's youngest daughter, Heather, had left her husband in Dallas and moved back home with her mom and dad. That was five months ago. Babee hadn't really said much about it, so something must be going wrong.

Had she been so engrossed in the Cottages, Rachel's Haven, and her own sorry love life that she hadn't even noticed that something was wrong in Babee's life? Cammy took a sip of her coffee, leaned back and asked, "What's up?"

With a sigh, Babee took a bite of her roll. "This *is* pretty good".

Cammy gave her a long, searching look.

"Okay, okay! Here it is in a nut shell. Danny thinks that Heather should get a job so that she can get a place of her own. I think she needs more time. And to top that off, Danny wants to swap houses with old man Paterson. Or in business terms, Danny wants to *sell* our house to Mr. Paterson and buy his. At least Mr. Paterson wants to do it, and Danny is considering it."

"Wow! That's a lot to take in! Let's start with Heather. Danny likes having her and the grandkids home, right?"

"Sure, he loves that girl, probably too much. But he doesn't want her to move in with us permanently. He says that she just can't keep sitting and doing nothing." Babee blushed. "And he says he misses me."

"Okay now! So passion has blossomed in the Sinclair household! Really! Aren't you and Danny a little too old for that?"

Babee blushed again. "You know we had that scare a couple of years ago with prostate cancer. I didn't care if we were ever intimate again as long as Danny was okay. Well, he's really come back. All the way! You know what I mean? Some men don't you know."

"Thank God for early screening! That can be a death sentence for so many men who wait!" Cammy grinned. "So the house is rocking, huh?"

"Well, it rocked until Heather and the children came back. I mean, how can you get your groove on with kids in the house?"

"Wow! Don't ask me. *Unfortunately*, I wouldn't know. What does Heather want to do? Has she talked about going back home? What about going back to school? I know the two of you talk. So tell me."

"Actually, I don't know much. I don't even know why she left Adam, her husband. She won't talk about it, and I don't push. She just says I wouldn't understand. I know that she talks to Adam, and he sent the kids an ipad so they could see him when they talk to him. He's also talked to Danny and me several times, but he won't say what happened to his marriage. Just says he misses us, and hopefully he'll see us soon. I've given up trying to figure it out. I hadn't said anything to you, but maybe you could talk to her? She looks up to you, and I could use all the help I can get with her. I should have asked you sooner."

"Of course I will. I'll take her shopping with me one day next week. We've always enjoyed doing that together, and I've been so busy lately I haven't taken the time to buy myself anything new. Now, it's time to take a little time for me. I'll call her. She and Melissa have become good friends. Maybe Heather's shared something with her, but I doubt if Melissa would share. I know I wouldn't share anything *you* told me unless you'd given me the 'OK'. So, the house swapping thing. What's *that* all about? Surely Danny would rather build his own home."

"Danny's father built the Paterson home, and Danny's always loved it. Why build a replica when you can have the real thing says Danny the builder. And Silas Paterson says he and his wife are getting old……."

"They are," Cammy interrupted with a smile.

"Yea, well, the Patersons think that they need a smaller home which we have, and we need a larger home which they have and which we don't need. Well, not really. Although with Heather and the kids there, our house does seem rather small, and Jeremiah can't spend the night like he used to. And I *have* always wanted a bigger house. When you think about it, their house is really close to the shop. Heather and her family would live upstairs above this shop, and she would work for me. It's so confusing and stressful, but it'll probably happen. I know Danny. He says that I spoil Heather. He wants her to 'stand on her own two feet'. There's been a little tension between us lately, too much tension for me. I love him so much. We'll work it all out. That's what we do." Babee took a brief pause. "So, how are your kids? At least how's Kim? I get to see Frank all the time."

"Oh, she's fine. Or, at least I think she's fine. I don't know. It's hard to tell. I…."

Babee's heart ached for her friend. She touched Cammy's hand. "I wish I could do something to make this all go away. You've carried that secret for a very long time."

"You have always *done* something. You listened to me, you didn't judge me, and you didn't tell my business. If I hadn't had you, I don't know what I would have done or how I would have survived. And hopefully, I'll carry *that* particular secret to the grave with me."

Babee studied Cammy for a long moment.

"You would have survived with or without me. You're strong," Babee replied. "I guess it's that Collins blood in you. You have that natural instinct to survive no matter what."

"But what did it cost my children? I know it's hard for you to understand. You know what the problem is, don't you?" Cammy groaned. "It's my name! It's a curse to me. Believe me, it's giving me nightmares!"

"Oh, please!" Babee said as she took a sip of coffee.

" Oh, yes it is. Just think! Look at their lives, Sadie Mae and Camilla, and look at mine. And don't look at me as if I'm crazy. It's true that Sadie Mae ended up with the man she loved, but she didn't get the *ring*! She could never *marry* him! Our family got his last name because he *owned* us."

"But he freed her and her children just before the Civil War was over, right? Come on, Cammy. What's *really* bothering you? I know it's not your name! Didn't sleep well?"

Cammy frowned at Babee. "Will you please let me vent? And I told you! They're giving me nightmares! The two of them! Listen! Just see if this doesn't make sense! Sadie couldn't marry the man she loved, and look at poor Camilla. She loved a man who did not love her! Beaufort left *her* for Sadie Mae! Sounds familiar? *Ralph and Viola*? Hell! Ralph never should have married me just like Beaufort never should have married Camilla! No, *you* can't possibly understand."

"Hey," said Babee, a little offended. "Why do people keep saying that?! I've never ……."

"I know." Cammy stopped her friend. She looked at the roll in her hand, and then she met her friend's eye. Her own eyes filled with tears. "That came out wrong. See, you got the 'love song' kind of love. You married your high school sweetheart, your first love, and he's never stopped loving you. You're his world. I married my college sweetheart, my first love, and my marriage was *hell*! Like Camilla, I loved him, but he didn't love me, and he finally left me for another woman! Danny loves you like Beau loved

Sadie, like dad loved mom, like Grandpa John Parker loved Grandma Sadie. I wanted *that* kind of love. I thought I had found it. But all I got was Ralph! And I *really* wanted the 'love song' kind of love. You know. The kind of love song that makes your heart pound and makes your knees go weak when you hear it; that makes you shiver and makes your blood boil all at once; that makes you feel faint and energized at the same time. The kind of love song that lasts for eternity! But all I got was Ralph!"

"Ralph was an ass, and why you stayed with him so long is a mystery to me. I'd have taken a stick to him a couple of times before I divorced him. You were a saint!"

"I don't know! Damn it! I didn't know. I didn't really know *him*. And I sure as hell didn't know what to do. I was so *sure* I loved him. And that he loved me. Look how wrong I was! By then we'd had Frank. I owed Frank a proper family, didn't I? And then Kimberly came along. Caleb was gone, and I really didn't know what to do! I thought that I was giving Kim a name and my children a family. As it turned out, I made their young lives hell!"

"No, Ralph made it hell! He was an ...."

"I know. An ass!" They both laughed together. "Well, even though Kimberly seldom comes home, we talk two, three times every day, and you know I get to see Frank all the time. So I'm blessed."

"Yes, you are; your kids are great! I was so glad when you finally divorced Ralph." Babee paused. "And you did find that kind of love, the 'love song' kind of love. Remember?"

"Please don't," Cammy whispered in an anguished voice.

"But Caleb did love you, Cammy. I know he did, and you know it, too. He really loved you. Totally! I really believe he loved you with all of his heart."

"See, that's that Sadie name at work. I finally had the man of my dreams, but *I* didn't even get to keep the man. No man, no ring, no name! Yes, I had the true love of my life, and what did I do? I lied to him! I cheated him! I broke his heart! I drove him away! Please," Cammy begged. "Let's not talk about this anymore."

"Just tell me one more thing. Do you still play *that* record or did you finally play a hole in it?"

"Don't be cute, and no, I don't still play it. And there's no hole it. I have it on CD now! But as strange as it is, I found myself humming it on my way here. I guess it's just this mood I'm in." Cammy's voice shook. "I can't seem to shake him, Babee. Look like I've spent my whole life trying to forget him and nothing works. Maybe I should stop trying to forget him. Just accept the fact that I'll always love him. Maybe then I'll be able to move on with my life."

Babee leaned back in her chair. She hated to see her dearest friend still so upset and hurt. Twenty-six years ago the pain and anguish had been even worse. She had wondered if Cammy would survive, but she had. And she'd survive the news that Babee had to tell her, but for the moment, she'd let it go.

"Kim hasn't been back since Ralph's funeral, right?"

"She says she's so busy with her job at the law firm that she can't get away. She claims she doesn't even have time to date much even though she keeps nagging *me* about dating. The nerve! But I wonder if all of this working is an escape for her. Sometimes she was so embarrassed by Ralph, so ashamed of his drinking and his women. How awful it must have been for her! All of her classmates gossiping about her father! And I let it happen to her. I should have told her the truth when she was old enough to understand. I just didn't have the guts to do it. You know, I always thought that Kim would live in Two Plantations. I thought that I'd turn all of this stuff over to her. Now I realize that I've never really talked to her or Frank about our finances or anything. I spent too much time focusing on trying to correct the mistake I made when I married Ralph! I scarred her."

"No, Ralph's behavior scarred them both! Ralph was ...."

"An ass!" They both said in unison and then laughed.

"You do need to start dating again," Babee said.

"*Really*? So here we go again. Why? Have you been talking to Jazzy?"

"No, not today anyway. But don't you *miss* it, Cammy? The companionship? Hell, girl, the intimacy?"

Cammy sighed. "Lately, yes. I've thought a lot about it, but I haven't dated in a long time. And who would be interested anyway?"

"Maybe Langston Mitchell? Remember him? President of Mitchell Federal Credit Union in Tallahassee? He came in earlier to special order a birthday cake for his sister, Kaye. He asked about you."

"So that means he wants a date? I don't think so. He's always been a nice guy. I'm sure he was just being polite."

"Please!" Babee nibbled on her roll. "He wanted to know if you were seeing anyone special. Told him no. So he asked for your number."

"You didn't!"

Babee smiled. "Yes, I did. And it's about time, too. You need a life! And I know you don't have a problem dating outside of your race."

Cammy laughed. "No, I don't. Remember that I grew up here. My first little boy friend was red headed Tommy Spears in first grade. He had freckles and the palest face; we called him carrot top. I thought he was so cute! So you gave Langston my number huh? Like I'm really ready to date! Thanks a lot! And if it goes wrong, it's your fault, and I'll remind you of it for the rest of your life."

6

"Uh! oh! Don't look over your shoulder, but Brian Yates' about to come into the shop."

"Please, not Brian!" The bell on the door jingled as Attorney Brian Yates came into the shop.

"Good morning, Camilla," he hesitated for a minute and then included Babee. "And you too, Babee."

"Whatever. What can I get for you today, Yates?" Babee and Brian had never liked each other. Brian and Ralph had been really close friends through law school and after. Babee always thought that they were birds of a feather. Time proved her right.

Brian pulled out the chair next to Cammy. "I'll take a couple of those famous cinnamon rolls and a cup of coffee to go, thanks."

Babee rolled her eyes at Cammy as she got up and went into the back.

"I thought that was your car out front, Camilla. How are you? You've heard that I've moved back to the family home, right?"

Brian Yates was short and round. Goodness! Everything seemed to be round on him - his stomach, his head, even his eyes. Cammy smiled. If he only knew how she, Jazzy, and Babee had called him 'frog' behind his back. His dark skin always looked a little dull, no shine to it, and he'd started to bald.

"Yes, I'd heard something about that. You've lived away from Two Plantations a long time. Sure you'll be happy here?"

"Shoot yea! Martha Sue and I can't live in the same town. She still wants me back, but I'm through there. Anyway, this gives me a chance to see you a little more. Maybe I can call…"

"Your to-go is ready," Babee said as she placed the coffee and bag containing his rolls on the table in front of him and took her seat in front of Cammy again.

Brian glared at Babee. "Camilla and I were trying to have a private conversation, if you don't mind."

"Why should I mind? By the way, Brian, you remember Leafton Davis? The attorney that represented Martha Sue in your divorce? He's a good friend of mine."

Brian stood abruptly. "Anything he or Martha Sue said to you is a lie!" he snarled. "I don't know how you keep any customers, Babee, with your sharp tongue and smart mouth! Listen, Camilla, I'll give you a call." He looked at Babee. "Keep the change!" He threw a five dollar bill on the table and stormed out of the door.

"Thank you, girl! He's so disgusting! You know he was supposed to be Ralph's friend and actually tried to hit on me when Ralph and I were still living together! The rat!"

"And you know why he's back here, right? Martha Sue finally got tired of him cheating *and* beating on her. She got just about everything he had to keep her mouth shut about that! Why do women stay in situations like that?"

"And why do men hit on women? Jeez, he gives me the creeps! But you watch him, Babee. I don't trust him at all."

Babee laughed. "I'm not Martha Sue. If he ever tries to do anything to me, there won't be enough left of him for Danny to sweep up! Now that the 'frog' has left, I have some news for you. Some gossip and some, well, we'll see if it's good news or bad news for you."

"Start with the gossip. Make it good!"

Cammy smiled at her friend. Thank God for Babee.

"Sapphire Grant passed through this morning on her way to Pensacola. You probably don't remember her; she's a classmate of mine. Remember, baby boomer, that I'm younger than you." Babee ducked as Cammy threw a small piece of cinnamon roll at her. "Missed me! Anyway, she works for Western Electric and said that someone is having the lights turned on at White Oaks."

Cammy groaned and shook her head. "I hope that this is not the beginning of another series of law suits from our dear Collins cousins. It's been what, about seven years of peace and quiet? Did she say a name?"

"Couldn't remember. I just thought I'd pass it along."

"You know, I think it's time for a city manager for Two Plantations. We need someone who can take some of the load off of John and the Foundation which, of course, means me. All of the necessary permits and other legal documents necessary for this town to run efficiently seem to be doubling. Just ask Danny. The town's growing; we have to catch up with the 21st century. It's long overdue. I'm giving Mayor Palmer a call today. And thanks for the heads up! Now, what's this other thing?"

Babee decided it would best if she just rushed in and prayed that this could be a miracle for Cammy, a second chance to get the love she so richly deserved.

"Well, you know the committee to select the new police chief to replace our beloved Chief Roscoe? The committee *you* refused to be a part of? The one my sweet husband decided *to* be a part of? You really should have been on that committee. Then maybe you could have avoided this. Anyway, Danny called just before you arrived. They've made their offer, and it's been accepted. Mayor Palmer is making the announcement this afternoon, but you have to know *now*!"

Cammy looked confused. She'd chosen not be on the committee, but she and many of the residents had met each candidate at the small reception given after each interview. In fact, she had organized each reception. What was wrong with Babee? Had she forgotten? Impossible! *She* had provided the desserts!

"I met all of the candidates."

"Not all," replied Babee. "Remember the telephone interview? No reception for that. That's who got the job!"

"Wow! That is something. I'm surprised that John and the committee would hire someone without actually meeting the person. That must have been some interview."

"They didn't need to meet him. Already knew him. Had his resume; it was excellent! Had the phone interview; it was excellent! The committee made the offer; he accepted. Done deal!"

"Okay, so who is it?" Cammy asked. "He must *really* be something special!"

"Oh, he *is*." Babee leaned forward and whispered. "Cammy, *Sug* got the job! Caleb Kimble Wellington is our new police chief. Sug Wellington is coming to Two Plantations."

Cammy was stunned; she couldn't breathe. Her eyes got big as saucers, her chest heaved as she tried to catch her breath, and her face paled. "Damn! Damn! Damn!"

****

After Cammy had rushed out, the bakery had gotten really busy. Otherwise, Babee would have closed up shop and chased after her friend. As it was, she had only had a couple of minutes to call Cammy on her cell to make sure she was alright.

Cammy's reaction had really frightened her. She'd looked as if she was going to pass out! And Babee blamed herself. She hadn't handled things right. She'd certainly made a mess of that! The look of anguish on Cammy's face broke her heart. And all of the pain that had flashed on Cammy's face still had Babee a little shaky.

When Danny entered the shop, Babee was wiping down the counter. She looked up as the door opened, and a slight smile crossed her face. Her heart

80

skipped a beat as it always did when she saw her husband's face or heard his voice.

Danny Sinclair still looked good to his wife. He wasn't tall, around five feet nine, but boy, was he built! He had worked in construction since he was a little boy helping his father in his own construction business, and it showed in his muscular body. He still looked liked a linebacker for a football team! He'd never been afraid of hard work, and the success of Sinclair Construction Company was the result.

Even though they had attended the same high school, Danny and Babee hadn't met until she'd moved to Two Plantations. They'd sat together on the school bus one morning, and it was love at first sight! And boy, did she love the sight of him!

Babee's smile widened as a lock of his sandy brown hair fell into his eyes, those sexy honey brown eyes that twinkled when he was full of devilment, which he obviously was tonight.

"Hi, good-lookin'!"

Danny Sinclair put the lock on the door, walked over to the counter, leaned over, and kissed his wife. "Nice."

"That all you got, lover boy?"

"Come from behind that counter, and I'll show you what I've got." He sat on one of the stools.

Babee walked around the counter and stepped between his open legs. "I think I see what you've got. And you seem to have it bad." She wrapped her arms around his neck and kissed him, mouth open and tongue seeking, finding, and playing back and forth. Danny pulled her even closer. Babee slowly broke the kiss.

"Play with fire," Danny whispered as he nuzzled her neck. "We're staying here tonight?"

Babee leaned back in Danny's arms. "Why should we? We still have a house don't we?"

"Well, here we'll have some privacy. Something we haven't had at home for a while."

Babee stiffened. "We're not going to get into that tonight, are we?"

Danny pulled her close again. He nibbled on her ear. "Babee, I miss you. I miss this. Don't you?"

Goodness, yes, Babee missed the carefree evenings she and Danny had shared once all the children had moved out. And after his bout with cancer, they had become even closer, even more intimate if that was possible! Oh, the sex games they'd played! They'd discovered a new kind of intimacy, a newer, freer passion, and they had enjoyed making love in every way they could imagine. They'd felt young again. That was until Heather had moved back home. With children in the house, well, that kind of stifled Babee's free love spirit.

She kissed him again. "Yes, I miss it," she whispered against his lips. "But I don't have any clothes here."

Danny laughed. "I packed a bag for us." He nipped her neck as her head fell forward. He reached up and his hand settled on her breast. He squeezed.

"You think of everything," Babee moaned into his ear. She stepped away. "I'm through down here. Let's go upstairs while we both can walk." They headed upstairs and entered the apartment.

"I love the way the old folks thought. I guess their idea of a small town was a few stores and lots of farm land. Putting a place for families to stay above the stores was a great idea. Made sense then; makes sense now." Danny had remodeled the apartment when he had remodeled the store below to accommodate a bakery. "How did it go with Cammy today?"

"Now you ask? Finally your mind is on something other than that piece of equipment in your pants."

"Oh, my mind is still on my, uh, equipment, but it's not going anywhere soon. How *is* Cammy?"

"Devastated. She literally fell apart. Then she seemed to pull herself together and rushed out. She's home crying her eyes out. I called her, and she could barely talk! I'm so worried about her. I think I really screwed up by telling her. And I didn't have time to tell her about Mayor Palmer's wife. Matilda is so young to have cancer; they don't even have any children yet. How he's handling all of that and this town too is beyond me. And now Cammy's so devastated; she probably hates me."

"Hon, she had to know and who better to tell her than her best friend. My goodness, girl! A twenty-six year old secret? It's about time for it to come out. Poor Sug. Man, I feel for *him*. Now that's a real homecoming surprise!"

"I just wish that there was something we could do for them."

Danny sat on the sofa and pulled Babee onto his lap. "There is," he mumbled as he ran his hand under her blouse. "We can be there to support them both. I've always liked Wellington; he was a good cop." He nibbled at her neck and caught her moan in his mouth while his hand caressed her breasts. "You feel good."

"So do you," she sighed as she rubbed her hips along his erection.

"Is this going to be a game night?" she whispered as she slid back and forth against him.

Danny smiled. "Yea. Tonight, the name of the game is the pastry tester. I'm the tester, and you're the pastry." He raised her blouse, lifted up her bra, and placed his lips on her already tightly puckered nipple. He sucked. Hard!

Babee groaned. "I think I like this game. I like it a lot."

7

    Who knew there were so many stars in the sky? Delphine Buckley sighed, a very contented sigh. She was actually standing on the porch of White Oaks. She still could not believe it; she would actually be living in a plantation mansion! And if she was having a hard time believing it, her husband, Timothy Buckley, was in total shock! Oh, yes, they both knew *what* they had purchased from her brother, Ethan, but neither had seen the house before they had arrived a few days ago.

    Well, *she* had seen it few times when she was a very little girl. When she was about four or five, her parents, Felicia and Ethan Dodd, would take the back roads from Pensacola to Jacksonville just to show her and her brother the two plantation houses. They would always pull into the drive of White Oaks, and they'd just sit in the car for a few minutes. Her mom and dad would take the whiskey bottle from under the front seat and pour themselves a drink. They always traveled with a bottle. Sometimes they'd even be drunk by the time they reached their destination.

    Her mom, Felicia Chancy Dodd, was a direct descendant of Camilla Harpson Collins, and she'd hated Two Plantations and all it stood for. But she wanted it, too. All of it! The town, White Oaks, and Peaceful Sands.

So Delphine and Ethan, Jr. would sit and sit and wait and wait while their parents passed the liquor bottle back and forth. Then their mom would point to the larger white house across the road with the sign *Peaceful Sands* hanging on a post at the front of the drive.

"That should have been ours," she'd say bitterly. "How Beaufort Collins could leave his wife and children in *this* dump, I'll never understand. Hell, I hate him! Him and his sorry colored family! The nerve of him! My grandparents said that something wasn't quite right in his head. Had to be crazy! Who would let his wife and children starve in this piece of trash, this little house and forty lousy acres, while he went off and lived with a slave and her brats? Who ever heard of it? Colored people living better than white folk! And they think they're smart, too! Every time any of us tried to sue 'um, they always had some legal paper, some fancy lawyer that kept us from getting what was rightfully ours!"

There'd be some more drinking. Then she'd make all of them get out of the car no matter whether it was day or night, sunny or raining. She'd march them down the drive, Delphine, Ethan, and Ethan, Sr., all the time fuming about the injustice heaped on Camilla Harpson Collins and her offspring. She'd walk back and forth, kicking at any sticks, rocks, or even leaves that were unfortunate enough to be in her way.

Waving her hands, she would scream, "This whole damned town should be ours. Ours you hear? And them damned colored asses across the road stole it from us. And they have the nerve to call us family! We'll never be family with coloreds. I hate 'um all!"

Then she would lean over and get directly in her children's faces. "You can't trust colored people! Can't trust them! They lie and cheat. They'll steal you blind if you don't watch them. They stole your heritage! All this should have been yours one day, and they stole it all. Never trust any colored people! Never!"

Then she'd spit on the drive, march everyone back to the car, have another drink, and then they'd head on to Jacksonville.

Delphine could only remember this happening a few times. She never did understand what made her mother and all the Harpsons so angry about White Oaks. It was really identical to the house across the road, only smaller. She'd liked it. But they'd stopped coming to White Oaks. In fact, they'd stopped traveling. As Delphine grew up, she realized that relatives had stopped inviting them to visit; people just got tired of the way her parents acted when they were drunk, and they were drunk a lot.

Yes, they'd stopped traveling, but it didn't stop Delphine's mom. The older she got, the meaner she got. Every time she got drunk, which was often, she would go on a rampage about colored people. She hated them, her husband hated them, and her children were supposed to hate them. They'd better or she'd make them sorry they'd been born.

"Be glad you were born white," she'd yell. "I want my heritage. I want what's rightfully mine, and I expect you both to marry rich, so we'll be able to hire a fancy lawyer and get what's ours! But you'd better never bring one of those coloreds home. Don't even think it!" And then, if they were lucky, she'd pass out.

Delphine sat on the front steps of White Oaks. Memories of her childhood kept emerging. All through her childhood, she had heard the story of Camilla Harpson and her marriage to Beaufort Collins. It was such a sad story and had shattered her mother's family. They blamed everything they didn't have on black people. The way the Harpsons told the story, when Camilla died, her offspring, Samuel Beaufort Collins, and his sister, Suzanna Belle Collins, had been forced to leave White Oaks. According to the Harpsons, they both managed somehow to go to college and were quite successful in their chosen professions, but they couldn't get over the way their father had treated their mother. And they hated black people.

Neither would live at White Oaks even though it legally belonged to them. What, after all, were forty acres and a little white house when they should rightfully have it all? Eventually, Suzanna had married and settled in Pensacola. Her brother had married and moved to Jacksonville. But neither could let go of the past. They became vindictive and plotted to get even with their father. Together, they'd tried to have him committed, said he was insane, but the judge in Tallahassee threw out the case. Samuel was so angry that on the way back to Jacksonville that night, he lost control of his car, hit an oak tree, and died instantly. He and his wife had no children.

By all accounts, Suzanna had grieved for her brother, and her hatred for her father and his colored family controlled her life and, unfortunately, the lives of her descendents. It became an obsession with each generation. They were all bigots, at least all of the Harpson family that Delphine had known. They hated black people. And that's how Delphine had been raised. She had hated black people, too.

Delphine could hear Tim moving furniture around in the front parlor. Imagine, she thought as she got up from the steps and headed inside. A front parlor!

"Want something to drink?" she called to Tim as she entered the room. Tim was leaning against the huge fireplace that dominated the room, sweat running down his face.

Timothy Buckley grinned at his wife of twenty-seven years as he wiped the sweat from his eyes. Every time he saw her, he knew how lucky he'd been to have found her. She was a beauty with her long, dark brown hair, bluish-green eyes, and creamy white skin. She didn't look like a woman who had had five children. Man, she looked good, and Tim just wanted to stop everything and take her out to the RV for some moonlight R &R.

He blew her a kiss. "I brought the cooler in and put it in the kitchen. You can bring me a beer."

"Your wish is my command." She walked into a kitchen that hadn't been changed in over one hundred years. Tim had put the cooler on the counter by the window and as Delphine looked out of the window, memories kept flooding in.

****

After high school, she couldn't wait to leave for college. She had waited for this day it seemed forever. She was eighteen and could finally make her escape. Ethan had gone to college in New York a couple of years before. She was going to school in New York, too. Her mother thought that they had the best chance of finding a rich husband and a rich wife in New York. After all, that was where all the rich people lived.

      She couldn't wait! Living at home had been hell! Her parents drank more and more, and as they drank, they became abusive to each other and to Ethan and Delphine. They couldn't keep jobs, and they'd even had a fight in the aisle of a grocery store. They'd both been arrested, and Ethan had had to use some of his money he had been saving for college to get them out. Luckily, both Ethan and Delphine were extremely smart and had received full scholarships to college.

      Luck was still smiling on them when Ethan met a girl during his senior year of college, and it seemed like love at first sight. She was from a wealthy ranching family out west, and Ethan couldn't wait to marry her. But no way was he bringing her to Pensacola. He flew his parents to New York for one day to met Marilyn, his fiancé. He picked them up from the airport, took them, including Delphine, to lunch where they were introduced, let them have one drink with lunch, then rushed them back to the airport and sent them home.

      Over lunch, their mom had asked several pointed questions about the wedding, the date, the place, what could they do to help, but Ethan had avoided answering the questions, and his fiancé, Marilyn didn't try to provide any information, either. She probably could tell that Ethan wasn't anxious to have his parents a part of that precious event. They got married the next month. A beautiful occasion.

Delphine was a bridesmaid; their parents were not there.

Delphine had great hopes for Ethan's marriage. Maybe her mom would get what she wanted, and Delphine could live her life the way she wanted to. She had changed so much in the few years that she had been in New York. She had been exposed to so many different people, many of whom were black. Being around them, interacting with them had shown her how wrong her parents had been. People really were not that different. Yes, there were color differences and some cultural differences, but Delphine discovered that those things did not change the essence of a person. She became more accepting, more open-minded. She even had some black friends. Ethan's marriage had to work. She didn't want to marry for money; she wanted to marry of love.

But Ethan's marriage didn't work. He was too much like his parents. He had a drinking problem and a terrible temper. He'd thought that he had married a woman whose money he could control. Turned out that wasn't the case and, boy, did that make him angry. He hit her one time too many. Within two years, they were divorced, and Ethan was back home in Pensacola.

Now the pressure was back on Delphine. The truth was that she was already dating a guy from a very rich family from upper New York. She'd been dating Steve Parkings for about two years; she'd met his family on a number of occasions, and they seemed to like her – a lot.

Unfortunately, she wasn't in love. He was a good, kind person, but there was no passion, no sparks flying when he kissed her. There was no burning need to be intimate with him. He was more like a very good friend, but Delphine did believe that he loved her, so when he proposed, she accepted.

Delphine's parents were excited!

"You won't do us like Ethan, will you?" They had never forgiven Ethan for his wedding and, later, mucking up their chance to get their hands on the land in Two Plantations.

"If you're drinking, we won't bother with a wedding. We'll just go to the courthouse and get married," Delphine had warned.

"Oh, baby, you know we just drink socially," her mom had laughed. "But if you think it'll bother your future family, we won't touch a drop."

So Delphine's mom started planning what she called the wedding of the year. It was going to be the biggest and grandest wedding Pensacola had ever seen, an expensive wedding that her mom and dad could not possibly afford.

"Mom, you have to stop spending so much money," Delphine had chided her on more than one occasion. But her mother just ignored her.

"Why are you worrying about money? Steve is rich. He'll pay for everything. Just tell him that you really want all of this; he'll give it to you. And once we get what's ours from those black Collins, you'll be as rich as he is."

Delphine knew they wouldn't be getting anything but what her mom had inherited and refused to sell, White Oaks Plantation, but she had a pretty good part-time job, so *she* sent money as her mom asked for it and just followed along with all the plans. That is until three weeks before the wedding.

Just three weeks before the wedding. Invitations had been mailed and gifts had started arriving. Just three weeks before the wedding. That's when she'd met Timothy Paul Buckley, a black bank manager from San Francisco. In New York for a meeting of minority bankers, he was having lunch in the coffee shop a block from Delphine's office, the coffee shop where she went every day on her lunch break. When she entered the shop, he was already there, sitting at *her* favorite table. He looked so amazingly sexy, he took her breath away. Confidence radiated from him. He seemed so self-assured, so fearless and proud - like an African warrior, smooth mahogany skin, thick black hair and piercing dark eyes. So sensual, so sexy, so alive! Their eyes met, and she knew. She knew instantly that *this* was the one. This was the man she had been waiting for her whole life – and he was black.

They'd shared a table that day and talked so long that Delphine was late getting back to work. She'd put off a dinner date with Steve and his family that night and met Timothy for a late dinner. The next day, they'd met for lunch, and again she was late back to work. She'd avoided Steve that evening, too, and went to dinner with Timothy again. That night she didn't go home; she'd stay the night with Tim, and they had made the most unbelievable love. By the end of the week, they'd married and were on their way to San Francisco.

Breaking the news to Steve was the hardest thing in the world. He had called her every name in the book besides a child of God, but Delphine accepted everything he'd thrown at her. She'd broken his heart and embarrassed him and his family, but she had found her true love, and she couldn't settle for anything less.

Her parents and brother had disowned her, and all the Harpsons in the universe stopped speaking to her, but Timothy's family was welcoming and accepting of her, and soon she had a new and, and for the first time in her life, loving family.

Twenty-seven years and five children later, she and Tim had decided to retire. They had purchased Ethan's share of White Oaks about six years before. Ethan wasn't really speaking to Delphine, but he was broke and she was the only one who would help him. Their parents had signed White Oaks over to Delphine and Ethan when Ethan had gotten married. It was supposed to be their bargaining tool to use to get Two Plantations. After his divorce, Ethan had spent most of what little money he had suing the owners of Peaceful Sands for what he called his fair share of Two Plantations. Their parents died within two years of each other, bitter and broke, from illness caused by alcoholism. So now White Oaks belonged to Delphine.

Delphine and Tim really had never thought of using the place, but when they'd decided to retire in Florida, they considered Tallahassee because they could travel to Atlanta or Orlando in a few hours, and yet enjoy living in a city that wasn't too large or too small. That's when they remembered White Oaks.

"Do you really want to do this?" Delphine had asked. "It's still the south you know."

Tim had laughed and given her a big, wet kiss. "Times have changed everywhere, honey. Remember, we have our first African-American president! And if it's still the old south, who cares?

We've been happy all these years. We'll be happy where ever we are as long as we're together."

****

That had been six months ago. Now they were in Two Plantations and settling into their new home.

Dephine smiled as Tim called to her.

"Hey, baby, are you lost?"

Delphine took two cold beers from the cooler and walked into the parlor. She found Tim leaning back in the antique sofa.

"This sofa is hard. It's in good condition, but hard. Come sit beside me."

"If it's so hard, why do you want me to sit on it?" Delphine laughingly asked.

"If I have to be punished, you have to be punished, too," Tim replied as he took his beer in one hand and pulled her down onto the sofa with the other.

"Imagine me, a black man, owning a southern plantation house. God does have a sense of humor, doesn't He? It's a neat place, huh? Someone's taken the time to keep it up. That's a relatively new roof up there. It had to cost somebody a pretty penny. I asked Sinclair about it. Said we needed to talk to Cammy Jackson; she'd explain everything. I like Danny Sinclair. Think anybody will stop by this evening? People have been so friendly to us! Wanna bet someone stops by with some food?" He asked as he turned his beer up, swallowed, and sighed. "This is so good! So cold!"

"I'm glad the beer pleases you; it's my pleasure to serve you in your southern mansion." Delphine laughed. "I don't know if we have room for any more southern dinners. There's just no room of it. But I do like meeting the people in this town, and everyone has been really nice. Ms. Moby is a hoot! And I like Danny's Sinclair's ideas for the place. I'd never thought of opening a bed and breakfast. After all, we did come here to retire."

"Yea, it's been running around in my head, too. I guess it's something to think about. Danny mentioned the Cottages at the Lake, but I gather they are only rented to the rich and famous. Right now, there is no place for the average tourist to spend the night in Two Plantations. A B&B could be profitable. I wonder if your *cousin* will let us take a look at the renovations that's been made in her place. Danny didn't seem to think it'd be a problem, but well…….."

"Yes, my side of the family hasn't been very kind to Cammy's. Danny, Ms. Moby and this entire town sing praises about Cammy Jackson, my *cousin*." Delphine laughed with her husband. "I hope they're right. I'm not here to make trouble for her and her family. Ethan and the others did enough of that. I think I really want to be a part of this little town, so I hope she's as accepting as the rest of the people we've met. I would have gone over and introduced myself already, but I understand that she's not feeling well. I can't wait to meet her though. I think she'll like us, don't you? *We've* certainly brought the Collins' family full circle."

8

Serenity Cottage, one of several cottages located at Peaceful Sands, hadn't changed in the three years that Brad Morgan had been coming to Two Plantations. The Cottages at the Lake was the best kept secret in the world, and for a sometimes frustrated artist, it was a perfect haven for rest, relaxation, and inspiration. No reporters. No cameras. Just peace and quiet! And this year, he needed peace and quiet more than he had in the past. The fame and fortune that went along with being a world- renowned artist was both a blessing and a curse, and lately it seemed more curse than blessing.

That's why he needed to come to the cottages. He always looked forward to coming to this charming little town, and he'd painted some of his best work here.

As he drove up to the cottage, he noticed that the small red flag had been placed on the white picket fence, the signal that the cottage was occupied. He always asked for this particular cottage even though there were eight others that surrounded the lake. There was something comforting about the small, white two bedroom cottage with the Kelly green shutters, slanted tin roof, and wide wooden front porch. All of the cottages had detached garages in back; that added to the privacy that the Cottages at the Lake provided for its exclusive clientele.

Each cottage was situated so that the only time renters saw each other was at the lake itself. Otherwise, each cottage seemed to be secluded in the woods, and all were a long way from the main house. In fact, the only time he saw Peaceful Sands was when he turned onto the almost invisible road that took him down to the lake and the cottage. He'd never been to the Serenity Cottage when anyone else was in resident. Or if they were, there was no indication whatsoever. But then they paid a hefty price for seclusion, and it was worth every penny!

Brad removed the key from under the welcome mat on the back steps and unlocked the door to the back porch before moving on to the back door. The back porch was a wall of floor to ceiling windows that could be raised or lowered to let in the fresh air but screened to keep out the bugs. The security alarm went off if someone entered the door or any of the windows. Brad knew he had forty-five seconds to unlock the back door and disarm the system. Peaceful Sands had thought of everything to instill a sense of privacy and security. There were security cameras all over the property, and without the right code, no one could enter the area.

So far there hadn't been a need for security guards. The Cottages at the Lake was the best kept secret in the world! Only a select group of people stayed at the Cottages and not one of them wanted to share the peace, quiet, and seclusion that the Cottages provided. No, for the time being, the Cottages ate the Lake was safe from the outside world.

It only took five minutes for Brad to unload his car. Cammy Jackson, as always, had thought of everything. He knew without looking that the freezer was stocked with his favorite frozen dinners and pizza, and he'd find his favorite beer and wine chilled in the refrigerator. He'd find the tortilla chips that he loved in the pantry along with the dry ingredients he needed to make his own pasta dishes.

She'd changed the décor only slightly, but the changes seemed to brighten the cottage even more – the new curtains were white, bright floral paintings now hung on the walls, a soft woven rug covered the wooden floor boards.

He'd probably take the new mirror off the wall. He didn't need it. He only bothered to look at himself when he had to attend some formal affair. Otherwise, his reflection was a living portrait of his parents. They'd never been able to move out of their hippie years, and his creativity had been nurtured by their beliefs in exploring the inner self. They'd encouraged his artistic nature; in fact, they'd encouraged it more than they had encouraged his formal education. When he painted or sketched or just wanted to be himself, he dressed the way he had when he was young and was exploring the use of colors, learning the feel of a paint brush. He'd put a headband around his long, sun streaked blonde hair, slip into his oversized cotton shirt and baggy jeans, and if the weather permitted, slide his feet into a pair of sandals. He spent so much of his time outdoors that his face was tanned and weathered by the sun, and his physique was superb.

As he looked around, the only thing that was significantly different was the missing bowl of fresh fruit and the vase of fresh flowers. They were Cammy's personal welcome gifts. She'd never missed those in the three years that he'd been coming. Something must be wrong. But he'd give her the same privacy that she afforded him. They'd become friends, sort of, and if she needed to talk, he'd be here. At least for two weeks.

He looked down at the painting that he'd leaned against the sofa. His pulse rate accelerated as it always did when he looked upon *her* face. The Mystery Woman! That's the name he'd given this particular painting, and he carried it with him where ever he went. He'd been offered unbelievable amounts of money for this painting; he'd shown it several times as he'd tried to discover who she was. But he refused to sale it. He didn't need the money, but for some reason he couldn't understand, he needed to find *her*. To make sure she was real and not a figment of his imagination. That red hair, those green eyes, that flawless skin! She had to be real; he and Jody had broken up because of her.

So now he was back in Two Plantations where he'd seen the Mystery Woman for the first and only time. He'd find her again. Just to prove to Jody that he wasn't crazy, that she *was* real and that there was no way that he was in love with a woman he'd only seen once in his life.

"You can't be serious," Jody had screamed when Brad had once again refused to remove the painting from their bedroom. "You are choosing a painting over *me*?! Are you in love with a *painting*? All those paint fumes have finally affected your brains!"

Jody Ashterbee was a pretty, successful daytime soap star, and Brad was never sure when she was really sincere or upset or when she was performing. They'd met at one of his showings.

"Two creative geniuses. We're destined to be together," she'd declared at a late dinner that first night. She was beautiful and sexy and he'd been by himself for a while, so they just sort of hooked up.

He'd fought the living together thing for quite a while, but she'd found a way to stretch the overnight stays into days and sometimes weeks, so he'd reluctantly given in. Being rich had its drawbacks and finding someone he could trust was one of those. He wasn't sure he trusted Jody that much, so he'd made sure that she kept her apartment and that her mail went there instead of his place.

Even before she'd moved in, she'd wanted Brad to remove the Mystery Woman from his bedroom.

"It's like she's looking at us making love. I don't mind an audience if you don't, but I'd rather it be real people, not a spooky painting. And you hold back. It's as if you don't want her to see us together."

"She's not spooky; she's beautiful! And don't be ridiculous. It's just a painting."

"Then move it."

"Can't. And won't!"

"Can't?!! Why not?? It's a painting for God's sake! You don't even know who she is. You've said so yourself. It could be your imagination. Not a real person at all."

They'd had that argument for the three months that they'd lived together.

"I can't take it anymore, Brad. I'm competing with a painting. You won't even leave town without it. How sick is that?!!"

Brad didn't understand it either. He'd seen the Mystery Woman once in a grocery store in Two Plantations. They hadn't spoken a word to each other. She'd been at the register when he'd walked into the store. She'd looked over her shoulder at him and froze. He'd just stared back until he realized that he was standing in the open door. He'd walked over to the vegetable section, and when he turned around, she was gone. He'd rushed out the door behind her, but she had disappeared. No sign of her.

He'd gone back to the cottage and painted her portrait. He hadn't needed her to pose for him. No! Her face was stuck in his mind, and he'd only needed his memory of her to complete the painting in only one night.

He'd taken the painting back to the grocery store to question the owner, but he denied knowing her. Brad knew he was lying, but he understood why. He'd gotten to know many of the residents on his first stay at the Cottages. He walked freely around the town because he didn't worry that someone was going to leak his location to the press; people in Two Plantations were friendly and minded their own business. They didn't talk about anyone else's business either. He'd shown that painting to every store owner in Two Plantations, but he'd gotten the same answer every time. No one would admit to knowing who she was. So when his week was up he'd left, carrying the portrait with him. And he'd slept with it in his bedroom and carried it with him whenever he traveled.

And now he was back. He'd find her this time for sure. He just had to!

Maybe Jody was right! Maybe he was a little in love with the woman in the painting even though that was impossible. He was a romantic at heart, but there was no way he believed in love at first sight! That was his parents' love story, and although he didn't really believe that they actually fell in love the moment they saw each other, *they* believed it. That's what counted for them. But for him? No way!

He just wanted to prove that she existed. That was all. Then he could go on with his life – with or without Jody.

****

The afternoon sun was warm against Megan's arms as she worked the soil in the small garden behind Rachel's Haven. When she'd left Cincinnati, she hadn't known anything about gardening. She'd been raised in a home where someone else cared for the grounds and gardens, and she had married a wealthy politician, Glynn Dover, who had someone else to tend the grounds and gardens. For him she'd been a trophy wife by day and a battered wife at night.

Megan shivered even though the sun was shining brightly. She'd pay for not using enough sun block. With her fair skin, the sunshine was her enemy. But sunburn was nothing compared to the bruises she'd worn for eight years as the wife of the revered mayor of Cincinnati. How shocked and angry everyone had been when he'd finally sent her to the hospital with so many bruises and broken ribs that the hospital staff and police officers could no longer remain silent.

But the anger had not been directed at him, the abuser. Oh, no! Everyone was angry at *her*! *Why did she have to go to the hospital for a few scratches? She'd probably fallen down the stairs. Clumsy fool! Nobody's fault but hers! Glynn Dover was a kind, gentle man. Look what he'd done for the lower income families on the south side! How dare she accuse him of something so terrible! He wouldn't do anything so awful! And he loved his wife so much! Look at all of the pictures in the papers! She was always smiling! Didn't look like a battered wife at all!*

Even now, after six years, she was still fearful of Glynn Dover. He hadn't fought the divorce, didn't want the negative publicity, but he'd threaten her every chance he got - through emails, private detectives, text messages. She'd changed phone and cell numbers and email addresses but he'd always discovered them. Then the state attorney decided that there was enough evidence to charge him with assault and battery. Boy, did that piss him off!

He'd caught her in the parking deck of her apartment building one day. If some of the men in the building hadn't pulled him off of her, who would have killed her. By the time she was released from the hospital, he'd pleaded guilty to a reduced charge of aggravated battery with a $10,000 fine. He'd been sentenced to twelve years in prison with the chance of parole after seven years of good behavior. He'd promised to finish the job on Megan when he got out. So she'd left town, moved to a little town in South Dakota, gotten a job, and gone into therapy. But a private detective had found her there with a message from Glynn.

She'd felt so helpless and hopeless. Her ex-husband was just too powerful, and she'd had nowhere else to go. Until her therapist told her about Rachel's Haven and Camilla Jackson. Coming to Two Plantations and Rachel's Haven was the best thing that had happened to Megan. For the first time in years, she felt free and safe!

And Rachel's Haven had given her a new purpose in life. She'd taken over or at least had been given the management of the haven where she'd worked hard to help Cammy update the technology and the security systems for both the cottages and the haven. She also helped Cammy decide who would best benefit by coming to the haven and if the Haven couldn't help them, she always found another safe place for them to go.

The barn itself was a form of security. It looked like a barn, a real barn. Looking at it, no one would believe that inside it contained all of the features of a home including seven small bedrooms and three full baths. And a person would really have to come down into the property to even see it. It couldn't be seen from the highway, and there was no drive or road that led to it. It was isolated, and even the visitors to the cottages were not aware that the barn even existed.

She'd lived in the renovated barn with the other residents of the Haven until Cammy had decided that she, and the counselors who sometimes spent the night, needed a space of their own. So Cammy had had a smaller replica of the barn built that had three bedrooms and three full baths.

That had been five years ago! It was a move she'd never regretted. Rachel's Haven was home to her now. Cammy paid her a very generous salary that she had nothing to do with but save and invest. She loved what she did, and she got the chance to help other women who had been abused. She was finally happy, and life had been good until she'd made the mistake of going to the grocery store without her disguise.

  She reached up to touch her flaming red hair and then thought better of it. She'd be washing it anyway, but there was no need to add more dirt to it. Her hair had always gotten her in trouble. Glynn had said that it was her hair that had drawn him to her. Later he'd said it was a whore's hair, and that made her a whore. He'd ordered her to not just color it, but he even went further and ordered her to shave her head. When she'd refused, he beat her. Yea, her hair was trouble.

  And one year ago when she'd gone to the store and hadn't worn her brown wig to cover all of that red hair, it had gotten her in trouble again. That day she hadn't worn the wig or the brown contacts to hide her emerald green eyes! After all, she was just going to the store, and most of the people of Two Plantations had now seen her with and without her disguise. She knew she could trust them. They were another layer of her security. But the moment that artist had seen her, she knew there'd be trouble. And she was right!

  The crazy man had painted her portrait that night! Thank God for the people of Two Plantations. He'd shown that painting to everyone in town. But he was out of luck! No one in this little town was going to tell him anything.

  Now he was back! Megan hoped that he had burned that painting. If Glynn ever saw it, he might be able to find her. But she'd never let him touch her again. She was stronger now. No man would ever again hit her and live to tell about it!

9

Caleb Wellington had finally returned home, and his sisters were trying to fix him up already. He couldn't believe it! Two days in Tallahassee, and he knew that he had been introduced to at least thirty women. No joke! Two days! Could a city the size of Tallahassee have so many single women? And did they really all want to meet him?! His six sisters were on a mission. Get Caleb hitched. Well, it wasn't going to happen!

When that plane had landed and he had seen all of his family waiting for him, well, Caleb didn't have words to express how he felt. His six sisters, his older brother, Milton, Jr. and his wife, and as many of his brothers-in-law, their children and grandchildren that could make it had come with Candice to the airport to welcome him home. It felt good. In fact, it had felt great. He was the baby boy of the family, and they were all so proud of him. He could tell.

They had left the airport in a caravan of cars headed to his mom's house; his oldest sister, Amelia, lived there now. It was now a ranch styled house that sat on an acre of land just outside of town on Thomasville Road. They had all been born in the first little house that their father had built, delivered by a midwife, Ma Betty Lee. It had been a two bedroom house with an outhouse out back. His dad had never been good at much except getting children, so the floor boards in the house had had gaps in them, the windows were drafty, and the ceiling was warped. In the winter it was too cold, and in the summer it was always too hot. The electricity was shaky at best, and the four older girls and his brother often had to do their homework by kerosene lamps.

His dad, Milton Wellington, never could hold a job long, so his mom had had to take in ironing for many of the wealthy white families in the area. Totally unreliable, his dad had never been a very good provider for his family.

But Caleb's mom, Sue Ellen, had been a very smart, Christian woman. She'd made sure that they all attended Sunday school and church every Sunday. Most of their Sunday clothes had been 'hand me downs' from the families that she worked for. She was also a hard worker, and she knew how to pinch a penny. Using every penny she could stow away, she'd managed to keep life insurance policies on everyone in the family. She'd always believed in insurance, and she probably knew that she'd have to bury her husband some day.

And she'd been right. He'd had a fatal heart attack at one of his girlfriends' house. Caleb's mom had given him a decent funeral and then used the rest of the insurance money to have a Jim Walter's home built right next to the old home. As soon as the new house was finished, she had the old house torn down and hauled off.

"Well, that's the end of that," she'd laughed as she watched the truck loaded with the wood from the old house drive away.

109

"God's really got a sense of humor. Milton finally put us in a decent house! Ain't that something! Children, that's the past driving away," she'd said as she waved the truck away. "Now you all can start livin' in the present. And so can I." Every time that Caleb came home, he remembered that day. He marveled at the fact that his mom had raised eight children alone; his father hadn't stayed around the house long enough to help. He missed her and her words of wisdom so much, especially at family gatherings like the one they had had the day he came home.

Now here he was. Hadn't been home for two full days, and he was attending another lunch at another sister's house with all of his sisters and six of their friends - one for each sister, all women. And his sister, Faye, had the nerve to mention a dinner that evening. He knew what he needed to do. What he had to do! Caleb was going to run, head out of town. Hell, there was an empty apartment over the police station in Two Plantations. That's where he would be staying once he officially became chief of police there any way, so he might as well make use of it now. Now was as good a time as any to get to know the town. Now! Right Now!

He was surrounded by women at a dining room table, and he was the whole dinner. Only he wasn't turkey; he was chicken and he was about to fly the coop.

Across the table, Ms. Jacqueline Pettigrew smiled and licked her lips like she was looking at a piece of prime beef instead of a man. She was a petite African American accountant with a really fine body, Caleb had to admit, and a pretty young face,

110

but her teeth needed a little work. He was supposed to remember her, but he couldn't. He guessed that she remembered him though.

"Sugar," Jacqueline said almost purring like a cat. "It had to be so hard raising a daughter all by yourself. So dedicated! And you never remarried? It must have been tough on you. I mean, when you dated and everything. I hear she's a smart girl. Like you. I bet she's close to her daddy. And I hear you're just like your daddy! How many more children do you have?"

"I don't believe in leaving babies all over town," Caleb replied sharply. He hated it when someone implied he was like his dad. Then he forced himself to smile at her. It must have worked because she gave him a big smile back. Yea, she really needed to do something with those teeth.

A hand tapped him on his shoulder. "So, Caleb. I can call you Caleb, can't I?" asked the fiftyish blonde professor sitting to his right. He thought her name was Samantha Cole. If Caleb remembered correctly, she taught business at one of the universities in town. His sisters made sure he had his pick - from a bank manager, accountant, teacher, and whatever profession they could think of in any race, color, height, and size.

"Yea, sure." Caleb gave his sister, Velma, a look. An *I'm going to get you for this* look. She just smiled and took a bite of her salad.

"So, it must have been very exciting being a federal marshal and all. I mean, did you wear a uniform? And now you'll be the new police chief over in Two Plantations. I bet you look really sexy in

111

a uniform," she leaned close to him as she placed her hand on his thigh.

"Whoa!" Caleb jumped up from the table. "Sorry! Gotta take this call!"

"I didn't hear a phone," Velma said. She didn't look too happy.

"Vibrate," Caleb replied as he headed into the small hallway close to the front door and opened his cell phone. He pretended to be listening and couldn't believe it when he glanced over his shoulder and saw all six sisters standing in the hallway glaring at him.

"You'd better not," Velma whispered.

"Listen, I'm sorry," Caleb whispered to them. "Gotta go. Hate to leave during your lunch, Velma, but duty calls. A meeting I forgot in Two Plantations."

"We know you're lying, Caleb. You never were good at it. You know you're going to pay for this. We'll get you good," Patience, his youngest sister whispered as she looked back over her shoulder at the women still sitting at the table.

"I wouldn't do this, you know if............."

"Make your escape while you can, Sug. Come on, give us a kiss and make it quick. But you will pay, my dear, you will pay," whispered Amelia as Caleb gave each of them a quick peck on the cheek.

Caleb couldn't get out of the house fast enough. And he wasn't going back to Amelia's to get any of his clothes any time soon. He'd stop at the mall to pick up a few things on his way out. He'd go to Two Plantations. Get a feel for the place. There was no one *there* trying to fix him up.

****

State Road 373 hadn't changed that much over the years. Huge oak trees still lined both sides and formed a canopy over the road; it was a beautiful and relaxing drive. Caleb drove slowly into Two Plantations. He was driving his '65 Mustang, the same one he had driven to this town so many years ago. But today was one of the few times he had been to Two Plantations in the day time. Most of his trips out this way had been made in the dead of night, and there hadn't been any street lights back then. Now there were street lights from the welcome sign at one end of the town to the welcome sign at the other end.

He rolled to a stop in front of the telephone booth at the edge of town. Hell, it looked like the same booth he'd used all those years ago. Then it had stood all alone, no buildings close to it at all, secluded, isolated from the rest of the town. A person could make a call from that phone booth, and no one would have even noticed back in the day. Caleb had done it a lot. But it was obvious that Two Plantations had grown some in the years that Caleb had been gone. Now a new police station had been built on the empty lot where the phone booth stood, and a street light stood right between the booth and the station. No privacy now. Thank goodness for cell phones and ipads!

The new police station had been built using the same architectural style as the other buildings that lined the main street. It must have cost the town a pretty penny to match those bricks to the bricks on the older buildings. The station itself actually took up one block. Of course the block was a small block, but the station was impressive for a small town. Caleb couldn't wait to see the inside.

Caleb pulled into a park in front of the station. He eased his long frame from under the wheel and walked over to the patrol car that was parked there. Nice. Had all the bells and whistles! Pretty good for a little town like Two Plantations, but already Caleb was beginning to get the feeling that Two Plantations might be full of surprises.

He had been trained to know his surroundings, so he knew the moment Chief Roscoe Miller had walked out of the station and headed toward him.

"Nice patrol car, isn't it?" the chief asked as he walked up to the car.

"Sure is. I am impressed." Caleb leaned against the car. Chief Roscoe looked at least ten years younger than his seventy-seven years. He looked like he could have worked for another good five. If that's what living in Two Plantations did, he was glad that he'd be living here. It obviously breathed new life into people! People aged well.

"Welcome to Two Plantations, Sug. I hope you don't mind me calling you that. I've known you all your life. Don't worry. I won't embarrass you in front of folks. Just feels comfortable calling you how I know you best. You look just like your daddy. Never knew what your mom saw in him. She was a real beauty! All the guys wanted to marry her. But your dad, Milton, got the prize. He had to have some good in him; it was something more than his looks that your mom saw. Your dad, he just loved women too much. It was a weakness he couldn't overcome. Hope you've forgiven him."

"Well, first of all, I don't mind you calling me Sug, sir. I'm Sug or Sugar to all my family, and they

114

don't care if I'm embarrassed or not. I'm good with it. My mom called me Sugar because she said I was such a sweet baby. The name stayed with me. It's served me well; the women loved it. Anyway, it's who I am. And yes, I stopped being angry at my father a long time ago. My mother wouldn't let us hold onto it. Said the anger would just eat us up and take away our real chance for happiness." Caleb looked up and down the main road. "I'm glad to be here."

"Can't wait to get started? Or are you running from all of those women you sisters are trying to fix you up with?" Roscoe asked with a grin.

"Boy, news travel fast! And yea, I'm running fast from that, but not to start working before my official start date. I did think this would be a good time to get to know the town and the people who live here. By the way sir, I know you said that your deputy wasn't interested in the job of police chief here, but are you sure? I need to know who I'm working with."

"Yes, news does travel fast down here. You know black folk. Haven't forgotten your history have you, son? During our slavery days, drums and songs carried news to our people from one plantation to another." Roscoe chuckled. "Now, it's called gossip, and we use the telephone and cell phone! And don't worry about Deputy Simmons. He likes being a deputy and going home to that pretty, young wife of his. You know you get to hire another deputy? Well, Simmons is going to ask for the late night shift. That's the shift his wife works at the hospital in Tallahassee. That'll give them more time to spend together. Naw, he doesn't want to be chief. He's a

115

good, dedicated officer of the law. You'll like him. Come on in the station and share a cup of coffee with me. We can talk better in air conditioning."

"Damn! Who designed this place?" Caleb couldn't believe his eyes when he walked through the door. "This station is state-of-the-art."

"Yap! The town did us good. Got everything we asked for and more. We had a good committee. Cammy Jackson chaired that particular committee. Remember her? Well, anyway, you'll find that the residents of this little town have a lot of say-so about what happens here. They decided that it was time for a new station. Cammy Jackson, you said you knew her some? Well, Cammy formed a committee, contacted Danny Sinclair, hired an architect in Tallahassee, and well, you see the results. The Foundation paid for it all. Town had a new courthouse built a couple or so years ago around the corner on Moss Road. Even paved the road. The Foundation paid for that, too. Cammy heads the Foundation. You did know Cammy back in the day, right?"

Caleb hesitated. "I think so. If not, I'm sure I'll meet her soon."

Did the Chief know about those late night rides to Two Plantations that he'd taken all those years ago? Lord, he hoped not, but he just knew that his face had turned some shade of red.

"Don't know how soon," Roscoe replied. He gave Caleb a sharp look. "She's been under the weather for a couple of days now. That's really unlike her. She had several engagements that she cancelled at the last minute. Not like her at all. But she'll be back on her feet real soon. Never known the girl to be sick in the bed. Good girl, that one. So, that cup of coffee?"

"Before that coffee, sir. The apartment up stairs. Is it all right if I go ahead and move in now?"

"Scared to go back to Tallahassee for a while?" Roscoe grinned.

"Not scared exactly. Just don't need the pressure right now, sir."

"Go head, the apartment is yours as long as you want it. Both Simmons and I used the one over the old station from time to time, but we hadn't used this one yet. Brand new. Go get your stuff. Bet you bought some new digs. Didn't want to go back to Amelia's in case they caught you in time for dinner, am I right? Sisters can be hell, can't they? Miss mine, though. You treat them girls good. They just want to see you happy. Good girls, all of them."

Caleb was glad to discover that the apartment had two entrances. After Caleb collected his few bags from his car, Chief Roscoe directed him to a discreet staircase located inside near the rear of the station. He would also be able to park in the back of the station and use an outside staircase that also led up to the apartment.

"I'll be down in a minute, sir. Just want to put my things away."

"Take your time, son. I'm not going anywhere for a couple weeks, at least."

The door wasn't locked, and Caleb walked into a very modern, and as he discovered under closer inspection, very plush two bed room, two bath apartment. It looked like it had been designed for the rich and famous, not a small town police chief.

The living room, dining room, and kitchen had an open concept design. The apartment was tastefully decorated and had everything a person would need: silverware, pots, towels, linen, even soap. Whoever had done the decorating had had a man in mind - muted browns and beiges with just a hint of blue in the accent pieces. The masculine décor was pleasing to the eye. Caleb liked it. The sun entered through the pane glass windows that were designed to see out but not to look in, just like those downstairs in the station. However, up here, he'd be able to open the windows if he wanted to. He liked the safety precautions. Caleb liked the whole set up a lot. He was impressed. Very impressed. Someone had thought of everything.

The kitchen had stainless steel appliances and a large counter top with lots of cabinets. Down the hall he found the hall bathroom and the two bedrooms. The larger bedroom had an attached bath. Yes! This was going to be great. It was fixed up like a fancy bachelor pad. Good deal! Caleb wondered who had decorated the place. The chairperson of the committee, maybe?

He went back down to the station. Chief Roscoe was pouring them both a cup of freshly brewed coffee. "Let's have a seat down here at the front counter for a minute and talk over this cup of coffee; then I'll give you a quick tour of this here station. Love this view. I'm going to miss it."

Caleb gave Chief Roscoe a pointed look. He hoped it did not reflect the sympathy he felt. He knew what it was like to leave a job he loved even though he'd been ready to go.

"Sir, you're welcome in this station any time you want. You can volunteer some hours, work with us part-time, or simply come and keep us company. You're not being replaced. Know that. That would be impossible. You're just helping a man find his way home. And I thank you."

"Thanks, Sug. And don't get me wrong. Me and the wife are looking forward to my retirement. Give us a chance to do a little traveling. Already got some plans with the kids. But I've been doing this for so long, retirement will take a little getting used to. Now, back to business. You know that the sheriff department patrols this area of the county regularly, two or three times during the late night shift. Might seem a bit much for our little town, but you know these gangs have started venturing out into smaller surrounding towns."

"We, the Feds, have been watching the trend now for several years. Counties like Leon crack down right away; others, unfortunately, wait too long before major damage is done."

"I know what you mean. Most of the smaller surrounding counties have been having a lot of trouble with them because of that, so we work closely with the sheriff's department. Found some marijuana planted north of town a few years ago. Got rid of them right quick! Caught the fellows trying to harvest the stuff during the wee hours of the morning. Hadn't had a problem since, but we don't let up. And with Smitty opening up his café and selling alcoholic drinks, well that's gonna add a new dimension to our little town."

"Man, when I was a young man, we always knew not to come to Two Plantations with any foolishness. Shoot, back then you *were* the police force. Then when you got Simmons, well, no speeding down this little road!"

"Yea, we've had a good ride, Simmons and I. And we were rewarded. Look at this building! And we really owe it all to Cammy Jackson's leadership. She's dedicated her life to this town. Wonderful girl! Guess you haven't seen her in a while huh?"

Caleb's training clicked into place. He hadn't been an outstanding federal marshal for nothing. He knew when someone was trying to get information from him, but he had trained his face and voice not to reveal anything. Too bad he hadn't trained his heart. Hearing her name over and over again was driving him crazy.

He looked Roscoe straight in the eye. "I believe that she is around my younger sister's age. I was running the streets pretty hard back then if you recall. I didn't have time for nice little girls. But the apartment upstairs. It makes a great bachelor pad."

"Huh, well, Cammy hadn't planned it that way. She figured the new person, male or female, might have a family and would need some place to stay until they got settled. If it's too dark or something for you, I'm sure she……"

"No, no, no, no, no! It's good as it is." The last thing he needed was Cam Jackson prowling around in the rooms where he lived.

Roscoe gave him another one of those penetrating looks. "Just so you know, that place upstairs is pretty much sound proof. I mean, you can hear some outside noise, 'cause it's not natural not to hear some street noise, birds singing, that sort of thing. But you won't hear any noise from down here.

120

That kinda bothered Danny though. Thought the chief might need to know if someone was breaking in or something while he or she was upstairs and the officer on duty was out on patrol, so Danny and the architect put their heads together and installed a system where you can hear what's happening in the main area of the station when you're in the apartment. You can't hear anything from the cells. I'm sure you know why. But from in here, yes. You can turn the system on and off. Might not use it at all, but it might come in handy."

"Danny Sinclair. That's Babee's husband, right?"

"Yes. He built this place. He has this hugely successful construction company. Does work all over the southeast. Even these hard times haven't really hurt him much, and he hasn't had to lay off any of his employees. Look across the street. That's Babee's bakery there on the corner. She has the best cinnamon rolls in the state. You got to try them." Caleb knew that look by now. "So you remember Babee, huh? Strange that. She's younger than Cammy that you don't remember, but they've been best friends since high school."

Caleb drained the last of his coffee. "Ready for that tour now, sir."

10

During the tour of the station, Deputy Bob Simmons came in.

"Glad to have you aboard," Simmons said as he shook Caleb's hand. "Heard nothing but good things about you. I remember you when you were on the force in Tallahassee. I knew then that you'd go far in this business."

"Thanks. And I'm glad you're staying on. I'm going to need your expertise as I work my way into the community."

"Oh, I wasn't going anywhere unless the new chief didn't want me. Me and my wife, we like it here. Don't want to live anywhere else." He laughed a little self-consciously. "New wife. Third one, you know. But this one's going to work. Not every woman's cut out to be married to a law officer, but Effie knows what to expect. We've lived together for a few years now. I wanted to get married right away, but she wanted me to know that she was in it for the long haul. We got married last year." He grinned.

Caleb slapped him on his back. "Three times, uh? Brave man! Brave man!"

Simmons finished walking through the cell block with them, and Caleb could tell that there was no envy there. Simmons loved what he did, but he didn't want to be chief. Caleb felt that they would work well together.

Once the tour was completed, Caleb excused himself, moved his car to the back of the station, and walked down the street to the grocery store. He needed some food for his apartment. He figured he'd probably have to stock up on the things he really wanted the next time he went to Tallahassee, but the little store should have the basics.

He had done his homework on the town, so he knew that there were as many white residents as blacks living in Two Plantations during any given census. At least half of the businesses were owned by whites, all of whom lived in Two Plantations. Most people, however, assumed that the town was like Eatonville outside of Orlando, an all black community. But the founders of this town, Beaufort and Sadie Mae Collins, hadn't wanted that. They had wanted a town for everyone, and they'd gotten it.

Caleb opened the door to the store and a little bell tinkled. Caleb smiled. Small town USA. Then his smile grew wider as he stepped inside and looked around. Another surprise.

"Welcome to Two Plantations, Chief Wellington," called Michael Preston as he came around the counter to shake Caleb's hand.

"Not chief yet," replied Caleb as he responded to the firm handshake. "Just call me Caleb. Nice place, Mr. Preston. Well stocked." Caleb walked over to the cases that held the prime beef and various selections of fresh seafood.

"Just call me Mike. Most folk do. Surprised at the store, huh? Most people are when they stop in. As you look around you'll see that we do carry all of the best of the old fashioned candies and cookies that people expect to find when they stop at a small town grocery store. And we do want to please the tourist. But we stock for the residents of Two Plantations. I'll have you know that they expect the best, and my wife and I try to deliver. The seafood comes in fresh every two days and the beef, pork, and chicken every three. Something really special you want, we can get it. Just give us enough notice. And we sell most everything else that you find in the big stores in Tallahassee. We just don't stock as much. No need to. What can I help you with today?"

    Caleb grabbed the steak that had caught his eye, a potato for baking, some salad fixings, eggs, milk, butter, bread, sugar, and coffee. "This is all I need for dinner tonight and breakfast. I'll be back tomorrow to stock up for the week."

    Caleb paid his bill and stepped out into the warm southern evening. He had missed the South. He had gotten use to the cold winters of D.C., but he had always missed this. He hadn't realized how much he had missed the comforting heat of the winter's day and the chill in the evening air. Oh, and the clean, fresh air! Yea, he was glad to be back. He walked the short distance to the station, went up the back stairs to the apartment, and let himself in.

    He wished that Roscoe hadn't told him about Cam's hand in decorating the apartment. He could feel her presence everywhere. While he cooked his dinner, he wondered if she had placed the pots and dishes in the cabinets. Did she touch them herself? He could see her sitting in one of the dining chairs at the table to be sure each was level. Did she sit on the sofa? Which spot? Was he going crazy? Hell yes!

    The steak was really good! Caleb finished eating, washed his dishes and pots, and then flopped on the sofa and flipped on the flat screen TV that had been hung on the wall above the small gas fireplace. The master bedroom also had the same set up with the TV and fireplace. Had Cam thought of that, too? Had she lain on the bed in the master to be sure the TV was positioned correctly? When he went to bed would he lay where she had? Yes, he was crazy! Good grief! Why had he taken this job?

Caleb's cell phone rang.

"Hello, daddy. Boy, are you in trouble!"

"So you've heard. Are they really mad?" He really didn't want his sisters angry with him; he just wanted them to stop trying to fix him up with anybody.

Candice laughed. "You know they'll forgive you anything. They just don't want to see you by yourself. I don't either. I never understood why you never married again. I could understand when I was little, but by the time I was in middle school, well, I kinda thought you would."

"You're not trying to join my sisters are you? Trader!"

"No, dad, I'm on your side, whatever side that is. But I'm so busy with classes right now, and I know that you moved back home to be close to me. I just don't want you to be alone."

"I'm good, Candice. I *wanted* to move home. I would have come back if you had gone to school in D.C. or Texas. And then we would have seen each other even less than we'll see each other now. I'm so proud of you and want you to follow your dreams. I'd be mad if you let your grades drop just to hang out with me. Don't worry about me. I'm fine." Just going crazy, Caleb thought as he wondered if he could really smell the perfume that Cam used to wear. He knew he was losing his mind.

"Just think about dating some. It can't hurt. I gotta go now; I have a study session. Love you. By the way, Aunt Amelia said to remind you that you're gonna pay; you're *really* gonna pay." Candice laughed as she ended the call.

Caleb spent another two hours looking at nothing on the TV before he decided to call it a night. When he entered his bedroom, his eyes fell on the stack of CDs he had unpacked. He rummaged through them until he found the one he was looking for. He checked to see if the system had a CD player. Yea, she or someone had thought of everything. He hesitated before he put in the CD and stretched out across the bed. As the sweet sounds of *"I've Been Loving You Too Long"* filled the room, he flipped over on his back and covered his face. He couldn't understand why he kept torturing himself with that song. After Maggie died, it'd become his anthem. Cam! God, what was he going to do about Cam?

Caleb fell asleep thinking about Cam and his first full day in Two Plantations. He'd be up early for his first run of the day; it was a perfect way to get ready. If he was lucky he'd get in another run in later in the day. Then he knew that he'd spend the rest of the day meeting some of the good people of Two Plantations. And he hoped that sooner rather than later he'd meet Cam's son. At last!

11

"Cammy, it's time to give up the pity party! You've been in that house for two solid days! It's time to come out now. This town needs you! And turn that damned song off!" Babee could hear Otis Redding playing in the background.

Even over the phone, Cammy could hear the deep frustration and worry in Babee's voice.

"This shouldn't be happening to me. Finally, I'm ready to get on with my life, and he comes back! How could he?!!"

"Just because he's going to be the chief here doesn't mean he's back in your life. That can't happen unless you let him back in."

Cammy sighed. "I don't want him in; I want to move on. But how can I now? Would you believe that Langston Mitchell called? Twice!"

"Yes! You go, Langston! Did you talk to him, or did you just let the phone ring as you've been doing with everybody else?"

Cammy sighed again. "I wasn't going to, but I didn't think it was quite right, you know. To just let him keep calling. So I called him back."

"And? Do you have a date?" asked Babee.

"I guess I sounded sick or something, so he said he'd call me later in the week. But Babee, how can I go out with him now?! It's all going to come out! How can I show my face? I'm so ashamed!"

"Of what? Something that happened twenty-six years ago? I don't think there's anyone in this town who hasn't made some mistake." Babee gave a short laugh. "That's why most people settle here. This town gives them the chance to put the mistakes behind them and get a fresh start."

"But my mistake affects my children! How can I tell them? How can I face them?"

"Cammy, first of all, Kim was *not* a mistake. You and I both know that you and Caleb were in love. She was conceived out of that love, and she has been loved all of her life. Your children are adults. Will they be hurt that you didn't tell them before now? Maybe. Will they be mad with you or ashamed of you? Well, I doubt that! Trust them to be the adults you've raised them to be."

"But what about Caleb? What will he think? After all, I kept his daughter away from him. He'll never forgive me!"

"Do you want him to?"

Silence. "That's not what I mean. Have you seen him yet?"

"Girl, I thought you'd never ask! He's still gorgeous! Age has only made him sexier than he was when he was young! You should see the women! They are all over him. I understand that he came to town early just to get away from the single women in Tallahassee!"

"Humph! He can't look that good! After all, he has to have had his sixty-fourth birthday by now."

"Get real, girl! You still look great! Why can't he? And believe me, he does." Babee sighed, and Cammy could hear the compassion and concern in her voice. "Look, Cammy, there's not going to be a secret for long. Everyone that knows Kim will see the resemblance. She looks just like him. And he has a daughter from his marriage; I've seen her picture. She and Kim look like twins."

"Oh, my God!"

"You can't hide, Cammy. He's meeting just about everyone in town, introducing himself. Which means he'll meet Smitty at some point, and he'll get to the clinic soon. It's really out of your hands now, so you'll need to talk to Sug and the kids. Soon! But there's something else going on. Matilda Palmer has breast cancer! I'd planned to tell you the other day, but you know what happened there."

"Oh, no! *That's* why Frank has been calling. I thought he'd seen Caleb, so I told him I had a bad headache and just needed some time alone. I've avoided talking to him or Kim since. Boy, what a self-centered jerk I've been!"

Cammy's heart ached. Breast cancer! Cammy's mom, Abigail, had died from breast cancer. And that's why Frank had become an oncologist.

"Well, as your best friend, I have to agree with you on your personal observation! I know you've got problems of your own, but you've got Collins blood running through you. So straighten that backbone of yours and do what you do so well. The Palmers need your support right now."

"Don't I get at least a little sympathy?"

"Absolutely not! You've had twenty-six years to wallow in self pity! Now it is what it is, Cammy! You've never let hard times get the best of you. You've raised two wonderful kids! Let them show you that their adults! You've really managed this town and all of the other things that go on at Peaceful

129

Sands. And you've done it carrying this secret all these years because that's the way you wanted it. Now, Sug, Kim, and Frank will know, and believe me, things will not be as bad as you think. So there's my sympathy. But Matilda needs support, not sympathy. Get moving!"

"You're sounding more and more like Jazzy! What's gotten in to you lately?"

"I could have lost him," Babee's voice had become as soft as a whisper. "I could have lost my husband. Things had gotten really, really tense between Danny and me. I was choosing my adult daughter over my husband!"

"Surely Danny didn't expect you to do anything else, did he? After all, she *is* your daughter!"

"And *his*. We've had the biggest arguments over this. Do you really know what *you* would do if you and Caleb had raised children into adulthood? Would you choose them over your husband? Let me ask you what Danny asked me. *What are you going to do when she moves on, either back to her husband or meets someone else? Are you going to be one of those mothers who float between her children so she won't be lonely?* And he was right. She *will* go on with her life, and I need to go on with mine. I choose to go on with Danny in it."

"Oh, Babee! I didn't realize that things had gotten so serious between the two of you!"

"I couldn't talk about it then. In fact, I only came to a true realization of what was most important to me a couple of nights ago." She laughed. "Good sex will do that for you! So I'm telling you this because your children *are* adults. They may be angry, they may be hurt, but they *will* go on with their lives.

You've got to go on with yours. I say all of this with love."

"Okay! Okay! I still really want to hide away from the world for a little while longer, but I know what I need to do. Matilda means a lot to me, and I won't let her down. I've got a couple of calls to make, and then I'm going visiting this evening."

"Scared you'll run into Sug if you go to the Palmers during the day?"

"Hell, yes! Terrified! But that's not why I'm going over later. I'm going to cook up some chicken and rice to take them for dinner, and then I'm staying to eat with them."

"I figured as much, so I've already provided the dessert. Danny and I will be eating with you. I knew you'd cook too much!"

"You were really sure of yourself, weren't you?"

"I was sure I knew Sadie Camilla Smith Jackson. Make your calls and I will see you tonight!"

Cammy hung up and leaned back. Jeez, where had she been? Babee's marriage had been in trouble, and John Palmer had been going through this medical issue with Matilda! This all seemed so unreal, but it really was life. Reality! People had problems. She was no different. But they all work them out, and she would work hers out, too.

She picked up the phone again and dialed. Brad Morgan answered on the second ring.

"Brad, this is Cammy Jackson. Was everything okay at the cottage? I'm sorry about the fruit and flowers. I'll make it up to you before you leave, I promise."

"Hi, Cammy. Everything was perfect as usual. Don't worry about anything, but you can always make it up with a dish of your chicken and rice."

"Sure. Maybe I can cook you lunch or dinner before you leave. I just wanted to check on you and say 'welcome back'."

"I'm glad to be back. And painting already."

"Great! I can't wait to see what you've done. I'll call you soon!"

She hung up and called Megan at Rachel's Haven.

"Megan, it's Cammy. I'm not checking on Rachel's Haven. I'm checking on you."

Megan sighed. "I'm good. After all, I knew Brad Morgan was coming back, so I was prepared. He's been here for two days, and so far he hasn't been showing that Mystery Woman portrait to anyone. Maybe he burned it. I hope so. He walks around the town as if he belongs here."

"And this displeases you because….?" Cammy tried to hide the laughter in her voice. She was glad to have something else to talk about. Something other than Caleb.

"You're fishing, Cammy, and that's not like you."

"I'm sorry. You're right. It's none of my business, but I've been curious every since last year. I can't figure out what happened in that store a year ago. You do know that your safety is the most important thing for me. If you feel threatened by Brad, we don't have to have him back at the Cottages at the Lake."

"Not have him *back*? Why would you do that? I mean, no, I didn't feel threatened by him. Shoot, Cammy, let me give it to you straight. I've wanted to tell someone. When Brad walked into that store and our eyes met, a wave of desire washed over me like a tidal wave. It felt both sinful and deliciously right. I'd never felt that way before, and if anyone was in danger, it was Brad at that moment. I ran out of there because my body and mind was completely out of control, and I've promised myself that no one or nothing would control me again. So there!"

Cammy couldn't hold her laughter any longer.

"I'm sorry, Megan, but you're only, what, thirty-five or six? Feeling desire is natural. Now at sixty, well, it's a little freaky."

"So who are you hot for? Do I know him? And it'd better not be Brad! I can't have him, but he's still got to be available for me to lust after!" Megan laughed. "But to be serious, Cammy, somehow I've got to let him know that that painting could put me in real danger. I know that it's time I shared my history with you......"

"We never pry, and you know that, Megan. I've done too much of that today."

"No, it's time. I want to make Two Plantations my forever home. It's time you really knew me. I know that right this minute isn't the right time. I know you're as worried about Matilda as I am. But later, we'll talk, okay?'

"Anytime. I'm putting something on the stove for the Palmer's dinner tonight."

"Make enough for me, and I'll bring some the wine and grape juice that we make here at the Haven."

"Sounds great! I'm sure you'll have on a disguise, but we'll know you. You'll be the one carrying the wine. Who knew that Matilda's gift for makeup and disguise would be so beneficial to the residents of the Haven. Now the women can shop and visit around town without being recognized. There's no fear that an abusive husband would recognize one of them even if he passed his wife or ex-wife on the street. She taught us so much. Now we have the chance to give something back to her. See you there!"

This time Cammy headed to the kitchen. It felt good to be doing something other than moping!

Later that evening there was a big crowd in the Palmer's house. And since Cammy knew the residents of Two Plantation, she'd cooked enough for everyone. She'd spent a great deal of time talking to John and Matilda in their study. She hadn't been surprised to learn that Frank would be in the operating room during the surgery, and she was relieved to know that it was stage one cancer which meant that the chances for a complete recovery were even better.

Brad had even shown up with a painting for the couple. "If ever you're in need, I can always sell it for you. It'll give you quite a nest egg," he'd told them.

Everyone was fascinated by the painting. Very few people realized how expensive the gift really was. Most of the people in town thought of Brad as just a painter, not an artist and certainly not a very rich one. Cammy watched as Brad sat next to Megan on the piano bench. There was no recognition in Brad's demeanor, but Cammy could see the faint blush under Megan's makeup. Her disguise was perfect, and Brad had no idea that he was sitting next to his 'mystery woman'. What a joke!

Cammy and Babee had gone into the kitchen to clean up.

"Have you talked to Sug today?" Babee asked when she was sure they were alone.

"Jeez, Babee, get straight to the point will ya?"

"I'm not going to let you put this off forever. Any way, you don't have forever. So...."

Megan walked into the kitchen. "Can I help?"

"Saved by the bell," Babee whispered in Cammy's ear. Then she turned to Megan. "Sure, grab a towel."

Babee glanced at Megan. "So, what did Brad Morgan say to you to have you blushing?"

Megan gave a nervous laugh. "Blushing? I don't think..."

"Yes, you were blushing, and it looked so pretty on you, too," Cammy interrupted her with a grin. "I noticed. I bet some others did, too."

"Come on," Babee urged her. "At least give a little information. Was he flirting?"

Megan bit on her bottom lip for a moment. She was a little confused herself about the conversation between her and Brad Morgan. "He, um, he said that he felt like he knew me from somewhere."

Cammy stopped washing the pot in her hand and turned to her. "And he was referring to the 'incident'?"

Megan laughed at that. "No, not at all. He thinks that I'm someone's poor relative. At least I think he does. He started asking me questions that I couldn't answer. Like where did I work or if I was looking for work. He wanted to know if I could type. That kind of stuff, so I came in here."

"And we thought it was our company that you were seeking. So, was he flirting?" Cammy asked.

Megan looked thoughtful for a moment. "I'm not sure. I mean look at me. There's not much about me tonight that would make a man like Brad Morgan flirt with me. Maybe he felt sorry for me and was about to offer me a job. But the way he kept looking at me, I kind of think that he was sort of, you know, flirting."

Cammy and Babee looked at each other and laughed.

"Megan," Babee grinned as they went back to work. "You've got to get out more often!"

By the time they had finished clearing the house of trash and washed and stacked the dishes, everyone had left. Danny was waiting for the three of them by their cars.

"The police station is on your way home, Cammy," Danny said as he held her car door for her.

"You too, Danny?"

"He's a good guy, Cammy. He deserves to know."

"Wow! Caleb really has a growing fan club, doesn't he?" Cammy asked rather bitterly. Then she placed her hand over Danny's. "Sorry. This is hard for me, but I'm going to do what's right. It's long overdue. Just keep me in your prayers."

Danny leaned in and kissed her on her forehead. "Always. This will work out. Trust your heart."

As she pulled away from the Palmers, Cammy's hands were sweating. She slowed down as she got closer to the police station. She could see Caleb's mustang and Deputy Simmons' car parked in back. She pulled into a parking space next to Deputy Simmons' car and looked up at the apartment above the station. She knew that she wouldn't see anything at all, but if Caleb was in there, he could see her car.

She sat there for about five minutes trying to decide if she would climb the stairs, if she was brave enough to knock even if she did make it to the top. No, she'd use the stairs as an excuse; they were just were too much for her knee she'd say if someone had seen her. She'd come back tomorrow. That's what she told herself as she backed out, turned on to 373, and headed to Peaceful Sands. Yes, she'd come back tomorrow after she practiced what she'd say to Caleb. How was she going to tell him about Kim?

12

Cammy was tired. She hadn't realized just how tired she was until she'd gotten home. That the visit with the Palmers had gone well was an understatement. John and Matilda were so happy to be surrounded by all of their friends. And Megan's disguise! Cammy knew that it had added to the merriment of the evening. Everyone in the room knew that Brad Morgan was in the room with his 'mystery woman', and he didn't even know it. Yea for Megan! But now Cammy could barely keep her eyes open. She headed to the bathroom.

She had just stepped out of the shower when the phone rang. She threw on her robe and rushed to answer it, but she didn't pick up in time. Good thing, too, she thought, because she hadn't recognized the number. Just as she turned, the phone started ringing again. She answered without thinking.

"Hello?"

"Hi, Cam."

Cammy felt dizzy. She thought she was going to faint, and her legs got weak. She slumped on the edge of the bed. She couldn't make a sound.

"Cam, are you there?" That laugh. Then a whispered "Breathe, sweetheart, breathe." He paused, and then laughed again in that low, sexy voice of his. "I'm not a ghost."

"Caleb?"

"Yea, it's me. We need to talk, Cam. I'm at your front door."

"What?!!" Cammy couldn't believe her ears. "Are you *crazy*?!"

"Hell, yea, I'm crazy, Cam. I have to be to be standing on your porch talking to you on the phone. I'm not going away. I'm *not* parking in back. Been there, done that! We have to talk. I'll just sit out here all night if I have to. Boy, that'll give the good citizens of Two Plantations something to talk about. Let me in Cam."

God, she couldn't believe this. She wasn't ready for this. Not yet. Her throat felt tight.

"No, please Caleb. Can't we talk tomorrow?"

"To give you time for what? To think of a way to avoid me like you've done for the last two days? Listen to me. We have to talk. I'm the new police chief of this town, and we're going to be running into each other a lot. Let's just get this behind us. Now! We're talking. Tonight! Just open the door. I'm not leaving."

Silence.

"Okay. You win. Just give me a couple of minutes." Cammy didn't wait for him to reply. She hung up, scrambled into a pair jogging pants and a sweat shirt, stuck her feet into her slippers, and rushed to the door.

Caleb was leaning against the door jam. He knew that he had lost his mind, but when he'd seen her car parked behind the station, he knew he'd end up here tonight. He just hoped that when she opened that door, he'd feel nothing. That all of those years of yearning had been in his mind. That the stirring in the lower region of his body when he'd heard her voice was all in his imagination. That just the sound of her voice couldn't do that to him any longer. He needed to know that he didn't love her anymore. He needed to know that. He needed to prove to himself that she was out of his system for good.

The door opened, and Cammy stood there. And he knew he had been wrong. He was lost!

Caleb straightened slowly. His eyes roamed slowly over Cammy's face. Then over her body. He smiled. Did she really think that that sweat suit could hide anything from him? Hell, he knew her body as well as he knew his own. Damn! Where was his anger? He wanted to be mad! He needed the hurt, the angry, the bitterness that he'd carried around for so many years! He needed it to surface now! But all he felt was desire. A deep, burning desire that he couldn't deny or hide. He just hoped that it wasn't so obvious in the outline of his jeans. He refused to glance down to see. When he spoke, he hoped it was with more bravado than he felt.

"Does this seem familiar? Only twenty-eight years ago, we always met at the *back* door. How long are you going to wait this time before you let me in? And you are letting me in, Cam. So, go ahead and say it. 'Come on in, Caleb'."

Cammy couldn't find her voice. She just couldn't. She stepped back. Then turned and walked over to the fireplace. She stood with her back to the room and wrapped her arms around her body. She heard the door softly close. She wasn't sure if Caleb had come into the room or if he'd left until she heard his voice close to her ear.

"Cold?"

She shook her head. She still had not spoken.

His hand began stroking her hair. "You've always had such beautiful hair. I'm glad you didn't cut it." She could feel her body trembling. She hoped he couldn't.

He was still close to her ear, and she could feel his body heat radiating against her back. He was just that close. She could feel his erection, too. But she still didn't turn around.

"I have arthritis," she whispered breathlessly.

His hand stilled. He leaned even closer, if that was possible. Then his hand resumed that slow almost sensual stroking of her hair.

"What?" Cammy could hear the laughter in his voice. She cleared her throat, but she still didn't turn around.

"I have arthritis. It's just in my left knee. But that's why I didn't come up the stairs. I know you saw my car."

Caleb laughed now, that low sexy laugh of his. "Cam, we haven't talked to each other in years, and the first thing you say to me is that you've got *arthritis?*"

She could feel his body shaking with laughter against her back. Everywhere his body touched hers sent sparks shooting through her body.

"It's not funny!"

"The hell it isn't!" He was still laughing as he said, "Turn around, Cam, and look at me."

She sighed and tried to turn. But they were so close together, it was almost impossible. "How can I when you'll so close?"

"Sweetheart, I couldn't move if I wanted to," he whispered in her ear. "Wiggle a little bit. You'll get around eventually." And I'll be in total hell while

141

you're doing it, he thought, but, boy, did he want that hell!

So Cammy turned a little bit at a time.

Caleb clinched his teeth as Cammy slowly turned to face him. As her body rubbed against his, he stopped laughing. His hand, which had been stroking her hair, couldn't move. In fact, he thought that he had actually stopped breathing. His heart pounded in his ears and his body tightened even more. Torture! Pure torture! And he had asked for it!

Cammy was on fire! Everywhere his body touched hers as she turned to face him was ablaze! Sharp, sweet sensations spiraled through her. It seemed as if it had taken hours, but it was only seconds before she faced him. As she lifted her face to him, his arms clamped around her, and he lowered his head.

Their mouths met in a ravenously hungry kiss. It was intoxicating, and as Cammy wrapped her arms around his neck to pull him even closer, she felt like she was about to explode. Just from a kiss!

Caleb ended the kiss first. He laid his chin against her head. His breathing was shallow. Cammy could feel his heart beat. She couldn't tell who was shaking the most; it was probably both of them. That kiss!

"Caleb," she tried to compose her herself. "We need to talk."

"Hmmm. Are you hot in that outfit?"

Cammy smiled for the first time. She leaned back in his arms. "I'd just gotten out of the shower when you called. I grabbed the first thing I could find."

"Are you *hot?*" He was on fire!

"Yea, I guess. But Caleb, we need to talk."

"Okay." And his mouth swooped down to hers and caught her up again in that all consuming kiss. When it ended, Cammy's knees were so weak, she would have fallen if Caleb hadn't been holding her.

"Cam," he whispered against her lips. "You're killing me here."

"Do you think I'm not affected by all of this? Jeez! But we *do* need to talk!"

"Damn it, Cam, we haven't talked for years! Can't we do it later? Do you want my death on your conscience? I'm dying here, girl. Please have some mercy on me!" As he was talking, he'd started to remove her sweatshirt, but Cammy caught his hand.

She laid her head on his chest. He could barely hear her as she said very softly, "I'm sixty, Caleb. My body. It's not......"

"Shhhhhh. Don't worry; it's okay. Let me show you, Cam. I could give you a lot of pretty words, but just let me show you how much I want *you*. I didn't think it would be this way. I can't think straight. I thought we could talk, but I can't find the words. Not right now. I just have to touch you, see you. Make sure that you are real! Please, Cam?" And before she could answer, her shirt was on the floor. Caleb stepped back.

"Shit!" he choked out. "You're beautiful." And she was. If he didn't know for himself, he'd never believe that she'd had two children or that she was sixty. Her body would put a well kept forty year old woman to shame. He reached out and caressed

143

her breasts. She moaned. He moved even closer and kissed her again.

"I don't think I can make it to your bedroom," he muttered as he rained kisses on her lips and down her neck. "You won't be insulted if I just drag you over to the sofa, will you? I'm feeling like a randy school boy, here, and I need you. Really bad."

Cammy couldn't even remember answering. The next thing she knew, she was on the sofa and Caleb's hands were all over her, and his lips were attached to her breasts. Her body was on fire! He raised his head up and looked straight into her eyes as his hands kept massaging her breasts. Losing the feel of his lips almost made her scream!

"You've always liked that, haven't you? My hands, my lips on your breasts. Your beautiful, luscious breasts. They've always been one of your most sensitive spots. Tell me you like it. I want to hear it. I *need* to hear it. From you."

He never took his eyes from her face as his fingers slightly brushed her nipple. Her chest arched up. "Tell me, Cam." His fingers brushed her nipple again. Her body twitched and she moaned.

"Yes!" she moaned. "Yes, I love for you to touch me. Please, Caleb!"

He smiled that sexy little smile of his as he once again placed his lips around her hard, brown nipple. He suckled and nibbled and licked and pinched as he took her higher and higher.

"Caleb."

"Hmmm?"

"You still have on your clothes. I still have on my pants."

"Hmmm." He bit down lightly on her breast.

"Jeez!" Her head fell back as she sucked in air through her teeth and her whole body arched off the sofa. "Don't stop!" She held his head to her breast as her body quaked with need. She could feel his erection pressing into to her, and she clinched her thighs together! She was so wet!

"Please, Caleb. Please!"

He raised up and in seconds they were both naked, and Caleb was back on top of her. He held his weight up with his elbows. He leaned down and brushed little kisses across her forehead, her nose, her lips.

"What do you want, Cam?"

A tear rolled down her cheek. "Are you punishing me?"

He licked the tear from her cheek. "Naw, sweetheart. Have you forgotten our phone sex? The way we got started? How good *that* was for you? I'd tell you what to do to your body, and you'd do it. It felt good didn't it? Now I want you to tell me, and I'll do it. What do you want, Cam? Tell me."

"I'm scared."

"Of what?" He kissed her on her lips. He lowered his head and kissed her just above her nipple. Her body shuddered.

"Of disappointing you. It's been so long."

He kissed her breast. Then bit her nipple, holding it a little longer, pressing a little harder. Her body arched. He raised his head.

His voice shook. "What do you want, Cam?"

She pulled his face to hers. "I want you inside of me. All of you! Inside of me! Now! Please, Caleb!"

145

Caleb shifted a little to the side. He ran his hand down her body until his fingers rested in the curls between her legs. Cammy's legs sprayed, and Caleb's fingers found the slick, wet folds of her sex.

"God, sweetheart, I can't wait any longer!"

He rolled back over her and braced himself on his hands. Cammy's eyes were heavy with desire. His voice was husky as he whispered in her ear. "I'm safe, Cam. You know, no STDs or anything. I don't have protection with me. Is it okay? Please say it's okay, sweetheart! But I'll stop if you say so. It'll kill me, but I'll stop! I wouldn't do anything to hurt you, and I don't want you to be afraid. Oh, but Cam! I've waited a lifetime! It's been too long!"

Cam shuddered with lust. She was so caught up in the thongs of desire that his words barely registered. She moved her head from side to side as she rubbed her body against his. "Oh, Sug! Please! I'm safe too. Now! Please, Sug! Now!"

Caleb lost all control and plunged, deep. He caught Cammy's scream of pleasure in his mouth as he rocked his hips and plunged deeper and deeper into her. It wasn't possible that she could still be so tight, but he was in her and he knew. Damn did he know! She gripped and held him inside of her as they moved to a rhythm that neither had forgotten. Unimaginable pleasure swept through them as they moved higher and higher to that ultimate mountain top. And if history repeated itself, they would fall off of it together. And they did.

They were still throbbing as they landed. Him still inside of her. Both too tired to move.

"Are you all right?" He raised himself to look in her face.

"Hmmmmm." She closed her eyes, but her smile said everything.

Caleb chuckled softly. "I'll take that as a yes. Good! I know I'm too heavy for you, but hell, I can't seem to break this contact. You feel good!"

Cammy still didn't say anything.

"What's wrong? Cat got your tongue?"

She stretched a little, trapping him even more inside her.

She purred like a cat. "Don't want you to move. Can't we just shift a little or something?"

He kissed the side of her mouth and smiled. "Sofa's going to be ruined. And *well*………"

Cammy laughed then. "Forget the sofa. I feel good and comfortable. We'll shift a little. I'm good like this. Okay?" Then she fell asleep. Just like that.

Caleb smiled and held her close. So much for talking! He pulled her even closer. Why had he wasted so much of their lives? They should have been together; they could have been enjoying each other. He should have contacted her years ago. Or rather, he should have let her answer the phone all of the times he *had* called through the years. But he couldn't change any of that now.

He eased himself over her and used the throw from the back of the sofa to cover her. How she could sleep so soundly was beyond him. He didn't want to leave her, but his car *was* parked out front. He leaned over and placed a soft kiss on her lips.

"Hummmm," was her only respond.

Caleb smiled as he put the lock on the front door and let himself out. They'd talk tomorrow. But tonight was a dream come true! He and Cam! Nothing would separate them again!

13

The sunlight filtering through the curtains woke Cammy. She sat up suddenly and looked around.

"Caleb?" The silence in the house told her that she was alone.

She lay back down. She would have thought last night was a dream if she wasn't naked beneath the throw and if she wasn't as tender as she could be. She stretched and smiled. Yes, the sofa was probably ruined. She'd clean it as soon as she showered and then later start shopping for a new one. This time she and Caleb would pick it out together.

God, she couldn't remember the last time she'd been so loved and desired. And it felt so good! She shook her head as she sat up. She hadn't realized how much she'd missed being with someone – being intimate with someone. Over the years she'd gotten used to being alone. She'd filled her life with Two Plantations and her children. She hadn't needed anything else. But now she felt *alive*! More alive that she'd felt in years. God! She'd had one night of pure bliss! At least it was something to hold on to because she had to face reality. She and Caleb would probably never speak again once she told him about Kim.

The phone rang and she grabbed the throw to cover herself.

"Caleb?"

"Hell, no, sis. Caleb? Why would *Caleb* be calling you at seven o'clock in the morning?" Jazzy asked.

"My goodness, Jazzy. Why are *you* calling so early?"

"Nope! Can't do it! Can't change the subject that fast! Why are you expecting Caleb, let me guess, Caleb *Wellington* to call you this early? And you know I'll bug you until you tell me the truth."

Cammy giggled. "Oh, Jazzy! Caleb came by last night. We….we made love for the first time in twenty-six years."

"It's about time Cammy. So he wasn't mad when you told him about Kim? He really is a special kind of guy."

The silence seemed to last forever.

"You did tell him, didn't you Cammy?"

"I tried," cried Cammy. "I really did, Jazzy. But, I mean, it just happened. But I did try. I kept telling him that we needed to talk, but he kept kissing me and touching me, and well….. It was *so* good, Jazzy."

"Damn, I knew I should have come home when Babee called and told me that he was the new police chief. Don't worry, kid. David and I will be there tomorrow. All hell's going to break loose when you tell him, especially after you've been together again. And it was *that* good, huh?"

"Jazzy, is this normal at my age? I mean, Babee was just telling me that she and Danny are becoming more intimate, but she's a little younger than I am. What about you? We've not talked about anything like this in years, but shouldn't I feel weird or something?"

"Hell, I never brought up the subject because I thought, after Caleb, you'd become frigid. And you *always* thought I was fast, so I just took my lead from you. Yes, Cammy, it's normal. Why David and I……..."

"*David?* You and *David?* I thought you had banned him from your bed after his last affair, what, four years ago?"

Laughter filled Jazzy's voice. "Yes, David. You may not believe this, but I've never been unfaithful to him. I've let him think that I *would* be if I was pushed too far, but even when I'd reached my limit, I've never wanted anyone but him. I was leaving him, you know. After the last affair. But he promised he'd change. So we made a deal. He'd take an AIDS test every year, and I wouldn't sleep with him for the first year. He'd have to really prove to me that he'd changed. And he did! Most of the time I'm glad that we made the bargain, but there are some times when I wonder what was I thinking! He's on me like fleas on a dog! When he's not working, he's with me. He takes me with him on his business trips; I shop while he's in his meetings. When he says he's going to the store and he'll be right back, he comes right back. So different than in the past. Back then, he'd leave to go to the store, and I wouldn't see him again for two or three days. You have noticed that when I come home, he's with me."

"Yes, I noticed. But he's always could put on a good front; I just thought that was what was going on. Oh, Jazzy, I'm so happy for you!"

"Yea, I'm happy, too. Don't get me wrong. I get a chance to breathe without him every once and a while. We're not literally attached at the hips or anything, but it's usually David and me and sometimes the kids and grandkids. And well, I kind of like it. We've had so much turmoil in our marriage; now we've found each other again."

"And so, you're intimate? I mean really intimate?"

"Are you kidding? You know that I've always had a high sex drive. Thanks to you and your naughty phone sex experience, I learned how to please myself. Just think! *You* taught *me* how to find pleasure. That's kind of unbelievable. When you told me about the phone sex you had with Caleb back then, I decided to see what else was out there. I didn't want to talk to some stranger on the phone; it'd feel like cheating. I didn't like the sex movies, but I discovered that reading trashy books really turned me on. And boy, are they filled with all kinds of creative ideas. I try them out on David all of the time."

"Jeez! There must be something in the air for maturing women. Look out world! Here comes the new Golden Girls! I thought that it was only men who really had the desire to make love after a certain age. I thought women were supposed to forget desire ever existed."

"Don't kid yourself; read your AARP magazines sometime. There are all kinds of articles online and in medical magazines about it, too. So you're normal. That good, huh?"

"Yes! I'm sitting here still naked; that's how good! But I have to face reality. You're right! He's going to be angry, and he'll never forgive me for what I've done. But I'm telling him today anyway. My mind is made up. So I'll need you tomorrow. I'm going to need all the help I can get!"

"Don't worry, sis. Things will work out. Believe me!"

"Why does everyone keep telling me that?"

"Maybe because we all know you and what a good person you are. Our generation has had some rough times with love, but we have that Collins blood running through us. We're tough! Together we can survive anything."

"I guess I should tell Smitty. He's bound to see Caleb, and the minute he does, he'll know. I should tell him first."

"You're too late; Smitty already knows."

Cammy gasped. "How?"

"About six, seven years ago, Sug ate at Smitty's café in Memphis. The minute Smitty saw him, he knew. He called me, mad as hell, while Sug was still there; he wanted to 'knock his block off'. I had to quickly explain that Sug didn't know about Kim. I told him a shortened version of the story, and since then, well, he and Sug have sort of stayed in touch."

"And he never said a word."

"We support each other, Cammy; we don't judge each other. See you tomorrow."

Cammy wrapped the throw around her and headed to her bedroom and a shower. When she checked her phone, she had missed two calls from the same number. Her hand was shaking was she dialed the number.

"Morning Cam. You must sleep like the dead! I've called twice. Thought I'd have to come and check on you if I didn't hear from you soon. I didn't well…. hurt you or anything, did I?"

She giggled. "No, Caleb, I'm fine. Well, a little well, you know, but fine."

"You called me Sug last night."

"I didn't!"

"Yes, you did. You said, 'Oh *Sug*, please....'"

"Okay, okay, maybe, but if I did, it was an accident. I've *never* called you that!"

"Well, I liked the sound of it. In fact, if I didn't think I'd have to walk around with a permanent hard-on, I'd tell you to call me that all the time. But then *I'd* be walking like I had arthritis in my *third* leg."

"That's not funny, Caleb. And I don't walk like I have arthritis. At least not anymore!"

"The hell it isn't funny! But I won't tease you. I don't care what you walk like. And I couldn't tell that anything was wrong with your knees last night!" He laughed.

"I thought you weren't going to tease me. Caleb, we have to talk."

"I know. Cam, who's Langston Mitchell?"

"Langston Mitchell? Why? What makes you ask about Langston?"

"I saw his name and number on your coffee table when I left last night. Please don't tell me that I wasn't the only man on your mind last night. I don't think I can handle that without finding him and beating him to a pulp!"

Cammy laughed. "Are you serious? You were the only man anywhere on me last night. Langston is just a friend. But Caleb, we *do* need to talk about some things."

"I know. It's been a long time coming. Can I come over this evening? Chief Roscoe and I have a couple of meetings today in Tallahassee with their

153

police chief and the sheriff. I don't know how long they will take. Is it alright? About this evening, I mean? I can pick us up something to eat."

Cammy bit her bottom lip. She knew it wasn't a good idea for them to see each other at night, but she wasn't sure if day light would make any difference. She just had to insist that they talk. Then she'd see what would happen next.

"Nothing to eat because we are going to talk, Caleb. That's all we're going to do. Talk!"

Caleb laughed. "If you say so. We'll talk *first*. I promise. So I'll see you later. Think about me because I can't get you out of my mind."

14

Dr. Mario Franklin Jackson, Frank for short, was worried about his mother. A headache? He couldn't ever remember his mom being sick; Kim couldn't either. In fact, no one in the family had ever suffered from chronic colds or sinus trouble or headaches. When they got sick, they got really sick. The only thing that made Frank feel any better was that his mom had cooked dinner for the Palmers and had stayed at their house for several hours last night. But still, he'd feel better when he checked her out himself.

He'd been the man of the family for so long even though his mom never allowed him to really take on any of the responsibilities that could have fallen on his shoulders. But he'd wanted to. His mom had been both mother and father to him and Kim.

Why she had married a jerk like Ralph Jackson, Frank could not understand. Sure, Ralph was his father, but he had been a real jackass, a miserable husband, a sad excuse for a father, and a very weak man. On his sober days, however, he must have been a pretty good lawyer. People still talked about some of the cases he'd won before the drinking had taken over. Obviously, Ralph had had some brains at some point in his sorry life.

Frank had seen pictures of his father when his dad had been a young man. He'd been handsome; Frank took his looks after him. Maybe he had gotten some of his brains. But that was all he took from his dad. He had gotten his height from the Collins family, and thank God he had inherited their value system. Ralph hadn't had one. Frank knew he would never be like his father. Ralph had made his mom miserable, and he had been a real embarrassment to him and Kimberly. Who wanted a father who was a drunk *and* a womanizer?

Frank couldn't even remember his mom and dad living together. Not really. His dad preferred living in Tallahassee. Mom wanted to raise her family at Peaceful Sands. Dad hated Peaceful Sands and the town of Two Plantations. So he kept an apartment in town and came to Peaceful Sands on the weekends. And he didn't make it many weekends. After a while, Frank started spending a couple of weekends out of the month in town with Ralph; his dad said it was easier to be in Tallahassee because of his job. Frank soon realized that it wasn't the job but the women that his dad wanted to be near. Frank was so happy when Kim was born. Ralph didn't want to be bothered with a baby, so they spent even less time with the town drunk. They simply had to hear about him at school from their classmates.

Frank had good instincts. Something *was* wrong. He could feel it. That's why, after he'd finished with his last patient, he'd driven to Two Plantations. He would stop by the clinic even though it wasn't his day to staff the place, but then he'd go straight to the bakery. He really wanted to talk to Aunt Babee, his godmother and his mom's best friend. If anyone would know what was wrong, Aunt Babee would, her and Auntie Jazzy.

Jeremiah Sinclair was already at the clinic when Frank arrived. After all, it was his afternoon to man the clinic. He and Frank shared a medical office, and it was great! Some people had advised against the partnership; they thought that it would cause problems since they were such good friends, more like brothers, really. But each had his own specialty and his own patients. They did share their office staff and nurses, and everything was working out fine.

After their practices had been established in Tallahassee, he and Frank decided to open up a free clinic in Two Plantations. Frank staffed the clinic on Tuesdays and Jeremiah on Thursdays. They both helped at Rachel's Haven whenever they were needed. This way they were able to give back to the community that had supported them all of their lives, and it felt good.

Jeremiah enjoyed his time in Two Plantations. He got a chance to spend time with many of the residents; people stopped by to sit and talk, pass on the latest gossip, and try to discover why he hadn't married yet. Every so often, someone would actually need his medical expertise. There were days when there was not time for any socializing. He and Frank provided free physicals for everyone in the town. Physical exam days were always busy days.

He also got a chance to visit with his parents, Danny and Babee Sinclair. Nobody cooked and baked like his mom, so he always spent Thursday nights with them, ate a good home cooked meal, and left early the next morning to get to Tallahassee in time for his first patient. At least he stayed the night

157

until his little sister, Heather, and her kids moved back home. Now, sometimes he'd sleep on the sofa in the den, but usually, after the clinic and bakery closed for the day, he'd just spend a little time with the family and then head back home.

Jeremiah really wasn't surprised to see Frank walk through the door. Frank's wife, Janice, and their kids had stopped by the clinic for a minute after they'd left the bakery. They'd been to Peaceful Sands to check on Aunt Cammy. The children loved visiting Peaceful Sands, and Janice loved it, too. Jeremiah knew that she would move to Two Plantations tomorrow if the medical practice wasn't booming. She loved this town almost as much as Jeremiah and Frank did.

"Hey, man! Just missed the family."

"I know. She called while I was on my way. Said to take my time. She wants to have dinner ready when I get home. Oh, she also said we need to start looking for a good woman for you. Thought you looked a little lonely." Frank grinned at his best friend and buddy.

Jeremiah cringed at the thought of marriage. "You've got the best thing out there. And since Janice's sister is oh so married with a house full of children, I'm out of luck. Otherwise, I'd give it a try! Anyway, Tallahassee needs a young, single doctor. Who else will take out all of the ladies?"

"You're not getting any younger, you know. And I'd recommend marriage. It's great!"

"That's 'cause you have a great wife. You were made for each other."

"If you give it a real try, there's a great wife for you out there."

"How do you know I haven't been looking," Jeremiah replied carefully. "Maybe she's just out of reach. You know. Someone I just can't have."

"Shoot! You could have any woman you want. Is there someone special? I'm ready to listen if you're ready to talk," Frank suggested gently.

Jeremiah hesitated briefly. No way could he share his feelings for Kim with her brother. "Naw, there's nothing. I like playing the field. It keeps me up on my game."

Frank gave him a disbelieving look. "Well, I......"

Just then the little bell jingled as the door to the clinic opened.

Caleb stepped into the small clinic. The two young men standing there stopped talking and simply stared at him. It wasn't difficult to know who was who. The man in the doctor's jacket couldn't be anyone but Danny and Babee's son. Before leaving for Tallahassee for his meetings, he'd talked to Danny Sinclair. It was easy enough to recognize his son. With his short sandy brown hair and deep blue eyes, he was a cross between his mom and dad. No, there was no mistaking him. There was also no way to wonder about the other young man standing there in his jean outfit and gator cowboy boots. Frank Jackson looked exactly like his father, Ralph. No, he knew who they were, but they must have mistaken him for someone else. Both looked like they had seen a ghost.

"Hi," Caleb regarded them with a puzzled expression. "I'm Caleb Wellington. I'll be the new police chief in a couple of weeks. I'm glad I found the two of you together. I wanted to introduce myself to you. It's a wonderful thing you're doing here."

For a couple of seconds the two men just stood there. Frank's face was drained of all color, and Jeremiah's was red as fire!

Caleb stepped further into the room. "Is something wrong? Is there a problem here at the clinic? Break in? Something missing?"

Jeremiah shook his head and stepped forward. "No, no. Everything's fine. Excuse us. Just a little in awe. Neither of us realized that *the* Caleb Wellington was our new chief. Man, you're a legend."

Jeremiah looked over his shoulder at Frank, then reached out and shook hands with Caleb.

Caleb studied them both. A little color had come back to Frank's face, but he looked rather uncomfortable. Caleb wondered for a moment if his mother had told him about….. No. No way. She wouldn't have done that. Not the Cam he had known. But something wasn't right.

"Look, if I came at a bad time……"

"No, not a bad time." Frank stepped forward, but he still looked slightly flustered. "Like Jeremiah said, we'll just surprised. *Really* surprised. We started hearing about you when we were still in middle school. Man! Do you still have your '65 mustang? Every guy who thought he was a player wanted a '65 mustang like Sug Wellington!"

Caleb laughed. For some reason, he liked these two young men. He still had the feeling that something was not quite right. There was something about the way they kept searching his face, as if they were looking for something. Maybe there was a look that an 'ol' player was supposed to have, and they

160

were looking for it. But no, it was something else. Something that he couldn't quite put his finger on, but there was something.

"Yea, still have it. In fact, I have it here with me now. And don't believe all that hype you've heard about me. You know how rumors can be blown out of portion."

"But where there's smoke, you know." Jeremiah grinned. "Come on. You can share with us. We're grown men now."

"Well, yea, I guess I did set a few fires but not as many as rumor has it. I talked to your father just this morning, Jeremiah."

"Now that's what you have to be careful about. He's a proud dad and has a tendency to embellish the truth. I'm no genius and definitely not the best doctor in the world. I guess he also told you that I need to settle down and give him some grandchildren. As if he doesn't have enough!"

"Well, he might have mentioned some of that. Also told me how the two of you went off to med school, came back and opened a successful practice in Tallahassee, and opened this free clinic for this town. It's a great thing to do. He has a right to brag. You're fine young men to give back like that. You both are a great example of paying it forward. Let me know if there's ever anything I can do to help around here."

Frank finally reached out and shook hands with Caleb. "It's just good to know that the clinic will still be in good hands when we're not around. We'll miss Chief Roscoe; he's known us all of our lives. But we know you, too. Well, indirectly. But we know

161

you have had an outstanding career in law enforcement. Two Plantations is still in good hands."

Caleb leaned against the edge of the desk. He didn't want to stare at Frank. It was taking all his concentration not to. Hell, they were still throwing glances at him and then at each other. But something in his chest, it must have been his heart, seemed to burst with pride. The boy had done well. He was a man any father would be proud of. Frank could have been his if only he had met Cam sooner.

He looked at Frank. "I knew your father back in the day. I heard he had passed."

He could see Frank tense up and could feel the anger radiating from him. His faced had paled again.

"If you knew Ralph, you knew that he was trash, a drunk. An embarrassment to me and my sister, and he made my mother's life a living hell. I don't miss him." *But I think I missed you*, Frank wanted to say. How strange that felt. He wanted to scream, '*You're the kind of man I could have called 'dad'*.

"I'm sorry if I'm rude, but if you really knew Ralph, you know why I feel the way I do." Anger still vibrated in Frank's voice.

"Son, I'm going to step in here with some unwanted advice, but I'm going to give it to you anyway. It's advice that my mom gave me years ago about my own father. Ralph was a saint compared to *my* father. My dad would make yours look like an angel! And I was real mad at him for a long time for everything he was and everything he wasn't. But my mom wouldn't let me hold on to that angry. She said the anger would just eat me up and take away my real chance for happiness. She said it'd end up killing my heart. Without a heart, what's there to live for? I loved my mom and believed whatever she told me because I knew it would always be the truth. So I let it go. Once I did, I was able to find that happiness."

"Did you really find it sir?" Frank held his breath.

Sadness washed over Caleb's face for a second. "Yes, for a while, I found the greatest happiness a man could have."

Frank took a deep breath and visibly relaxed. He had heard that Caleb's wife had died some years ago. He wondered if Caleb had been talking about his deceased wife or Frank's mom, Cammy. "Thank you sir; I'll remember that."

Caleb knew it was time to change the subject. "Now, let's talk about my favorite pastime. Are those fishing rods I see back there?"

It was almost two hours later when Caleb left the clinic. After all these years, he had finally met Cam's son. Once the boy had gotten comfortable around him, they had gotten to know each other pretty good. They both enjoyed cars, jogging, and fishing! No telling what else they had in common. Caleb shook his head. He had no idea what he was doing! He was really moving too fast! Trying to get to know Cam's son! Was he crazy? Yea, he was way out of control with this thing. But when he looked at Frank, he didn't see Ralph. He saw Cam's son. A son *he'd* never had. He saw a young man he knew he could love as his own. And now he finally had Cam back in his life. He couldn't wait to see her again.

Frank and Jeremiah were quiet after Caleb left the clinic. Neither spoke a word. Shock still registered in Frank's face and tears gathered in his eyes.

"Holy shit!" Frank shuddered.

"Oh, damn, man," Jeremiah said when he saw Frank's face. "My God! I don't know what to say. Hell! You didn't know did you? Don't *do* that, man. I mean, I don't know what to do or say. How can I help? Frank, don't cry or we'll both be crying! I guess you're mad, huh? Mad with your mom or with Caleb or both I guess. Man, what can I do?"

Frank wiped his face with his hands. He took a deep breath and his body shuddered again. He tried to pull himself together. "I don't know what I am. I'm confused. Not mad though. I guess I should be, but no, I'm not mad. I wouldn't know who to be mad with! It was a shock, alright."

Frank still couldn't grasp it. His mom and Sug Wellington!

" Isn't this crazy?! My mom, Sug Wellington, and Kimberly! Jeremiah, I don't believe he even *knows* about Kimberly. I mean, how could he *not* know? But I don't believe he does. Could he?"

"You think he just ditched your mom when she got pregnant? But didn't Ralph claim Kim?"

"I'm not sure just what Wellington did. This is damned confusing. Ralph acted like Kim was his; he treated her just like he treated me if that's anything to brag about. He never, ever acted like she *wasn't* his. But now I know why Mom has been avoiding me; she probably thought that I had met *him*. He's Kim's father! What a secret to live with! Since Kim has always thought she was Ralph's child, Mom must be frantic trying to figure out what to do now that Wellington will be living here. But I'm actually happy for her. For Kim I mean. Anyone for a father is better that Ralph, and I get the feeling that Caleb Wellington is one hundred per cent better that Ralph. It's going to be a shock for Kim; once she gets over that though, I think she'll be happy. A really decent man to call father! I don't know; maybe I feel sorry for *me*. Something happened when I saw him. When I put two and two together. Seeing him, talking to him, man, I felt something. It's crazy I know, but I thought *'This should have been my dad'*. It's like a punch in the stomach. I've just realized how much I really missed not having one, a real one." His voice trembled. "I'm going to Janice and the children. I need them right now. "

As Frank headed to the door, he turned to Jeremiah. "Look, if by chance you talk to Kimberly, don't mention any of this yet."

"Frank. Brother. Man. No way would I do that. That's your mom's call, and she'll make the right one. I have a feeling that everyone who knows Kimberly and have seen Sug Wellington has figured it out by now. But nobody's going to say anything. This town would never do anything to hurt any of you. Your mom has to handle this, and she will. Aunt Cammy's a tough woman; you just need to be there for her and Kim. I'm here for all of you. You're family."

"Thanks."

Jeremiah locked the doors and sat down at the desk. Kimberly was like a sister to him, and they had been communicating regularly since he left for college. She had shared so much with him over the years. How was he going to keep this from her? She trusted him. Like a big brother.

But in the last few years, something had changed for him. When he talked to her on the phone or saw her, he didn't really think of her as a little sister any more. More and more, he saw her as a woman. A very desirable woman. And Frank's little sister.

15

How strange it felt! Kimberly Olivia Jackson was missing home. This had to be one of those rare jokes that God played, or something was really wrong with her! Maybe she was confusing being tired with homesickness. Maybe she was just missing her mom, which she did. But lately, she knew it was much more than that. She actually *wanted* to be in Two Plantations again.

She shook her head in bewilderment. All of this could be about the concern she was having for her mom. Cammy Jackson didn't get sick, and she certainly didn't have headaches. Something was wrong! Her mom needed her, and here she was, sitting behind a desk in New York, hundreds of miles from home.

Kimberly looked around at her office. It was really was plush. Three years ago, three new lawyers had been hired by the firm of York & York, and she had been one of them, increasing the legal staff to seven. For some reason that she still didn't understand, she'd been given *the office*; a corner office furnished with top of the line plush leather chairs, glass topped chrome tables, African mahogany bookcases, and a fabulous 18th century desk. Expensive art work decorated the walls; one piece was even by the famous Brad Morgan. Floor to ceiling windows provided plenty of sunlight and a fantastic view of New York City. The only people with a better view were the owners, Melvin York and his brother, Sydney.

Yes, it was a great place from which to work, but getting *the office* had caused some jealousy among the other attorneys. Particularly with Carl Young, who had been with the firm for over a year before Kimberly was hired. She had instantly sensed his dislike, and after some snide remarks about how she had gotten the *office* and her job – had to be her race or her sex or her looks or a combination of any of those - Kim made every effort to spend as little time around him as possible. He was always stirring up trouble in the office, and rumor had it that he wouldn't be around too much longer.

Kimberly didn't let any of it bother her. No really. She was proud of who she was and what she had accomplished. Graduating at the top of her class from law school, she'd had offers from firms from all over the nation. She'd decided to join York & York, and she'd never regretted her decision. They kept her busy, and they paid well. She enjoyed what she did. She'd even been able to take on some pro bono cases; it was her way of giving to those who could not afford good legal representation. But lately, all of it didn't seem to be enough. Something was missing, but she didn't know what. She really needed to take a break; she needed to go home.

The phone rang just as she was shutting down her computer.

"Hey, Kimberly. Are you working to the usual late hour? Some of us are going to grab something to eat about eight. There's always room for you in my car."

"Thanks, Tony, but I'm not working late tonight. In fact, I'm just getting ready to leave now."

"Now? Are you sick or something? We usually have to drag you out of here at eight! And you know that sooner or later you're going to have to go out with me on a real date. I won't give up. I can always come and pick you up from your apartment."

"Thanks, but I'll have to take a rain check. Tonight is just for me, and I'm looking forward to it. Thanks though."

She gathered her bag, checked to make sure she had her ipad, cell phone, and keys and stepped into the reception area.

Shelia Tolliver looked up, surprise written all over her face. She looked down at her watch and up again at Kimberly.

"So, is there a snow storm coming or something? You're not ill are you?" she asked, a hint of laughter in her eyes.

Kimberly laughed. It was very strange for her to leave the office before seven or eight in the evening. Sometimes it was even later. But today, she had decided that she was leaving early. She had some thinking to do, and she needed to do it away from the office.

"Cute, Sheila, cute! No snow storm and no illness. I'm just giving myself a break for a change."

"Good! It's about time. Do something fun! Get out of that business suit and into something sexy and go have a ball! You deserve some fun in your life."

"Thanks, Sheila." Sheila had been at York & York when Kimberly had been hired. In her late fifties, Sheila had that second mom vibe for all of the

169

young attorneys at the firm. "Just getting home early will be having a ball! Don't you work too late yourself! See you tomorrow."

The elevator was crowded at this time of day. Kimberly hadn't realized just how many people actually left work at five o'clock on the dot. Maybe that's why she had started working late. Today she knew she'd have a hard time getting a cab. But she wasn't changing her mind. Leaving work before eight o'clock in the evening felt good. Waiting for a cab was worth it, and the weather wasn't bad.

Luck was with her! Kimberly was home in record time! A shock for New York City!

It felt strange entering her apartment this early on a work day. It wasn't a very big apartment; it was large for New York but small compared to the apartment she had shared with her roommate, Joan, in Tallahassee. Nine hundred square feet didn't sound like much to people from the south, but it was considered spacious in New York City and well worth the price. Kimberly knew that she was lucky to have the space.

The 17th floor apartment was an end apartment which gave her windows in her living space and in her bedroom. And her bedroom had a door! The windows let lots of light into the apartment, which a southern girl really needed. She didn't have much closet space or washer and dryer, but the small space had forced her to be creative. She'd bought furniture that had storage compartments like her end tables, her coffee table, and her bed. Her mom had come to the city to help her with all of that stuff and had helped to turn this small space into a comfortable home.

The kitchen was tiny, but Kimberly usually ate out, sandwiches or salads at the office or a quick meal after work with some of the staff from the firm. She hoped that she had something to munch on today. She really didn't want to have to go out again. In fact, she had decided in the cab that she just wanted to shower, eat, and read a good book. Something she hadn't done in a long time. She also needed to think, so maybe reading wasn't going to happen.

Taking Sheila's advice, Kimberly quickly discarded the black silk Anne Klein business suit and Manolo Blanhnik ankle strap pumps and headed to the shower. She'd worry about food later.

The shower had been wonderful! Kimberly snuggled into the corner of her sofa, warm in her favorite cotton PJs and happily nibbled on some dry cereal she had found in the kitchen. She'd decided against the book and had flipped through the TV just to see what she had been missing. Nothing. But she left it on for the noise. For some reason she felt so alone tonight.

And she was. She hadn't dated much since she'd moved to New York. Not that she couldn't have though. She'd met several very nice guys who had a lot going for themselves, but after a date or two, they lost interest. One reason might have been that she wasn't giving up anything. She simply hadn't met the man that she wanted to give herself to, not emotionally and certainly not physically. But that was not exactly true. She secretly had a huge crush on someone, but he was not interested in her. So, she'd buried herself in her work. Until now.

Now she knew it was time to find the answers to the things that had troubled her most of her life.

Like just who was she? Oh, she knew she was Camilla Jackson's daughter. She truly had her mother's body! She was really built! If people back in Two Plantations saw her from the rear, they always thought she was her mom; from the neck down, they could be twins. No doubt she was Cammy's daughter. And Ralph Jackson was her father. But what did she have of his? She couldn't see it. She never had. Not his face; not his coloring. Nothing! She didn't look like her mom, and she didn't look like Ralph! It had always bothered her, and it was time she learned whatever truth there was to learn. She couldn't move forward with her life until she uncovered what was hiding in the past. And she knew there was something lurking back there and that something would probably hurt her mom. That's why she'd never questioned her. But before she could delve into those things, she had to find out what was wrong with her mother now.

She'd called her mom several times, but she'd claimed a headache and then wouldn't return any of Kim's calls. Kim had then called her Aunt Jazzy, but she had been rather evasive.

"If it's a headache, she'll be alright. They can be a bitch if you don't catch them in time. Maybe she'd taken something to make her sleep. I'm sure she'll call as soon as she feels better."

But Kimberly wasn't buying it. It just didn't sound right. Something was wrong. She'd call Frank again. As she reached for her cell, it began to ring.

"Frank! I was just about to call you! Great minds work alike, don't they?"

"Yea! And we have the greatest of them all, right? How are you, little sis?"

172

"I'm really good. I left work on time today, thank you. No working late today. Oh, and I'm really thinking about coming home soon; home to Two Plantations. Is mom okay?"

Kimberly could hear the hesitation in Frank's voice. "I think so. Janice and the kids saw her for a little while today. Her headache was gone, but Janice said she seemed a little nervous. Maybe a reaction to whatever she took for her headache. I had planned to stop at Peaceful Sands myself, but something came up. So what brought about this sudden urge to see Two Plantations?"

"*What?!!* What's this? After all the 'Kim, you should come home more often' lectures, when I say I'm finally coming home, you act like you don't want me to. Come on, Frank! Something's wrong. It's Mom, isn't it? What's wrong? Is she ill? Is that it? How serious is it? Tell me the truth, Frank!"

"Whoa, Kim! Calm down! If Mom's sick, I don't know about it. So just calm down. I'm sure that we'll all figure out what's going on together. We always have. Relax. So, you're thinking about coming home when?"

Kimberly inhaled deeply and gave a weak laugh. "Well, not tomorrow unless…..?" Frank didn't make a sound. "No? Well, like I just said, not tomorrow. I was thinking in a couple of weeks. I need to wrap up some cases that I'm working on right now. The rest I can rearrange. If I need to come home sooner……."

"If there's some serious illness going on with Mom, believe me, you'll be the first to know or at least the second or third. Right now, let's just let her come to us when she's ready."

"My wise big brother. Okay. But I *am* worried. Mom's always seemed so young, so full of life, but when I've talked to her these last few weeks, her voice seems to have aged. I can't handle that. She's been the best mom in the world, and I don't know if she realizes how much I love and need her. I haven't been around much. My fault. But I can't lose her."

"Kim, I can't tell you not to worry; I'm worried about her myself. But we're not going to lose her. And I honestly don't think she's dealing with a serious health problem. So let's just take this one day at a time. Anyway, she'll be overjoyed to know you're coming home. I'm glad too; I miss you."

"I miss you, too. Frank, I have a different kind of question. And don't laugh! Are we rich? I mean our family? Rich? Wealthy?"

All she could hear was laughter. Finally, when Frank could speak he said, "Girl, where do you get all of this stuff?"

"You remember Carl?"

"The clown that keeps giving you all the drama?"

"Yea. Well, the slime ball actually checked into our family's finances or so he said. Had the nerve to say my family bought me my position with the firm. Said we're rich. We aren't are we? I mean I know that our cousins over in D.C. and Maryland are wealthy and Uncle Smitty and Aunt Jazzy, too, but I always thought we were the poor relatives."

Frank laughed again. In fact, Kimberly wondered if he'd ever stop laughing.

"Poor? Well, I don't think that poor would be the word to describe us."

174

"Well, maybe not poor compared to some people, but you know what I meant! Poor when we are compared to the rest of our family. I just thought that we lived off of, well, you know, some sort of trust fund set up for Two Plantations. Poor like if we didn't live at Peaceful Sands, we wouldn't have a place to stay. That kind of poor. Certainly not *wealthy* rich!"

"Would it be so bad if we were? You were happy at home even if you thought we were the poor relations. We would have been raised with the same values if you'd thought we were rich. Do you remember that 1973 Beetle Mom bought me so I could drive to school and be able to stay to basketball practice?" Frank stopped laughing long enough to ask. "You were so ashamed to ride with me. You'd slide down in the seat and ease out of the door before I could even stop. I don't know why. It was a cool car."

"But not a rich kid's car, huh?"

"No, definitely not a rich kid's car. And if we are rich, that just goes to show how awesome Mom really is. Just think! We grew up as rich kids and didn't even know it! Kim, we have what's really important - values, morals. We've always known that there was money in the family. You know. Passed down from the first Beaufort and Sadie Mae. You haven't forgotten them have you? That's how Two Plantations has survived and prospered. If our little branch has a little money, too, well that can't be too bad can it? Listen, Sis, don't let that bum get next to you. You earned that job. Top of your class, remember? And you work your butt off for that firm. He's sour grapes. And he's mad 'cause you won't go out with him! Getting away from him will do you good. You're going to let me know when you get your plans together?"

Kim could hear Janice yell in the phone. "Hi, Kim!"

"Tell her hello for me and kiss the kids. I can't wait to see everyone. Love you. Good night."

Kimberly felt great! Boy, it felt good talking to Frank. She really should have spoken to Janice herself. And she hadn't asked about Jeremiah. Lately it'd gotten more difficult for her to talk about Jeremiah with Frank; she couldn't let her real feelings for Jeremiah show to anyone. She could always call him herself; she often did, but knowing him, he had a date. She couldn't wait to get home to see everyone. Including Jeremiah. Maybe he'd have time to take *her* out. And not as Frank's little sister.

As she went into her bedroom, she picked up a book that had been lying on the coffee table. Reading for a little while didn't seem like such a bad idea after all.

16

Secrets! Damned secrets! Cammy wanted to scream! How could her past come back to haunt her like this?! And she'd known. Those nightmares! All of them screaming for her secrets! This just couldn't happen! Caleb was never supposed to come back! He was supposed to be in her *past*! He wasn't supposed to *ever* find out about Kimberly! How was she going to be able to tell him now?

After last night, being with Caleb again, loving him again, Cammy knew that she would spend too much time today thinking, and that's just what she had done. *The past!* It had always haunted her, but she's somehow kept herself so busy, she'd managed to keep it at bay most of the time. But she couldn't today. It was the past that had brought her to this point. She'd have to face it to move on. Telling Caleb about Kimberly was going to be one of the hardest things she would ever have to do.

She had great kids, and she was so proud of both of them. Both had excelled academically since kindergarten and had finished at the top of their classes. Frank played basketball in high school, but in college had spent most of his free time studying. He had gone to college locally, attending FAMU as Cammy and generations before her had done. He'd then gone on to med school at Howard University in

Washington, D.C. and had completed an intensive internship at Shands Hospital in Gainesville.

He had received offers from hospitals all over the nation, but he decided to go into to private practice with his best friend, Jeremiah Sinclair, Babee's son. They were both excellent doctors and had a thriving practice. They also ran a clinic in Two Plantation, and they were two of the very few men that the women at Rachel's Haven trusted.

Frank had married during his internship. Janice was the best daughter-in-law in the world, and they had given Cammy two precious grandchildren. Frank and his family lived in Tallahassee but had decided a couple of years ago that eventually they would move to Two Plantations and were already looking at house plans. Until then, they spent at least two weekends a month with Cammy out at Peaceful Sands.

Kimberly had always been one of the most popular girls at school. She had been a cheerleader, her senior class president, and the homecoming queen. She, too, had attended FAMU and had gotten her law degree from FSU, following, Cammy supposed, in Ralph's footsteps. Unlike her brother Frank, however, when Kim finished law school, she couldn't wait to leave home. She, too, had numerous offers from law firms stretching from one coast to the other, and she'd decided to go with a firm in New York City. At least she'd stayed on the east coast, not that it made much difference. As seldom as she came home, she could have been working in Europe.

Cammy was proud of them both, but she knew that their childhood hadn't been easy. In fact, in some ways it had been traumatic. With Ralph as a father, what else could it be? Ralph! How could she have been so stupid! Yes, she had to face her past if she was going to make things right for the three people she loved the most!

****

She had been a junior at FAMU when she'd met Ralph Jackson at a fraternity house party. He was in his first year of law school. He was so good-looking. He wore a neat little fro, and he looked like a yummy Hersey bar, all milk chocolate. All the girls wanted a piece of him. He wasn't tall, no more that Cammy's height, but he was built like a receiver for a football team. Slim, solid, and sexy! And oh so popular!

She had gone to the party with Jazzy and her boyfriend, David. David had just graduated with his law degree, and he and Ralph were frat brothers.

The party was packed. Cammy and Jazzy stood along the wall and watched the dance floor as it seemed to sway to the swing and flow of the dancers. The music was loud and the drinks were flowing. David had stepped away to talk to some fellow graduates, but he'd kept a keen eye on both Cammy and Jazzy. Really, he'd kept his eyes on Jazzy; he had a jealous streak a mile long. Her sister, Jazzy, was a beauty and a bit of a flirt. Several guys had stopped to ask for a dance, but they'd both turned them down. But not without Jazzy flirting a little first.

David didn't stay away too long. When he came back, he had Ralph Jackson with him. Most of the crowd was drinking, so she wasn't surprised to see both David and Ralph with drinks in their hands.

"Hey, Cammy. This is Ralph Jackson. He wanted to meet you. Ralph, my future sister-in-law, Cammy Smith." He turned to Jazzy. "They're playing Smokey Robinson.

Come on, baby. Let's dance." He led Jazzy onto the dance floor and left Cammy with Ralph.

"Not drinking? Want me to get you something?" Ralph had asked.

"No, thanks. I don't really drink. But thanks."

"Oh, so you're a good girl. And a fine one at that." Ralph leaned closer and whispered in her ear. "I like good girls. Especially when they have a body like yours. Yea, you're one really fine woman. Girl, you turn me on. The things I could do to you. I'm parked out back. Come let me take you for a little ride. What do you say?"

Cammy didn't know what to say. She gave him a smile, but it was a little forced. She felt so stupid!

"Hey, relax, cutie. I was just teasing. But you are beautiful. Really beautiful. Can I call you tomorrow? Maybe the four of us can go for a ride or something."

"Sure," Cammy replied breathlessly. Someone as handsome and popular as Ralph Jackson really wanted to see her again. Boy!

A short time later, Jazzy and David got into another one of their arguments, and Jazzy was ready to leave. When Ralph saw them heading for the door, he left the girl he had been talking to and walked them out to the car.

He held the door as Cammy got into the back seat. "I'll get with David about tomorrow. Good meeting you, Cammy. I can't wait to see you again." He closed the door and stepped back. He hadn't even asked for her number Cammy thought. But she thought about him all the way to Peaceful Sands.

Jazzy was mad. She didn't even wait for David to walk her to the door.

"Come on, Cammy! I'm mad as hell! Let's just get inside and let this jerk go home!"

180

Dad had left a light on at the foot of the stairs and at the top. They turned them out as they went pass, but as Cammy turned to go in her room, Jazzy called to her.

"Come in my room for a minute, Cammy. I want to talk to you about something."

Cammy went in and closed the door. When Jazzy was mad, she could talk all night.

"Look, Cammy. Ralph isn't the guy for you. David shouldn't have introduced you to him. And before you go through all the bull shit about you're old enough to know what you're doing and the crap about you can date who you want to, trust me on this. You do not want to get involved with Ralph Jackson."

"Why not?"

"He's not for you, girl. He has a – a reputation."

"So does David, but you're dating him."

"Yea, and what a mistake that is. Listen to me, Cammy. I saw the way he was looking at you and the way you were looking at him."

"So?"

"Shit! You were looking at him like a worshiping little kitten, and he was looking at you like the big, bad wolf licking his chops for the kill!"

Cammy laughed. "Relax, Jazzy. You're over exaggerating. Anyway, he didn't even ask for my number."

Jazzy gave Cammy a penetrating look. "You're not going to listen to me. I can tell. Don't end up like me, Cammy. He won't be worth it. But if you ever need me, I'm here for you."

Cammy hadn't listened, and she and Ralph had become an item. Her mom had shared Jazzy's opinion of Ralph. She hadn't liked him at all. "Don't be too quick to give yourself to him," Abigail had warned her. "Promise me

181

you'll wait. He's not the one for you. Just take your time, baby."

By the end of Cammy's senior year, Abigail had been diagnosed with breast cancer. The day they'd gotten the diagnosis, Cammy had been distraught. That night she'd made love with Ralph for the first time. She hadn't known what to expect. But all she'd felt was pain. There was no gentleness. No words of love. Just pain. She'd thought it was her grief that had prevented her from feeling passion and love. She'd wanted to hear the bells and whistles that she'd read about in the many novels she'd read.

Sadly, Cammy never heard them with Ralph. A week after Cammy graduated, she and Ralph got married; she was twenty-one years old. Even though Jazzy and her mom were dead against it, Cammy just knew she was in love, and nothing would stop her from marrying Ralph. But the wedding wouldn't take place without some problems.

Abigail had insisted that Ralph sign documents stating that he would not try to get any of Peaceful Sands assets if the marriage didn't work. After all, they had the Cottages at the Lake and Rachel's Haven to protect. He was livid! As a lawyer, he'd studied those documents and realized that there were no loop holes in them, and he had refused to sign. Not that he wanted anything from Cammy, he'd explained. It was just the principle of the thing. Call the wedding off he'd said two weeks before the wedding day.

Cammy was devastated. She'd begged her mom to reconsider, but Abigail wouldn't bulge. But Ralph finally did. He'd invited all of his colleagues, his friends from law school, and most of the local politicians in Tallahassee. The wedding had to take place or he would become one of those jokes lawyers told over drinks. He couldn't have that. So he'd signed the agreement, and the wedding took place.

Her wedding night was like her first time. No bells! No whistles! No blinding explosions! But she had Ralph. She'd thought that was enough.

Two years later, Abigail died.

Five years later, Cammy gave birth to their son. She'd wanted to name the baby after Ralph, but the day Frank was born, she discovered that Ralph already had two sons; one already had been named Ralph Jackson, after him. That's when Cammy had learned that he had been seeing a woman named Viola Sutton long before their marriage. One son had been born two months before she and Ralph had gotten married; the other was just a year older that Frank.

Jazzy and her mom had been right all along. Cammy had made a horrendous mistake. She never let Ralph touch her again.

17

It was three years later when she met Caleb Wellington. Spring time in February! She'd been shopping in Tallahassee, and he'd stopped her for a speeding violation in a school zone.

As she rolled down her window, he leaned down and looked in. Cammy's breath caught. She was looking at the sexiest man she had ever seen. He was simply gorgeous. For a long moment they had just looked at each other. He had looked as stunned as she was.

He'd seemed frozen.

"Here's my license, officer." Her hand was shaking as reached into her purse.

He smiled. Damn, he was breathtaking. "No need. I know who you are. You're Ralph Jackson's wife, right?"

"Yes, and you are?"

"Officer Wellington, ma'am. Caleb Wellington."

"So you're…."

"Yea, I'm Sug," he said in a deeply sexy voice. Then he winked at her. "Cause I'm so sweet!"

Cammy laughed. "So it's all true! You really are a flirt!"

"Not when I'm on duty, ma'am, but if you'd like to find out when I'm off…. But then you wouldn't be interested. You're still married to Ralph."

For some odd reason, Cammy had felt a stab of disappointment.

"Are you writing me a ticket, Officer?" Irritation filled her voice.

His eyes slowly swept over her body. "No, ma'am. No today. You're free to go for now." He stepped away from the car. "But I promise you, I'll be talking to you real soon."

Cammy could hear his laughter as she pulled into traffic.

Whew! Caleb Wellington. Cammy couldn't believe her reaction to him. Caleb Wellington. She turned on the air in the car. Boy was she hot!

As she looked in her rear view mirror, she wondered for the first time why she and Ralph were still married. They lived apart, but they were not divorced. Ralph said it would hurt his career, and really, Cammy didn't want to have anything to do with another man. Staying married was like having a 'not available' sign. Ralph had been enough to turn her off from any serious relationships. She had her son, her job, her home and her town. She didn't need a cheating, lying man in her life. Having had one was more than enough.

But that man, Caleb Wellington, made her wonder. Damn, her body was still tingling from that look. She lowered the air. She wondered if she needed to take a cold shower when she got home.

As she cooked dinner that evening for Frank, she kept thinking about Officer Wellington. Sug. She had never felt such a strong attraction to anyone, not even Ralph. Yea, she really needed a cold shower. After she had played with Frank, she took him up stairs and put him to bed.

A shower would be good, she thought as she went down stairs and into her bedroom. Several years ago, her grandparents had changed one of the downstairs parlors into a master bedroom with an en suite bath. Now it was her bedroom. She had shared it with Ralph during their brief time together. *After they had separated, she'd replaced everything. She hadn't wanted anything that Ralph had laid on.*

But as she got ready for bed that night, she wondered what it would be like to share a bed with Caleb Wellington. She shook her head. Surely she had gone without sex too long.

The phone rang about 12:30 that night.

"Hi, Cam." Cammy stopped breathing for the second time that day.

She'd know that sexy voice anywhere. "How did you get this number? No, don't answer that. What are you doing? You do know that I am married." *Cammy tried to sound upset.*

"Want me to hang up? I will, you know, if you tell me to." *He waited.*

"Why did you call?" *She hadn't told him to hang up.* "Suppose I wasn't alone."

"Oh, I knew you'd be alone. I know Ralph. And I checked up on you. Won't date so probably haven't been with a man in what? Years?"

Cammy was mortified. "How dare you!?"

He laughed, that low, sexy laugh.

"Want me to hang up now? I will you know. Or I can do what I've been thinking about all day. I just want to talk to you. You turn me on; I know you could tell today. I want to turn you on. I've been thinking about you all day, Cam. Couldn't get you out of my mind." *He lowered his voice even more. It was so sexy.*

"I want touch you with my words. I want you to feel me like I'm there with you. I can tell you things that'll make your breast tingle as if my lips were there. My hands. I want to hear you moan. I want my words to touch you in that most secret place where my hands can't. I want my words to have you clinching those beautiful, long thighs together, wanting me between them. You'll be wet for me, sweetheart. Your hands *will become my hands, and my words will guide you. How long has it been, Cam? How long? Have you ever had phone sex, sweetheart? It can be really good."*

Cammy could barely breathe. No one had ever said anything like that to her before. "Why are you doing this?" she whispered.

"You know there's an attraction between us. You felt it today like I did. And hell, I want to hear you want me. I've thought about it all day long. Messed up a couple of reports because of you. You felt it; I know you did. You can feel it now, can't you?"

"Caleb, this isn't right. We can't do this. Why, you don't even know me, and I don't know you. And I'm still married."

"Don't you think I know that? But you can't deny what we both felt today. What we felt happens instantaneously. Like magic. Our magic, just you and me. Want me to hang up?"

She'd felt it alright! Cammy hesitated and then sighed. "So what exactly is phone sex?"

Caleb laughed. Then he'd started saying some of the sexiest, nastiest things Cammy had ever heard. And he was asking her to do some of those things to her body. And she did. Everything he said thrilled her, shook her to the core. He had her experiencing feelings she didn't even know she could feel in places she thought she had no feelings. His words had her trembling, shivering in delight, and she did end up clinching her thighs tightly together and moaning, begging him to stop.

He'd laughed and hung up with "I'll talk to you tomorrow night."

And that went on for a month. Phone sex every night. If he worked at night, he called early in the morning. It was driving her crazy, it was good, and it wasn't enough. Then for a week, he didn't call. Not once. Each night she'd had to take a cold shower, and she still craved his voice. Each sleepless night she'd waited for that phone to ring. And finally it did.

"Cam, I'm in Two Plantations. I want to see you."

God, just hearing his voice had her clinching her thighs together, had her tingling and even then she knew that she couldn't help herself. She was moist for him; his voice did that and more to her.

"Caleb, we can't. It's not right. What if someone sees you? You're not really here are you?"

"I am. Tell me to go back to Tallahassee and I will. But I'd rather see you. Tell me you don't want to see me, Cam, and I'll go away. Just tell me."

"Go away? You don't mean for good, do you? You mean just mean back to Tallahassee. We'll still talk, right?"

"Cam, I need you. You probably won't believe this, but I'm in love with you. I didn't expect this to happen so soon. Hell, I didn't expect it to happen at all. But it did, right or wrong, it did. And I need to be with you, to hold you, to make real love to you. To be inside you. Tell me to go away, Cam, and I will. And I won't bother you again."

Silence.

"Park in the back. I'll meet you at the back door."

Minutes later, her hands shook as she opened the back door. Caleb stood on the steps.

"Are you sure, Cam? 'Cause if you let me in, I won't be able to back away. So if you're not sure, tell me now, and I'll leave."

Cammy closed her eyes for a second and took a deep breath. When she opened them, Caleb stood directly in front of her. Her heart was beating so fast, she was sure that he could hear it.

He leaned in to her and brushed his lips against hers ever so lightly.

"We're standing in the door, Cam. Tell me what you want," he whispered against her lips.

"Was that our first kiss?" she whispered as she looked up into his eyes.

He laughed softly. "That wasn't a kiss. That was just a hello. I won't force you to let me in. I have to know that you want this, too."

Cammy backed into the house. Caleb pulled her close as the door closed behind them. He turned her face up to his, leaned down, and kissed little feathery kisses all over her lips. Cammy's body throbbed. Her breasts seemed to swell; her nipples hardened. Her legs grew weak. She went up on her toes as she tried to capture his mouth with hers, but he moved his lips to her cheek, then to her ear, and finally, when she stood trembling in his arms, he returned to her lips.

"Jeez, girl, I could take you right here I'm so hard!" He teased her lips with his tongue.

"When you open your mouth for me, Cam, our tongues will do the dance of love that our bodies will eventually do." He pulled her even closer. There was no more room between their bodies. Cammy could feel his erection pressed against her stomach. Desire flooded her.

"Do you want me, Cam?"

"Yes!" And his mouth caught the word as his tongue invaded her mouth. As their tongues wrestled with each other, in and out and whirling around, their bodies moved in rhythm.

Caleb broke the kiss first. He laughed softly. "That, my love, was our first kiss. Are we going to stand here all night? Your son's in bed, right? I'll never come here again when he's home, but I need you so badly tonight. I need to know that you want me as much as I want you. Listen, we don't have to rush anything 'cause it's not about sex with you. I want to make love to you because I'm in love with you. So what do you want to do? I can still leave."

Cammy took his hand and led him into her bedroom. Caleb was so gentle. He knew all of her sensitive spots. After all, he had guided her into discovering them when it was his words and her hands. Now it was his hands, and he took great pleasure in bringing her to fulfillment using his hands and his mouth. And when he caught her scream with his mouth as she reached her orgasm, he knew that it was her first real one and he had given it to her.

He eased into her before her orgasm had ended, and the feel of him inside her had her spinning out of control again. For the first time in her life, Cammy heard the bells, the whistles, and the explosions. Making love to Caleb was better than any phone sex! The way he kissed her, the way he touched her, the tender way he made love to her triggered such an exquisite, thrilling release that she became shameless in her desire for him.

She'd been hooked! For the first time in her life, she'd known what it was like to be with a man who truly loved her. Oh, she'd been head over heels in love with Caleb Wellington! And he'd been in love with her! He'd been a loving, wonderful, caring man, and for two years her love and passion for him had never dimmed. He'd made her feel beautiful! So complete! So loved!

And then she'd lost it all. Why hadn't she trusted him? Ralph had really done a job on her self-esteem! He'd left her filled with so many insecurities! Because of the way Ralph had treated her, she hadn't been able to trust the one man who deserved it the most! Oh, how stupid she'd been! She'd pushed the only man she'd ever truly loved away with a terrible lie that she'd had to live with for twenty-six years.

Until now! Now she'd held him in her arms again. They'd made love. She'd felt truly whole again! A woman loved! And with a few words, she was going to lose everything! One lie had lost Caleb to her twenty-six years ago, and the truth would lose him again. Was there no justice in this world?

18

Cammy found herself once again sitting on her sofa. She was so tired of thinking, of remembering, of crying. Now, she wasn't pretending; she had a real headache that was throbbing and a heartache that was killing her. She couldn't even remember how or when she'd showered and dressed. She'd tried to stay busy; she'd cleaned an already clean kitchen and remade the bed that she hadn't slept in. She'd gently cleaned her sofa. Then she'd cried again because it felt as if that cleaning was a foreshadowing of what would happen when she told Caleb about Kim. It would erase any hope that she'd had for her and Caleb.

"Caleb," she whispered softly. "Please be able to forgive me. God, please…."

There was knocking at the door.

Caleb! It had to be Caleb even though he wasn't supposed to come back until later in the evening! It seemed like an eternity since he'd been gone! Please let it be Caleb! But when Cammy looked through the peep hole, the woman on the other side of the door was a stranger to her. Someone must be lost. But this was 2012, and Cammy knew better than to open her door to strangers. At that moment, the phone rang.

"Hold on," Cammy yelled through the door as she reached out and grabbed the cordless phone. "Hello?"

"Cammy, this is Danny Sinclair. That white lady at your door is, well, she's your cousin. She and her husband have moved into White Oaks. I'm over here helping her husband with a project in their kitchen. He sort of suggested I call when she just got up and walked out of the kitchen a couple of minutes ago. She's probably still out there; you might want to go ahead and let her in. She seems like good people."

There was a soft knock. "Hello, in there."

Cammy hung up the phone. A female cousin at White Oaks! That could only be Ethan's sister, Delphine. Goodness! The last thing that Cammy needed on her plate was another lawsuit! She took a deep breath and opened the door.

"I'm so sorry. I don't really open my door to strangers. It's not safe anymore you know. You'll find that that's the way it is these days. Safety first! Come on in. I'm Cammy Smith Jackson. Welcome to Two Plantations."

Delphine walked through the door and looked around. "Oh, yes! I like what I see already. Mr. Sinclair was right. Your family's done a great job with this interior. Oh, by the way, I'm Delphine Buckley. I'm Ethan's sister. And before we get into the family stuff, I've bought Ethan's share of White Oaks, and I'm not suing your family. *Cousin.*"

They both laughed. "That's a relief! Come have a seat. I have some cookies in the kitchen. Want some? Maybe something to drink?"

Delphine sat on the sofa. Cammy was glad that she had cleaned it as soon as she had dressed that morning. "Sure, I'll take a coke if you have one. And some of those cookies. Are they homemade? Smells like chocolate chips. They're my favorites."

"Homemade for sure. They're my favorite cookies, too. My daughter-in-law makes them. They're the best." Cammy grabbed a coke and a ginger ale, grabbed the plate of cookies, and returned to the living room.

"This room is great! I can't wait to see the rest of the place. My husband, Tim, and I are seriously thinking about turning White Oaks into a B & B. We're retired and weren't looking for a project, but, well, I think we've been convinced. Ms. Moby says that's what we need to do, and she doesn't seem to take *no* as a legitimate response." Delphine took a bite of a cookie. "Wow, these are great! Mind if I take some to my husband? I think you'll like him. Am I talking too much? Guess I'm a little nervous."

Cammy laughed. "No, you're good. I'm probably not the best of company today, but I'm glad there'll be no more law suits. It's gone on for much too long. So, are you sure you going to live at White Oaks? It's yours free and clear? If so, I think I may have a pleasant surprise for you. I'm really glad you came over, Delphine, and I really look forward to meeting your husband. I believe White Oaks has been waiting a long time for you to arrive. B & B, huh?"

"Yea. Mr. Sinclair thinks that a lot of the improvements your family has made to this place over the years would be ideal for a bed and breakfast. That is if you don't mind."

"Mind? No way. I'm happy to have peace within the family at last. And if you do decide to open a B & B, we'll know that you've decided to make White Oaks your home. Want to see the house now?"

Cammy rose, and Delphine did, too. "No, I'm not going to stay long. I heard that you've been ill, so I don't want to keep you too long. So, you were named for both of them? Sadie *and* Camilla? Wow! What a burden! My mom wanted to name me after Camilla Harpson Collins and Beaufort Collins' daughter, Suzanna Belle Collins, my great whatever grandmother. Dad didn't like the name. So they named me after his sister and added Belle. By the way, there are not many Collins left on my side; in fact, I think Ethan and I are the last. But there are plenty of hateful Harpsons around. They've all disowned me. I'm glad I came over here. Maybe we'll get to see the house tomorrow."

"You realize that there are some things that you probably don't know about your side of the family."

"You think? I guess my mother told us the story of Camilla and Beaufort so many times, I probably could repeat it in my sleep. Don't worry. That was their drama; it's not ours."

"Are you sure you're Ethan's sister? Same parents and everything? You are as different as day and night! He hates us!"

"Yes, he's my brother; we have the same parents. Both of my parents were alcoholics; they literally drank themselves to death. Ethan is one, too. They had to blame someone for their failures. Your family was handy. You had something they wanted. I hope Ethan has gotten some help. I hate to see him end up like our parents."

They stepped out on the porch and stood listening to the wind gently blowing through the oak trees.

"I'm going to like it here," Delphine whispered softly as she walked down the steps.

"I'm glad. I'm also glad you've come home to White Oaks."

Delphine turned and waved as she crossed the road. Then she actually skipped up the drive to her new home.

Finally! One of Camilla and Beaufort's descendents was going to live at White Oak, maybe for good. And no law suits. It was about time! The visit had gone well. It had been a surprise; yea, a surprise, but it had turned out to be a pleasant surprise.

Cammy rushed back inside. Where had the time gone? She had to get dressed; Caleb was coming tonight! *What to wear?* She thought. A sweat suit wasn't any protection. She remembered where that had lead. And she and Caleb needed to *talk*. After rummaging through her closet, she'd finally settled on a black sweater and a pair of black slacks. People always said that black was slenderizing, and even though she planned to *talk*, she wanted to look her best.

The sun was setting when Caleb knocked on the door.

"Come on in, Caleb." With her heart hammering in her chest, Cammy couldn't control her smile as she opened the door and he walked in.

As he pushed the door closed with the heel of his shoe, he pulled Cammy into his arms.

"I'd rather hear you say Sug," he whispered in her ear as he nibbled on her earlobe.

"Hummmm, Caleb. Don't." Cammy tried to twist away, but in doing so she rubbed against his erection.

He hissed. "Damn, Cam. Be still. I've been trying to hold this together all day. I want to be in you when I let go. Not in my pants."

"Caleb......" He slide his tongue into her mouth, and she automatically responded, grinding her body into his. "Caleb," she moaned. "We have to stop this; we have to talk. It's important."

"Okay," he whispered in her ear and continued to sprinkle kisses on her neck, her throat, her face as he slowly walked her backwards until she hit up against the arm of her sofa. "Talk."

Cammy could barely breathe. "I can't like this. I….I need some room."

"Can't happen right now." Caleb shifted his hip, and she could feel his erection throbbing against her stomach.

"Caleb, please! I'm begging you. We have to talk now. It's about……"

"Touch me, Cam." He took her hands that had been caught between their bodies and slide them under his shirt. "Feel how my heart is beating, sweetheart. It's yours. Oh, man, I love the way your hands feel on me. Yes, that's it."

Passion seized her as she allowed her hands to roam over his chest, over his muscles, pinching his nipples, touching his hard, flat stomach. She was dizzy with desire! So much so that she hadn't realized that Caleb had eased her back over the arm of the sofa. She gazed up at him with eyes darkened with desire. She didn't wait for him to take off her sweater; she snatched it off and threw it on the floor.

Before she could even ask, his hands were already touching, massaging, and squeezing her breasts. She cried out as he leaned over and gently nipped her nipple. First one and then the other, over and over again until her head spun. And all the time, he was removing her slacks and panties. And she couldn't stop him. Nothing mattered at that moment but the feel and touch of him. And her need!

As soon as her pants were off, she splayed her legs. How wanton! But she couldn't help herself. She was on fire for his touch.

He stood back and looked at her.

"Mine," he said as he slid a finger up her thigh. Her body trembled. "Beautiful!" He muttered as he gently slid his finger up and down her thigh, slowly, gently up and down, each time getting closer and closer to her moist core. And each time her body arched higher and higher, begging him to touch her at the center of her need. To end this exquisite torture.

"Tell me what you want, Cam."

She spread her legs even farther apart. "Caleb, touch me. There. Now. Please."

He eased his finger just below her wet opening. Her body leapt as he slowly eased his finger into her. As he moved his finger deeper and deeper within her, her cry split the air. Her heart pounded and her hips twitched as he used his hand to bring her to the brink of desire. Her eyes flew open and her body withered as she found release, and she spiraled out of control.

"I can't wait any longer, Cam." And then he was inside of her, building up another fire, stroking it as he withdrew and pushed in again, deeper and harder each time until they both leaped off that mountain top together. And the fall was wonderful!

He dozed off holding her close.

The sound of a car horn blowing woke Caleb. Cammy was still asleep. How they'd both slept on that sofa, he'd never know. He, at least, should have fallen off. He knew it was time to leave, but leaving was hard. He'd just take a shower and cook her breakfast before he left. Even though someone had probably seen his car out front, he didn't want to cause more gossip than necessary.

He loved Cammy! He smiled as he stepped into her bedroom and into the shower. He was still smiling after he'd dried off and put back on the clothes he'd arrived in last night.

He went into the kitchen. Would he remember where she kept everything or had time changed her and her habits? He found the frying pans in the same cabinet that she'd kept them in twenty-eight years ago. It was only when he turned to the sink to rinse out the pan did he see the pictures on the window sill over the sink.

He froze. He stepped closer. He couldn't believe his eyes. Candice? Why would Cam have a picture of Candice in her house? He reached over the sink and brought the picture closer to his face. It was Candice, but it wasn't. The girl in this picture was in a cheerleading uniform; Candice had never been a cheerleader. The pan dropped from his hand.

The noise from the kitchen woke Cammy. She looked around and realized that she was on the sofa. She pulled on her shirt and pants.

"Caleb?" she called as she walked into the kitchen. He was standing in front of the sink, his back to her. He turned slowly, and she saw what he had in his hands. He hands were trembling, this time in rage

"Who is she? No, no, don't answer that. What a dumb question! How *could* you, Cam? How could you keep my daughter away from me all of these years?"

"Caleb, let me explain."

"No!" he yelled. "You can't explain this! You had my daughter, and you didn't tell me! I've had a daughter, and I don't even know her. How could you?"

Cammy started toward him, but he stepped back. "Don't. Don't come near me."

He looked down at the picture. Tears were rolling down his face. His voice broke. "What's her name?"

Wiping the tears from her eyes, Cammy looked at Caleb. "Please let me explain."

"What's her name?"

"Kimberly Olivia Jackson."

"She's *not* a damned Jackson," he growled. "She's a Wellington. Where is she?"

"What are you going to do, Caleb? She doesn't know."

"What am I going to do?!! Hell, I have a daughter that you kept from me. A daughter that will probably hate me for being an absent dad! A dead beat! I've got to find her. I've got to try to explain. She has to know that I would never have left her had I known. Damn, Cam, how could you do this to me?"

He took several deep breaths and turned again to the sink. "You never slept with him, did you? Why'd you lie?" He turned back to her. "No, it doesn't matter now. Where is she, Cam?"

"She's in New York. Caleb, what are you going to do? I have to know."

"Why?" He took a menacing step toward her. "You didn't think it important that *I* know. What am I going to do? I have another daughter who's grown up thinking that she's an only child. Now, I get to tell her that she has a sister. A sister that *I* didn't even know about. I've got to try to make some sense of this to Candice when I can't make sense of it myself. Then I'm going to New York to find my daughter! And I'm taking this picture with me! Good bye, Cam!" And he stormed out of the door.

19

Caleb could barely remember leaving Peaceful Sands and Cammy, but he knew that getting a speeding ticket wasn't going to solve anything. It wasn't going to change anything either. He had another daughter! Caleb still couldn't believe it. If he didn't have her picture lying on the front seat beside him, he'd think it was a dream. But it wasn't bad dream. A shock, yes! But not something that couldn't be made into reality. No child of his would ever be considered bad or a mistake or unwanted. He and Cam had a child, a girl. And she'll never believe how badly he'd wanted to have a child with Cam.

He pulled to the shoulder of the road. Tallahassee was only twenty miles from Two Plantations, and yet this was the second time he'd had to pull over and stop. The first time was just before eight o'clock when he'd called Candice.

"Hi, Daddy," she'd chirped into the phone.

"Hey, baby, how long will you be home?"

The happiness went out of her voice.

"As long as you want. What's wrong?" She knew something was wrong. He'd sounded so sad. "Are you okay?"

"Sure, kid. I just need to talk to you. That's all."

"Well, I'm here, Dad. Always. See you soon?"

"Be there soon. You know that I love you, don't you Candice?"

"Of course I know that. Daddy, what's wrong?"

"Nothing that you and I can't solve together. I'll be there soon."

This time he'd pulled over because he couldn't see. Tears had flooded his eyes again. "Cam! Cam! Cam! How could you do this to me?" he cried as he laid his head on the steering wheel of the car.

How could this have happened? How could he have missed it? He knew to the day when Cam got pregnant. He just didn't know why she had lied to him about Ralph. And why he'd been so ready to believe her.

They'd been together for two years, but they'd made love on the phone more often than they had together. After all, Cam had a son, so they could only see each other when Frank spent the night with Babee or Jazzy or if he was out of town visiting his Uncle Smitty.

Then they'd come together and spend whatever time they could laughing and talking, and of course, making love. However, the last couple of months they were together, Cam had changed.

Caleb was working a case that involved Cam's husband, Ralph, and his live-in girlfriend, Viola Sutton. Ralph's drinking had gotten worse, and he had become violent with Viola and their oldest son. She'd wanted to press charges against him, but Caleb had intervened and convinced her to relocate to another city and start over. He had known a little about Rachel's Haven, but he couldn't even suggest sending Viola there. And having Ralph lose his license to practice law would have hurt them all including Frank; he and Viola's sons deserved to have a working father.

Somehow it always seemed that the few nights that Cam had free, he was helping Viola. He'd known the history between Viola and Cam, so he hadn't wanted her to know he was helping her husband's mistress. But it was during this time that Cam became so insecure and possessive.

"Why can't I see you any more, Caleb? Are you tired of me?"

"Lord, no, Cam. I love you. You know that."

"Then why don't we see each other anymore? Come tonight. Please?"

"Isn't Frank at home?"

"Yes, but I need you. I need you to hold me. I need to know that you still love me. I'll divorce Ralph tomorrow. Tonight if I could. Please don't leave me, Caleb. Please!"

"Cam, please. What's the matter? I know it's been about a month since we've actually seen each other, but it has nothing to do with us. It's just business. Lately when you're free, I just haven't been. But that'll change soon. Sweetheart, I love you. Don't you believe that?"

She was crying now. "I'll come to Tallahassee. I'll call Babee and ask her to come over. I'll come to you. I never do. I'll come to you this time. Caleb, oh, I love you. Please don't leave me. Please!"

"Cam, try to calm down. I'm not leaving you. I love you! Tell you what. I'll be out there tonight. It'll be late, but I'll be there. I promise."

Caleb had kept his word. And Cam had been all over him from the moment he'd walked through the door. When he'd reached for a condom that he kept in her night stand, she'd stopped him.

"Don't Caleb. Not tonight."

204

"Come on, Cam. I'm about to burst here. You know we have to."

"Not tonight," she'd whispered. *"I can't conceive. I really can't. And I love you. Love me, Caleb. I want to feel all of you inside me. Don't hold anything back from me tonight. Give me that something that you've never given another woman. Just me! No protection. Because you love me, only me! Please."*

And Caleb did. He'd wanted to believe that she was safe, but deep down he'd hoped that she wasn't. She'd have to divorce Ralph then. And they'd be a family. Cam, Frank, their baby, and him.

But then two months later she'd told him that she'd slept with Ralph. And he'd believed her. But why had she lied?

He arrived at Candice's apartment sooner that he'd wanted to. Before he could knock, she opened the door.

"Daddy, you look like hell! What's wrong?"

"Don't I get to come in first?"

"Sure. Come in, have a sit, and tell me what's wrong. I've been going out of my mind with worry."

He sat on the sofa and patted the seat beside him. He leaned his head back and closed his eyes.

"I don't know where to begin. It all happened some many years ago. Long before I'd even moved to D.C.; before I met your mother. Before I met Maggie, I was in love with…"

"A lady named Cam," Candice finished for him. Caleb eyes flew open, and he sat straight up.

"How do you know about Cam?"

"Relax, Dad. It's all right. I've known for four years now. Mommy told me."

205

Caleb looked confused. "Margaret? Impossible! Maggie's been gone longer than four years, and she'd never have told you something like that when you were little. Who's been talking to you?"

Candice laughed. "Believe me. Mommy told me. Remember the box you gave me on my sixteenth birthday? The one from Mommy?"

"Yea, your mother bought that box a month before you were born. She started putting little things in there for you each year. She'd planned to give it to you on your twenty-first birthday, but she'd made me promise that if anything happened to her, you should get it on or after your sixteenth birthday."

"Well, Dad, one of the things she had in it was a letter; it was written when I was four years old. In it, she told me all about her first love, Peter, and how abusive he was. She also told me that she'd never stopped loving him, and if she hadn't met you, she probably would have gone back to him even though she knew what he was. She also told me about you and Cam. She said even though you denied it, she knew that you still loved Cam and that she hoped that by the time I read her letter, either she'd still be married to you or you'd made it back to your first love even though she'd never get back to hers. She also assured me that two of you had a good marriage and that you loved each other, that you were the best thing that ever happened to her. It was if she knew that something was going to happen to her; I've accepted that. But she wanted both of us to be happy. So I know about Cam, Dad. Is that's what's wrong? Do you think I'd be mad or hurt because you've found her again? Don't worry. I think it's great. Just like in the movies!"

"Jeez! Women!" Caleb shook his head. "I wish it was as simple as that, Candice. But since you know all of that, I guess it might be easier if I just showed you this."

Caleb gave the picture to her. She was quiet for a good minute. Then she smiled. "Who is this?"

"It's your sister. A daughter I fathered with Cam. A daughter I didn't know about until this morning."

"Wow! I have a sister. What's her name? How old is she? Where is she?"

Caleb was so wary. He didn't even notice Candice's excitement. "That much I can tell you. Her name is Kimberly Olivia. Her last name is Jackson, but that's not going to last. Hell, she's a Wellington, and no child of mind is going to carry another man's name. Jeez, this is a mess! She's grown. I can't make her change her name. She probably won't want to. She'll probably hate me." Caleb shook his head as if to clear his thoughts. "She's twenty-six, and she's an attorney. I know that from her older brother. He's a great guy! No wonder he and Jeremiah looked at me so strangely. What a mess! Anyway, she lives in New York, and I've got to find her and talk to her. I need to explain."

"So let me get this straight. I have a twenty-six year old sister who is an attorney in New York City? I'm not an only child anymore." Candice threw her arms around her dad.

"Candice, I never lied to you. I didn't know. If I had known, I'd have never left her. I'd have

207

stayed and been a part of her life. I wouldn't have deserted her if I had known."

Candice went stiff in his arms. She slowly pulled away and turned her face away from Caleb.

"Baby, I know I've hurt you. But I've never lied to you; I really didn't know. Please say you understand. Your respect and trust mean the world to me. I'm not a deadbeat dad. I don't get children and leave them. I shoulder my responsibilities. Look at me; talk to me, Candice."

Turning to face her father, Candice felt insecure for the first time in her life. She searched his face. Tears filled her eyes.

"Do you now wish that I hadn't been born? Now that you have another daughter?"

"What!?? What are you saying? I would give my life for you, Candice. I love you! How can you ask something like that?"

"Well, if you had known about her, you wouldn't have left Tallahassee, right? Which means you wouldn't have met and married Mommy, and you wouldn't have had me. What am I to think? That you're sorry now that Mommy and I happened."

"Damn, I'm really screwing this up! Come here." Caleb pulled her into his arms. "You're my baby, and there has not been a second that I wished for anything else. I'm trying so hard not to lose your respect that I'm not thinking and speaking clearly. This is a mess! And I don't know what to do to make any of it right! But I couldn't live if I lost you or your love or your respect! You mean the world to me! You believe me, don't you?"

She wiped her eyes. "Yes, I do. But, Dad, think about this. This is more than just about you.

This is about me, too. I have a sister! A sister! And she might not even want to get to know me! Just think. There's no way we can grow up together; we're both already grown. Just like there's no way you can make up for all of those years you've missed. I'm sure there's a better way to handle this, Dad. You're too emotional right now."

Caleb stared at his daughter in amazement!

"When did you grow up and get so smart?"

"I've been an only child. Only children get smart fast; that's how we survive! So this is what I want you to do. Go spend the day with Aunt Amelia. Tell her you've come to get some of your clothes which you really need to do. Then, Dad, I want you to spend the night here with me. I kinda need you near me tonight. Reassurance, you know, that you are not going to run off and leave me."

"Are you telling me to forget all that I've learned this morning? I can't, Candice."

"No, don't even try to forget it. But Dad, it is what it is. You can't change it. So you've got to figure out how to live with it and move on to the future with two daughters instead of one. Spend the day visiting and spend the night here. Promise me you'll do this for me." Candice's voice trembled.

He hugged her tightly. "I promise. What time do you want me to return? After your study session?"

"Yea, that's a good time. Around eight. Bring some pizza when you come. And Dad, everything will turn out okay. I promise you that. Now, I've got some work to do before class, and you need to get into some running clothes so you can work off some of that stress. Let me take care of you for a change."

"I don't deserve a daughter as understanding as you."

Candice giggled. "I know, but you're stuck with me."

As soon as Caleb closed the door, Candice was on her computer. In less than five minutes she had located three email addresses for Kimberly Olivia Jackson.

God, she whispered. Please let me do this right. Then she typed an email to all three addresses. "Hi! My name is Candice Wellington, and it's very important that I talk with you. Click on the attached picture, and if you want to talk, skype me at 850-777-3256." She hesitated briefly, then clicked 'send'.

20

Kimberly was sitting at her computer at work when the email came through. At first, she didn't open it. Junk mail! And she didn't have time. She had a very busy schedule. She was in the middle of a pro bono case, and she needed to get court papers filed immediately. But she kept coming back to the email; curiosity finally got the best of her.

Wellington. That was the name of the new police chief for Two Plantations. At least she thought that's what Jeremiah had said when she'd spoken to him earlier this morning. But it couldn't be Candice; that's a girl's name. She held the cursor over the attachment for a moment. For a moment she felt chilled. Something close to fear assailed her; her hand shook as she clicked on the attachment, and a picture appeared. She stared. Why would this Candice person have a picture of her? Then Kimberly gave a small cry and started choking. She couldn't breathe. Her chest hurt, and she couldn't get air into her lungs. She leaned over gasping for breath. Tears gathered in her eyes.

She couldn't remember how long she'd stayed that way before she could breathe again. It was impossible. That picture had looked like her when she was younger. But it wasn't a picture of her; it was a picture of someone who looked just like her. Oh, yeah, she wanted to talk to this Candice person. She just needed to clear her head and calm down.

Candice looked at the clock again. 10:05. It'd only been ten minutes since she'd sent that email, but it felt like an eternity. Well, if Kimberly didn't respond, she'd just send another one. She had a sister, and she wasn't given her up without a fight!

The phone on her ipad rang.

For several long seconds, they just looked at each other.

"Who the hell are you?" Kimberly finally choked out.

A shadow of a smile lurked on Candice's lips.

"I don't have time to play, little girl! Just who the hell are you and what do you want?!!" This time Kimberly was literally shouting.

"Whoa! Calm down, please. My goodness! I can see why you're such a successful attorney; you must scare the hell out of a jury. I'm Candice Wellington......."

"I know who you are; I *can* read, you know. And you know what *I* mean. I want to know just who you are and what do you want from me! Now!!! And just so you know, you're not going to blackmail me or my mother! So get on with it! Now!"

Kimberly noted the shocked look on Candice's face. That was one good thing about skyping. They could actually see each other's expressions.

Candice was angry. "Now *you* just wait a damned minute. I'm your *sister*! Why the hell would *I* want to blackmail you *or* your mom?!! I'm glad I have a sister or at least I was until a minute ago!"

"My *what*?!!

"*Your sister*! Yes, I said it, and I'll say it again. *Your sister*! Are you *blind*? What is it you can't see, Ms. Attorney?!! Damn! This was a mistake. I should have left this up to my dad – *our* dad- and your mom. Who's going to mess up *everything*. They will you know. Old people don't know how to handle things like this. They're too emotional; too caught up with each other to see what they'll do to us. But let 'em. I don't care anymore. I just thought if you and I had a chance to talk before….. Well, just forget it. Go answer your phone; it keeps ringing. And have a good life!"

"Wait! Wait! Don't hang up! I mean, *please*, don't hang up! Let us both calm down. Oh, my goodness! Jeez, I'm sorry! I just don't know…….Do you know what a *shock* this is? It's like looking at me reflection in a mirror. Only I know it's not me! Oh, my goodness! This is *not* the way I thought I would find out!"

"Your phone's still ringing. Aren't you going to answer it?" Candice was still angry.

"It's my mom. But, I think we, you and I, should talk before I talk to her. If you don't mind."

Candice relaxed a little. "I think you're finally thinking right. What did you mean? About the way you would find out? You already knew?"

Kimberly sighed. "No, not really. But deep down I knew that Ralph couldn't be my father. I mean, look at me. I don't look like anyone in my mother's family. Mom always assured me that it was our white ancestor's bloodline coming through. I always wanted to believe that, but I just felt it wasn't true. And I don't look like anyone in Ralph's family. Now, I know who I look like; I look like you."

"And my – *our* dad, Caleb Wellington. All of the Wellingtons look alike, but we look just like our father, who is a very good looking man. He'd have been a beautiful woman. If he wasn't a man. That's why we look so good. Sorry, I'm rambling now."

Kimberly laughed. Laughed! "Are you always so, so……."

"Talkative? Positive? Pushy?" Candice laughed. "Only when it's something I really want. Then, I've learned, it's better to take things into your own hands. And especially when it involves things of the heart. It doesn't seem to me that old people handle stuff like that too well. And I really want us to be sisters. You really called your… your father Ralph?"

"Yes, both Frank, my older brother, and I did. He didn't mind. He thought it made him seem young. Ralph was a drunk. He never lived with us. It was a strange situation. He's dead now, but he and my mom divorced about two years after I was born. But you know, now that I think about it, he never treated me any differently than he did Frank. He spent a little time with us when he thought about us, but most of the time he was too busy chasing women to pay either of us any attention. But when he did, he had both of us with him, not just Frank. Weird, don't you think? I mean, he had to *know*."

"I guess. Especially if he knew our dad. I'm sorry that I pushed this on you. I know I should have let your mom or our dad tell you all of this first, but you see, he's all upset because he didn't know about you until this morning! Boy is he pissed! He wanted to come to New York to find you *today*. He probably already has all of your information; he's a retired federal marshal you know. Or maybe you don't. Anyway, he's got all kinds of connections. But I sort of talked him into staying put for a day. He's so emotional over all of this; I just knew he wouldn't handle it right. You know; he'd get his words all wrong and stuff. And he's so mad with your mom right now, even though he still loves her, that he might have made you mad instead of understanding. Then you might not have wanted to meet *me*. I've been an only child; my mom died when I was seven, and I've always wanted a sister so bad. And now I can have an older sister, and since you have a brother, maybe I can get a sister *and* a brother out of this deal."

Candice stopped to catch her breath.

"You *are* a talker, are you?" Kimberly laughingly said.

Candice giggled. "Well, yes, mostly, but more so when I'm nervous or scared. And I'm really scared that you won't want me for a sister because of what our parents did, your mom and our dad."

"He had to know about me, didn't he? I mean, he left my mom pregnant, moved on with his life, and never looked back. He never tried to contact me. All these years and he never once tried to contact me, to see me."

"He didn't *know*. Not until this morning! That's why I wanted to contact you first. It's a very crazy story. I told you, old people can't handle this kind of stuff."

"Candice, they weren't '*old*' twenty-six years ago. And what do you mean, he still loves her? I thought you said that he was angry, pissed I believe you said."

"Well, yea, he is. He's always had this code of honor thing about having children out of wedlock. His father had plenty, so he, our dad, made sure that he didn't."

"Well, he sure messed up one time!"

"Guess that can't be denied. *They'll* have to tell you that part of the story. I'm too young to hear that kind of stuff from my dad. Jeez, that's creepy! But he does still love your mom; I can tell. He calls her 'Cam". You should hear the way he says it. I hope someday I can find a man who says my name with such reverence in his voice. Oh, yea, he still loves her."

"But does my mom still love *him*?"

"Kimberly, just think! What was he doing in her kitchen before seven o'clock in the morning? Come on! I'm *not* that young! And I've got a plan. Maybe we can get a whole family out of this, brother and sisters, mom and dad. But we've got to work fast."

"Hey, hold on! A plan! I'm still reeling from you!"

"Listen, we've got to work quick on this! That's your mom calling again, right? Listen, you've got to meet my – *our* dad first. Your mom's probably in so much pain right now, so *you've* got to be the one to help her! Meet Dad first; decide if he's someone you'd like to get to know better. That'll help you when you talk to your mom. I've already booked you on a 1:30 flight today to Tallahassee."

"What? Girl, I can't just......"

Kimberly stopped. She'd gotten her own emotions so caught up in this drama that she'd forgotten what had made her such a top notch

216

attorney. The girl was right; emotions had a way of sidetracking sound logic. She was good at what she did because she could read people and could tell the truth from a lie. Candice was telling the truth, at least as much truth as she knew.

Candice was also right about something else. It was time for Kimberly to take control of her life. If she'd allowed *her* feelings to get all messed up in this so that she couldn't think straight, she could imagine how her mom and Caleb Wellington were handling all of this stuff. Not well! Not well at all!

"So, you say he was in my mom's house *early* this morning? My goodness! My goodness! Maybe I'm too young for all of this, too. Okay, tell me your plan."

****

It had taken only half an hour for Kimberly to talk with both partners, had her cases distributed throughout the staff of lawyers, filled out leave forms, and was in a taxi headed to her apartment. Everyone had been so understanding, and she hadn't had to say anything more than 'a personal problem at home'.

"Take care of yourself and your family. You're too important to this firm to lose you," Melvin York had told her as he gave her a big hug. "Every so often, our families need us. You take care of yours and don't worry about this place. You're needed here too; your job is secure."

Kimberly texted Frank on her way home.
"You with mom?"
"Yea. Why?"
"I know about them and me."
"How? Did Wellington contact you? Are you okay?"

217

"No, not him. His daughter. And, yes. I'm okay. What about Mom?'

"A mess! You wouldn't take her calls. Mad?"

"No. Strange isn't it. Listen, I need your help. Get her out of the house. Keep her busy. Where's Aunt Babee?"

"Here with Mom. Yea, I can do that. What about you?"

"I'll call you within the hour. Be somewhere where you can talk."

"Okay. Be safe."

It took Kimberly another half hour to throw a few things in a carry-on and was back in a cab on her way to the airport. Once inside, everything moved pretty swiftly, and Kimberly had a few minutes to relax. She called Frank. He answered on the first ring.

"His *daughter* called you?"

Kimberly laughed. "Yes, actually sent me a picture of her through email. You can't imagine how shocked I was! But not really surprised. I always knew that there was something. I just didn't expect to find it out quite this way. Have you met him, Frank?"

"Kim, are you alright? You sound way too calm."

"Once you meet her, Candice, I mean, you'll understand. She's a whirlwind, and believe me, you'll get caught up in her enthusiasm. Hard to be negative, sad, or mad around her! Have you met *him*?"

Frank hesitated for a second. "Yea, he stopped by the clinic shortly after he arrived in Two Plantations."

"So tell me about him."

When Kimberly closed her phone, she was smiling. She trusted Frank's judgment. She was going home.

21

Cammy thought that her heart had been broken before, but she couldn't remember *any* pain as bad as the pain she was experiencing now. It just wasn't fair; it wasn't right! She'd been so close! Cammy and Caleb! Together! They'd touched! They'd kissed! They'd laughed and talked! For a little while she'd thought that they'd have the rest of their lives together! They should have had forever! Now, instead of finally getting her 'love song' kind of love, her heart was singing the blues. God!

She had wanted to lock herself in her house. But Frank and Babee wasn't having any of that. She really shouldn't have called Frank, but she was half out of her mind. He'd rushed right out to her, and Babee had arrived at Peaceful Sands about an hour later. Frank had met her on the porch.

"Thanks for coming, Aunt Babee. Mom's a mess, and I really don't know what to prescribe for a broken heart. Especially my mom's!" Frank looked so confused.

"So she told you? About Kim?"

"Oh, she told me alright! About Kim and *everything* else!" Frank shook his head and then grinned. "Please tell me I won't have to listen to my daughter's confessions. It's a bit too much!"

Babee laughed. "Talk to Danny so you'll be prepared. He's had an ear full over the years! Are you all right?"

"Well, at first, I just wanted to find Sug Wellington and smash his face in, but two things stopped me. One, I knew he could probably beat me to a pulp, and two, I actually feel sorry for him. That's a hell of a secret to discover after twenty-six years. But I hate to see her hurting. It's killing me, but I don't know exactly what I'm supposed to be saying to her. Thanks for coming. She needs a woman's ear right now. I've already called Aunt Jazzy, and she and Uncle David won't be arriving until later tonight."

"Don't even think about it. I would have been mad if you hadn't called. Besides, I have been given the day off, so I need to be doing something useful!"

Heather was running the bakery for the day, and both Danny and Heather were happy about it. Babee wasn't that sure, so being with Cammy was good for her. It would keep her mind off of the mess Heather was sure to make in her shop.

A few minutes after Babee had arrived at Peaceful Sands, Delphine had called and invited them to breakfast at White Oaks. So Frank had handed his mom into Babee's capable hands and had returned to town.

Cammy could understand why he'd been so anxious to leave. She'd told him *everything* about her and Caleb, even about the last two nights. *Everything!* She just couldn't stop crying and talking. Poor Frank! He had listened so patiently. No wonder he was so popular with his female patients. But to have to listen to his *own* mom talk about her broken heart, her affair, even her ……, well, he was a good son. That's all she could say. And now that she looked back on it, it was rather funny. Especially when she was telling him about last night! Poor Frank!

    She and Babee had walked across to White Oaks to have breakfast with Delphine and her husband. Boy was she surprised when she was introduced to Tim Buckley. Who would have thought that one of Camilla Harpson Collins' descendents would be married to a black man! Would wonders never cease! God truly does have a sense of humor!

    "It is so nice to meet you," Cammy had said once she could get her eyes back in their sockets.

    Tim gave her a big hug. "It's a pleasure to meet you too, *Cuz*. You're not too shocked, are you?"

    Cammy laughed. Earlier she'd thought that she'd never laugh again. "Well, to be truthful, yes I am. And Delphine set me up. She just said I'd really like you. I just assumed you were white."

    "So I guess we're the flip side of Beaufort and Sadie Mae for our generation. You can imagine my surprise when we pulled up here about a week ago. Me living in a plantation house. My family thinks it's one big joke. Wait 'til they visit."

    "I'm so glad you're both here. And you'll have to share this love story with me some time. So, how *do* you get along with the Harpsons?"

    "Ha! Disowned Delphine; don't even acknowledge me! The happiest day of our lives, besides, of course, the day we met! Love at first sight! I'm a lucky man!"

"Hey," Delphine called from the kitchen. "Do you both expect Babee and me to do all of the work around here?"

Cammy and Tim made their way into the kitchen where the table had been set and the food was all prepared. It had been a good and distracting way to spend the morning.

Kimberly still hadn't called back, but Cammy didn't have much time to dwell on that because Delphine and Tim decided that there no better time than the present to see Peaceful Sands. Babee had called Danny while they were eating breakfast, and he was waiting for them when they crossed the road.

The afternoon passed swiftly as the five of them walked through every inch of Peaceful Sands, including the dusty attic. They stopped from time to time to get something to drink and to eat a snack. They sat on the floor of the attic and talked and laughed while Danny sketched and made some temporary changes to the plans that he had used in the renovations for Peaceful Sands.

Then they'd walked back across to White Oaks and walked it from top to bottom.

"How's that knee?" Babee'd asked on several times throughout the day. That had started a lengthy conversation about arthritis and carpal tunnel, which Tim had, and other ailments that seems to follow folks into their golden years.

"Caleb laughed when….." she couldn't go on.

"When what?" asked Delphine.

Cammy gave a shaky laugh. "Well, he laughed when I told him I had arthritis in my knee. He's a retired federal marshal you know. He's stayed very fit."

Delphine and Tim smiled at each other. "So you've noticed our new chief of police, huh?"

The knock on the door stopped Cammy from answering. Thank goodness! It was Frank.

"Frank, you've come back!"

"Sure, mom, you're going to dinner with us. Janice and the kids are over at the house now. Hello, everyone! Did you enjoy your day? Every time I called Mom she was climbing stairs or going down stairs."

"It was a great day," Delphine answered, it seemed, for everyone. "We can't wait to get started on the renovations."

"So you've decided?" Cammy asked as she, Frank and Babee headed out of the door.

"Yes! We'll stay in the RV while it's being done. It'll give us time to think about advertising and all of the other stuff involved."

"Well, let me know what I can do to help. Now, I'm off to dinner."

When they stopped on the porch, Cammy turned to her friend. "Thanks for everything, Babee."

"Don't thank me, girl. That's what family is for. You're in good hands now. If those two grandchildren can't keep you occupied, nothing can. Stay in touch. Love you!"

Cammy hugged Babee and whispered in her ear, "I don't care what you say. Thank you for being the best friend ever."

Cammy smiled up at Frank as they walked down the steps. "It's been a strange day. Thank you, Frank, for being such a wonderful son."

"Ah, Mom. Don't thank me. But the next time you want to talk about, you know, your *sex* life, please call Janice!"

Cammy laughed. "On, come on Frank. You're a big boy now."

"Yea, Mom, but not *that* big!"

22

Caleb had finally made it back to Candice's apartment. He arrived much earlier than he'd planned, but his family had worn him out; he needed some down time so that he could think.

Once he'd gotten to Amelia's house that morning, he'd changed clothes and gone for that five mile run that he'd needed so badly. Then when he'd returned, Amelia had put him to work fixing any and every thing that she could find that was broken. She didn't ask any questions, that's what he liked about his oldest sister, but she must have known that something was wrong. She'd kept him busy most of the day.

She'd also called every Wellington that did not have a job, and all of them had converged on her house which meant that by the time Caleb had finished and showered, a Wellington cookout was in full blast! He'd called Candice to come out, but she never returned his call. Finally, he'd been too tired to even try to hold conversation, so he'd started home – home to Two Plantations. He didn't know when he'd started thinking of it as home, but he knew it was now. Even when everything was turned upside down, that's where he wanted to go.

But he'd promised Candice, so he turned around and gone to her apartment. He was happy that Candice hadn't come home yet. It had been a long day; he needed a little time alone. Caleb had found a couple of cans of beer in her refrigerator. Boy was he going to give her hell about that, roommate or no roommate, but those beers were good and cold, so he decided to help her out and drank both.

Once he'd finished both, he put the cans on her coffee table so she'd see them when she came in. Then he leaned back with his heads behind his head, his feet on the coffee table, and his eyes closed. He fell asleep.

Kimberly paid the taxi driver and with her overnight bag in her hand, climbed the stairs to the apartment where her real father waited for her. How could she do this? She was so afraid! She'd jump on that plane and hadn't given herself enough time to process everything, to decide if this was really the right way to handle this situation. Uncertain, she stood outside with the key in her hand. Candice had left it under the door mat just as she said she would. Her real father was on the other side of that door! All she had to do was just open it. But did she really have the nerves?

It was the key in the door that woke him. But he didn't open his eyes. He wanted to hear her reaction when she spotted those beer cans.

Caleb waited but all he could hear was the door closing, a gasp, and then soft crying. His eyes shot open! "Candice, don't……."

Then he shot out of the sofa. Shock covered his face! "You're not Candice; you're Kimberly. My God!"

Tears ran down her face as she stood with her back to the door.

"Oh, God, Kimberly! I'm so sorry. I would have done anything not to hurt you. Please forgive me! I'm so sorry!" By this time, Caleb was crying, too, but neither had moved. He wanted to take her in his arms and hold her tight, but he was afraid to move. He was so afraid of her rejection. Even though he deserved it!

"Kimberly, please say something! Say you hate me! Tell me you never want to see my sorry behind again! Say something!" Kimberly could hear the anguish in his voice. Her father! This was really her father! She wiped the tears from her face, gave him a little shaky smile, and took a small step forward.

"Candice was right. She said we couldn't leave it up to you to say the right thing. She said you're too emotional." She took a shaky breath. "And she thinks that you're too old to handle all of this. Maybe she's right about that, too."

"Candice? What does she know? I don't even know what the right thing to say *is*! I just don't want to run you away. And I'm *not* old."

Kimberly couldn't seem to stop staring. She now had a face that looked like her. She moved farther into the room. In a slightly unsteady voice she replied, "Well, if you don't want to turn me off, don't start putting ideas in my head like hating you and all that other stuff. Let me find out if I should or not. Don't make those decisions for me. Okay?"

Caleb stared at his daughter. Except of the tears, she was definitely composed, in control. He could see the attorney in her. Must be why she was so successful in her profession. But he could also see the nerves, the uncertainty, the hesitation.

"Okay. Then, let's not just stand here. I have pizza in the kitchen. If you're hungry, let's sit and talk while we eat. By the way, why are you here? You should be in New York! You've spoken with your mom already I take it."

"No, I haven't spoken with her yet. I wanted to meet you first. Talk to you first. I already know my mom. I know anything she did, she did out of love. I need to get to know you a little bit. And I'm here because of your more than assertive daughter, my little sister, Candice."

While she was talking, Caleb had put the box of pizza on the table along with paper plates and sodas. He stopped. The look of shock had been replaced with genuine surprise.

"Candice?"

"Yes, that little sister of mine something else. How did you get her to be so full of confidence?"

Caleb shrugged. "Her mother died when she was young. I owed it to her to help make her as strong and independent as possible."

Kimberly laughed. "You certainly did a good job of that!"

"You sound exactly like your mother when you laugh. You're beautiful like her, too."

"You think my mom's still beautiful?"

"Think? Cam's the most beautiful woman I've ever known. But I don't understand. If you haven't spoken with your mom, how did you meet Candice?"

"She emailed me. It must have been as soon as you left her this morning. She sent me a picture of herself. I suppose you can guess the rest!"

"I should have known Candice was up to something. But I was so upset this morning, so mad. Kimberly, please believe me when I tell you that I would not have left Tallahassee if I had known about you. I'm not that kind of man. I stand by my responsibilities."

"But how could you *not* know? I mean you, mom, no protection?"

Caleb was silent.

"She told me she was safe; I took it to mean that she on the pill. It was the only time in my life, except with my wife, that I'd ever done that."

"But you did because……?"

"She asked."

"Just like that?"

"Yea, just like that. I loved Cam. I'd have given her anything I had."

Kimberly's laugh was shaky and ended with a sob. She inhaled deeply. "Well, you sure did that. And she didn't tell you about me?"

"No, I didn't even know she was pregnant when I left."

"Then why did you leave? I'm sorry about so many questions, but I'm trying to understand. I really need to understand."

"I left because she told me she had been with your … with Ralph. I couldn't handle that; I was crazy in love with your mother. So I was devastated. I felt like a fool, so I left. I swear I didn't know about you, Kimberly. When I heard she was pregnant, I was already in D.C.; I thought you belonged to Ralph. I didn't know."

Kimberly looked down at her empty plate. She couldn't even remember eating any of the pizza. Tears had gathered in her eyes again.

"Frank likes you. Say's you're a good man. He's a good judge of character."

Caleb was afraid to know where this was leading, too afraid to hope. He realized that he'd stopped breathing. At least, he thought he'd stopped. But his heart was pounding, so he knew he was still alive. He watched as Kimberly stood and walked around to where he was sitting. He slowly got to his feet.

"It's hard to take this all in. Everything's happened so fast. I *know* I like Candice. And it's so strange, but I think I like you, too. I've wanted a real father all of my life. I've given *this* part a lot of thought, and I don't think it's too late to have one now. What do you think... Dad?"

"Dad?"

"Yea, if that's okay with you."

Caleb pulled her into a hug so tight, he was afraid he'd hurt her. He loosened his hold a little, but he didn't let go. "Oh, yes, Kimberly. It's definitely okay."

"*Yes!*" Candice's scream from the door startled them both. "I couldn't wait any longer! You're both still alive which means you didn't kill each other! Which is pretty obvious, right?! I knew it! I told you, didn't I Kimberly?"

Caleb and Kimberly laughed.

"Is there no half measure with you, Candice?"

"Not when there's something I want, big Sis! What's next on the agenda?"

231

"Could you take me to Frank's house? I have to see my mom now. But Candice, you can't come in tonight. And it has nothing to do with you meeting them. You will; I know I wouldn't be able to stop you even if I wanted to. But I have to talk to her first. Let her know that everything's okay. I'll call you tonight. We probably have some more things to discuss."

"I can take you," Caleb offered.

"No!" Both girls answered together. Then they laughed, but Caleb didn't find it funny. He looked a little put out.

"Dad," Candice said as she kissed his cheek. "We love you, but you're not really good at this. You don't choose your words well. You mean well, but you'll let your emotions take over. Believe me when I tell you this with love. Let Kim talk to her mom. You wait here for me. Oh, and order another pizza."

She and Kimberly were almost out the door when Candice yelled to her dad. "And that wasn't my beer."

Caleb could hear his daughters giggling as they went down the stairs.

23

Kimberly let herself into Frank's house. She could hear the laughter and noise coming from the family room at the back of the house. She stood there and listened to the fun and gaiety for several minutes.

Talking with Caleb had been easy compared to what she would face now. She still couldn't believe how natural it felt to call Caleb Wellington 'dad'. How wonderful it had felt for him to hug her! She almost felt dizzy with relief! God! How one picture could change her life! But she felt good about the change!

Now she had another hurdle to leap. She had talked with Frank several times, so she knew the pain her mom was in. Interesting though, that Frank had a hard time dissecting which was causing the most pain – the truth she'd been hiding for so many years or losing Caleb for a second time. After talking to Caleb, her father, Kimberly was leaning more to the losing Caleb idea. Jeez, they really loved each other. It was tragic and wonderful at the same time.

But it was their love more than anything else that told Kimberly how to handle this with her mom. Take charge! She could finally have a real family at last, she and Frank. No way was she going to let her mom and dad mess it up for them again. Candice was right again! Her mom and dad were just too old to get this right without some help!

Frank, Jr. was the first to see her standing in the door to the family room.

"Aunfie Kim! Aunfie Kim!" he shouted as he ran to her.

She picked him up and swung him high over her head as Yvette hugged her knees. "It's Auntie not Aunfie."

"Not!" shouted Jr.

"Is too, isn't it, Auntie?"

Jr. put his hands of her cheeks and looked into her eyes. *He's a romeo already* Kimberly thought. "I'm saying it right, ain't I Aunfie Kim?"

"No! No! No! You're too little to say it right! It's Aun*tie* Kim. *I'm* saying it the right way. *Right?*"

Kimberly laughed as she put Jr. on the floor. "It sounds as if you're both saying it right!"

"Told you!" Jr. yelled to Yvette as they raced back to their game.

Kim walked over to the game table where Janice, Frank, and her mother were sitting playing scrabble.

"Hi! My! It's good to be home. At least it's good to be back in Tallahassee. I won't be home until I get to Two Plantations. I've really missed you all so much!" Then she looked down at the game board. "And *that's* not really a word, Mom! Are they still letting you cheat?"

Cammy literally bounced up from the table and caught Kimberly in a tight hug.

"Kimberly! When did you get home? Oh, my God! Oh, my baby! I'm so glad you're home, honey! I've been calling you all day! How are you? Are you okay? You look great! Why didn't you return my calls?"

Over Cammy's head, she smiled at Frank and Janice. "I'm fine, Mom. Let me look at you. You look great yourself! Now sit back down; don't let me stop your game!"

"Take my place, Kimberly. I have to put the kids to bed anyway." Janice gave Kimberly a hug and a quick look of sympathy before she gathered her two protesting children and took them upstairs.

"I'm right behind you, babe," yelled Frank as he pecked Kimberly on the cheek and dropped a set of keys into her hands. Then he leaned closer and whispered in her ear. "Be prepared to learn a lot about sex tonight! Good luck!" Leaning over, he kissed his mom on her forehead and, with a quick grin at them both, sprinted up the stairs behind his family. Silence settled over the room.

Cammy reached over and took Kimberly's hands in hers. She was trembling.

"Kimberly, I have something I have to tell you. It's so hard for me to admit such a terrible secret, but I've kept it much too long, and it's cost me far too much. I hope you can forgive me."

"I can forgive you anything, Mom. I love you. You've been the best mom in the world to Frank and me. Nothing you could have done will ever change that!"

"I don't know, Kim. I pray that you are right." Cammy took a deep breath. "Well, Kim, I'm sorry, but Ralph Jackson is not your father. There. I've said it. How you must hate me. I'm so sorry!" Cammy began to weep.

235

Seconds passed. Kimberly knew she had to play this out so that her mom could put this guilt behind her. After all, Kimberly had already accepted her real father into her life. Maybe she could help her mom finally have her once in a life time love.

She squeezed her mom's hand and handed her a napkin from the table. "Don't cry, Mom. It's okay! Believe me; I'm not surprised. Actually, I'm relieved to know he's not my father; he was an awful excuse for one! I always knew that I didn't look like him. I just didn't know who I really did favor. So, who is my real father? I'm not going to ask if you loved him; you wouldn't have been with someone if you hadn't loved him. Did he love you?"

There was so much pain in Cammy's eyes as she looked at her daughter. "Oh, Kim, why didn't you ever say anything? All of these years! Although I probably would have lied to you at the time. I'm so ashamed of what I did to you. Your real father's name is Caleb Wellington; he's the new police chief of Two Plantations. And yes, oh, yes, we were in love!"

Kim took her mom's hands in hers. "But he couldn't have been much better than Ralph! He had to be a bum. Look how he ran off and left you!"

Cammy shook her head. "No! It wasn't like that at all. He didn't know about you!"

"Come on, Mom. You loved this guy, and he ran off when he discovered you were pregnant! It's alright. You can tell me; I can handle this."

"No! It wasn't like that. We, Caleb and I, well, we didn't go out anywhere. You know. Out in public! Remember, I was still legally married. But we spent a lot of time together at Peaceful Sands. Then I started hearing rumors about Caleb and Viola Sutton.

Well, you know my history with Viola. I was distraught! So I didn't let him use protection one night. That's when I knew for sure that he really, really loved me. He'd had a strict rule about that, and he broke it for me. For *me*! I really wanted you. Our child – Caleb's and mine. And I knew he would want you, too. I knew him that well! When I missed my cycle, I couldn't wait to tell him. So I went to the police station in Tallahassee and waited for him to get off. But when he came out, he was with Viola. They got in his car and drove off. He didn't even see me! I was furious! How *could* he? And with *Viola*!! When he called later that evening, I told him…. Well I told him that I'd been with Ralph. You know, intimately. I'd wanted to hurt him like I was hurting. And I did. I really hurt him! I broke his heart! Within two weeks he was gone. By then I'd realized that I loved him too much to lose him, but it was too late. And since no one knew we were seeing each other, I couldn't ask his family or friends where he had gone."

"Wow! But what about Ralph? He *had* to know that he wasn't my father."

"He did! But he didn't say one thing. It was only after you were born, and he realized that Caleb was your father that he told me what had happened."

"And that was………?"

"Caleb had stopped Viola from pressing criminal charges against Ralph. In a drunken rage, Ralph had hit her and their oldest son. Caleb helped her move from Ralph's place and then found her employment in Daytona. It took about two months. His guess was that Caleb didn't say anything to me because Viola was involved. But I'd heard the truth too late; Caleb was already engaged. I couldn't tell him then, Kim! He'd moved on with his life because I had lied to him. I broke his heart; I didn't deserve a second chance. But he wasn't a bum! He's the greatest man in the world!"

"You still love him, Mom?"

"Oh, yes! Last night was so wonderful, Kim. When he touched me….."

"Mom! Please! That's just too much information. I get the picture, okay?!!"

Cammy smiled at her daughter as tears rolled down their faces. "Why are my children so shy about intimacy? Anyway, I was given a second chance last night, and I blew it again. He hates me now. But you have to meet him, Kimberly. You'll love him. He's wonderful!"

"I've already met him," Kimberly said as she leaned over and kissed Cammy on her cheek. "And if first impressions are reliable, I think he might be wonderful, too! Get your things, Mom. I'm ready to go home to Peaceful Sands. Everything's always clearer there. And if Frank has his information right, Aunt Jazzy and Uncle David are already there."

Cammy couldn't move. "Already met him? How? Where?"

Kimberly laughed. "Come on, Mom. I'll tell you all about it on the way home.

****

Kimberly was glad that Aunt Jazzy was at Peaceful Sands when they arrived. It had been a long and emotional day, and she still had some things to do before she could go to bed and, hopefully, to sleep. So she'd left her mom in Aunt Jazzy's capable hands and gone up stairs to her old bedroom.

As soon as she removed the silence mode from her cell phone, it rang.

"Hi, Candice. Goodness, you must have ESP!"

"Well, I'm not good at waiting as you should know by now! How did it go?"

"She still loves him! It's amazing! You probably don't know this, but we have this legacy in the Collins' family about this true love thing. Passed down through generations. Before, it's always seemed like a make believe story, but hearing them, mom and Caleb....I mean Dad, talk about each other, I'm a believer now. Can you imagine? After twenty-six years! That's a powerful love."

Candice sighed. "Yea! I hope I find a love like that. But I want to find it and keep it. No separations!"

"I'm with you there! I know you already have a next step to this plan of yours so what is it?"

"Well, a lot depends on Two Plantations. I think that that's where they should reunite. You know, add to the romance and everything. This is what I've been thinking. What's more natural than to get you together will your Wellington aunts and uncles? If there's some place in Two Plantations where we could hold a small gathering, you know a sort of welcome to the family thing, then we could set them up so that Dad would have to take Mom home. And yea, I called her mom. How awkward is it going to be for you to call her mom and me call her Cammy or Ms. Cammy or Ms. Camilla or whatever? Really!!

I hope she won't mind. Don't you worry; I'll talk to her about it. So is there some place?"

"Yes, now that you mention it. My Uncle Smitty is about to open up a café here; that would work. My Aunt Jazzy and Uncle David are already here. We have a new cousin who has moved into White Oaks, and we can add Heather and Jeremiah, Aunt Babee's children. Yea, I can see how this could work. But Dad's family. They're not going to be mean or anything to my mom. *That* I will not stand for!"

"Don't worry about that! It's all taken care of! They were shocked for sure! But they love Dad, and they're always in his corner. He's a Wellington, and Wellingtons take care of their own. You'll love them! They're a bit over whelming, but it's all with love. So are we set?"

"Yes! We'll plan for Saturday night. I'll let you know what time. Okay?"

"Sure! And Kim, have her wear something sexy. You know, we want that sensual tension in the air kind of atmosphere. I'll bring a boom box or something just in case your uncle's place doesn't have any music, and we can have some Marvin Gaye and Whitney Houston playing softly in the background."

"Candice, where do you get this *stuff* from?"

She giggled. "I read romance novels. Doesn't everybody? They teach you a lot. If you don't, you ought to. Got to prepare yourself for the unexpected and so on. See you tomorrow."

Kimberly stretched out on the bed. She hadn't expected to fill so relaxed and contented. She should have been an emotional wreck. But since her mom and dad were already wrecks, it didn't leave her much room to join them. Wow! A real family! It was so close. She couldn't let anything stand in the way. This had to work. Yes, she, Aunt Babee and Aunt Jazzy would take her mom shopping tomorrow. Those two aunts will have her sexy in no time. She smiled as she dozed off to sleep.

24

The knocking at the front door brought Cammy awake. Could it be Caleb? She was too afraid to hope, but she quickly put on her robe and rushed to the door. She didn't even bother to look out of the peep hole; she just opened the door and there stood a miniature Kimberly.

"Hi I'm Candice. I know it's early and everything, but I just couldn't wait, you know. I kept thinking, you know, that it just wasn't fair. After all, Kim had met Dad, but I hadn't met you......"

"Candice, slow down," Kimberly said from the stairs. "Let her in, Mom, because she won't go away."

"Are you trying to be funny, Kim? Boy, is that how you dress for bed?"

Kimberly looked down at herself. "And what's wrong with my PJ*s*?"

"Nothing much. Just looks a little drab for someone so young. Is that your Aunt Jazzy behind you? Now *that's* how you dress for bed."

Kim and Cammy looked up at Jazzy who had on a very sexy red and black lingerie set.

"She's married," Kim and Cammy said in unison.

"Yea, well, you have to practice these things. You just can't wait until you meet someone special to practice. By then, you need to have it right."

"And just what do you sleep in?" Cammy asked.

"Well, something like Aunt Jazzy's wearing. I can call you Aunt Jazzy can't I? Only not quite so provocative."

Kimberly and Jazzy sat on the stairs and gazed at Candice in wonder.

"And Caleb knows this?" Cammy just wouldn't believe that Caleb would be happy with that information.

"Sure. I mean, I've always liked that kind of stuff. Since I was in middle school and saw some in a fancy magazine. You know there is some decent lingerie out there. Not that yours is indecent, Aunt Jazzy. But I *like* frilly, feminine. It makes me feel good!"

"God, Candice." Kimberly shook her head as she and Jazzy stood up. "I'm going to have my hands full with you. I guess I'd better wash up and dress. Looks like our day has begun."

"I'm right behind you, Kimberly. Indecent huh? No wonder David insisted that I bring it."

"She's not mad at me is she?" Candice asked as Jazzy and Kim disappeared at the top of the stairs. "Aunt Jazzy I mean. I *liked* her night stuff. She looked cool in it."

"Come and have a seat while I start breakfast. And no, she's not mad. She's flattered. She'll probably buy two or three more now."

"Can I help? I'm sorry I woke everyone up. I'm just so excited, and I wanted to speak to you. I just couldn't wait. What can I do?"

"Nothing right now. Let's just sit and talk. I guess you want to talk about me and your dad."

"No way! I know about that. No, I wanted to ask you….."

She couldn't seem to get her words out, and tears welled up in Candice's eyes.

"What's wrong, honey?"

"You know that my mother died when I was seven. I'm twenty now. That's a long time not to have a mother, don't you think?"

"Oh dear! It must have been so hard on you. I was a young adult when my mom died, and it was the most difficult time for me."

"It was for me, too. But I had Dad, and he was wonderful. It was just the two of us from then on. But now I have a sister *and* a brother. I've already talked with Frank this morning, and he said he'd be happy to have me for a little sister, too. It's really the only logical thing to do since Kim and I are sisters, don't you think? I *should* be a part of the equation. But see, you're Kim and Frank's mom. They *call* you Mom. What am *I* to call you? Certainly not Cam; that's Dad's name for you. It would be disrespectful to call you Cammy or Camilla. Do I call you Ms. Cammy or Ms. Camilla or Mrs. Jackson?"

Cammy was speechless. How was she to answer such a question and give the right answer? One thing she did know. She did *not* want to be called Ms. Cammy or Ms. Camilla or Mrs. Jackson. But if Candice wanted to use either one of those, she'd deal with it. After all, Candice was now as much a part of the Jackson family as she was the Wellingtons. And she was a great kid; Cammy could tell.

"What do you think you'd feel most comfortable calling me?"

"Mom."

"What?!" Cammy was stunned.

"That's what I'd feel most comfortable calling you if you don't mind. I miss having a mom; I want one again. I'll never forget my mommy, but God's given me another chance at a real family. Even though you and Dad can't seem to get it together, I've dreamed of a brother and a sister, a mom and a dad. But if that would make you feel uncomfortable, I'll understand. I know I can't have everything I want."

"Oh, Candice," cried Cammy as tears rolled down her face.

Candice came around the table and kneeled beside Cammy. "I'm sorry. I'm sorry I upset you. Please don't cry. Forget I said anything. It was stupid of me. Don't cry!"

Cammy reached down and hugged Candice to her. "Oh Candice, that's the nicest thing anyone has said to me in a long time. Of course you can call me Mom. I'm honored to have you as a daughter."

Jumping to her feet Candice shouted. "Yes! A family! This is great! Can I go and tell Kim?"

There was no need to answer because Candice was already running up the stairs.

"Tell her breakfast will be ready soon," Cammy yelled after her.

Wow, that girl is really something, Cammy thought as she started preparing breakfast. Now if only Caleb would forgive her. Then they'd be a complete family. But that wasn't going to happen. He hadn't even tried to contact her since he'd walked out on her.

"We're going shopping," Kimberly announced after breakfast. "Go get dressed, Mom, and wear something easy to get out of. We're going to be trying on dresses for the party tomorrow night. And before you tell me again that you don't need to be there, this party's important to me. I need you there."

"Of course, honey. I'm sorry. Don't pay me any attention. Most of the time I can't believe that you and Frank have handled all of this so well, especially you! I keep waiting for the ball to drop. You know, the blame, the tears, the looks of disappointment and shame."

Kim caught her mom's hand. "Mom, I've spent most of my life filled with questions. A lot of time and a lot of questions! And nothing changed; none of my questions got answered. I spent all that time, and only got the answers to my questions when God was ready. Now that I have the answers, I guess you expect me to spend *another* life time trying to figure out why things happened the way they did? I refuse to waste any more time doing that. I can't change the past, and you can't either. I'm really sorry that you and Dad want to spend so much time rehashing the past and won't move forward, but Candice, Frank, and I have decided to learn from the past and make each day we have together the best days of our lives. And we're beginning with the party tomorrow night. So get dressed. You're going to have a marvelous time today, believe me."

An hour later, Cammy, Jazzy, Babee *and* Delphine were on their way to Tallahassee. They were headed to Desiree's, a new dress store that sold the latest after five fashions. They were giggling like teenagers when they entered the shop, but Cammy stopped immediately. She wanted to sink through the floor! All six of Caleb's sisters and his sister-in-law were already there, looking at dresses.

Amelia was the first to spot her. "Camilla, we've been waiting for you. Candice said that they already have a couple of dresses picked out for you and that we shouldn't buy anything until we see what you're wearing. Well, don't just stand there; I'm Amelia, the oldest of the brood. Welcome to the family."

Within minutes everyone had hugged and shared names. Cammy knew Justine, Velma, and Patience from junior high school, but after integration, they had gone to a different school. Desiree, the owner of the store, gave them a few minutes to get to get to know each other, and then started showing them some of the dresses she had just gotten in.

Cammy held an ankle length, floral dress in front of her. "How does this look, Jazzy?"

"Like you're old. Put that away, please. Look at something like this." And she held a sexy strapless dress up for Cammy to see.

"No way! I have too much up top for that!" Everyone laughed. Then there were a series of 'top heavy' and 'flat chest' jokes. And as they passed dresses from one to another, a few dirty jokes were passed around as well.

The other shoppers in the store kept looking at them and smiling. A few thought they were a little too loud, but Desiree didn't seem to be bothered. Maybe she was used to older women on a shopping spree. And really, if they all bought their dresses from her, she'd make a lot of money in one day; her dresses weren't cheap.

Jazzy clapped when Kimberly, Candice, and Janice walked in. "Finally, the voice of authority!"

" Put that back," Kim said as she walked up behind her mom. "That's frumpy."

"Tried to tell her, Kim," Jazzy yelled across the store, "but she wouldn't listen to me."

"Well, Candice and I have selected several dresses that we think you will like. All of you. But we'll start with Mom, and the rest of us will be her back up group. Desiree, we'll start with the candy apple red strapless with the sweetheart neckline."

When Desiree brought the dress out, everyone went wild!

"My goodness! I love that dress!"

"*You* Aunt Amelia?" asked Candice.

"Shoot yes! It's too short for me at my age, but if it was longer...... Well, Wyatt would get a kick out of seeing me in something like that. And after all, tomorrow night will just be family and close friends. What's the harm? We all deserve a little fun every now and then. Anyway, we're just older; we're not dead!"

"Amen to that," an elderly woman in the store yelled, and then everyone was laughing again.

"No, Kim. I can't wear that. Why, it's strapless and I'm, you know, well endowed."

"Which means she has big boobies as if we can't see," chimed in Babee.

"Try it on. The top will stay in place, and it's won't be too short. I promise. If you really, really hate it, we'll look at something else, but we think once you see yourself in it, you'll love it. I already have one just like it in a different color; believe me, the top stays up."

"Let's just look at something else, children. I'm too old for this."

"Oh, no," Velma said as she caught Cammy's arm and nearly dragged her into the dressing room. "No way am I settling for some old ladies' dress if I can have something like *that*. Since we can't choose until you do, you're trying on that dress."

While Cammy was in the dressing room, Desiree brought out a rack of clothes. "Candice and Kim went on line and chose these particular styles and colors for all of you to try on. You are all so lucky! These young ladies have great taste, and they want you to look as young as you obviously feel. So have a look and let me know when I can help."

For the next few minutes there was *'I want this one!' 'This color would look great on you!' 'That's not too long, Velma! How short do you want it?' 'Hope everyone's stocked up on their blood pressure pills!'* and amid all of this, giggles and laugher. Most of the other customers in the store had stopped shopping and were simply enjoying all of the fun. Then Cammy stepped out of the dressing room.

"Wow!"

"Hot damn!"

"That's no grandma there! Damn, girl, that's it! That's your dress!"

"I can't wear this. It's too short, isn't it? And the top! I look like Betty Boop in this!"

"And the problem with that is? Hump! Betty Boop is fine! Yea, so you've got a pretty good double D going on up there, but you're nowhere near Betty!" said Teresa. "We Wellingtons are bean poles. It's not that we don't have anything up top, but you wouldn't believe the rolls of tissue we used to stuff in our bras when we were teenagers."

"You did that, too?" asked Delphine. "And I thought that I was the only one who had to do it. Mother Nature wasn't as kind to me as she was to my friends. After I got married, I actually bought some fake ones. Tim threw them out. He said they gave him nightmares!"

Even Cammy, who'd been looking so serious, had to laugh at that.

"Mom, it's not too short. We made sure of that. Yea, it's about a couple of inches above your knees, but you have the legs to carry it off," said Candice. "I'm more like my Wellington aunts. I'd pay money to have the legs you and Kim have."

Kim could see the hesitation on Cammy's face.

"How do you *feel* in the dress, Mom? How does it make you feel?"

Cammy thought for a minute. Then she smiled. "I feel great. So feminine! So sexy!"

"Whew! Thank God that's settled," Velma piped in. "It's our time now, girls. Let's go!"

25

Saturday had gone by too fast for Cammy, and she was dreading this 'welcome to the family' get together at Smitty's. She *had* enjoyed shopping with the Wellington sisters. She'd been surprised at how welcoming they were to not only her, but to Delphine and Babee. There was no need to worry about how Jazzy would be welcomed; she had the kind of personality that could not be denied. But Cammy was still so ashamed of her actions all of those years ago, and she *had* kept the Wellingtons away from Kimberly. And even if the sisters were willing to forgive and forget, there was no way Caleb would, and he would be there. The evening would be a nightmare!

Cammy had given up talking Kim out of the party, and she'd stopped trying. After all, the party really was for Kim and not for her. Yesterday had proven that Kim would be embraced by her father's family. She and Candice were so excited about tonight, and if Cammy was honest with herself, she was a little bit excited too. But the dress that Kim had bought for her to wear! It was shameless! How her breasts would stay in that top, well, she'd tried to tell them! They'd just laughed. Cammy hadn't been surprised at Jazzy and Babee, but her daughters and the Wellington sisters!

And she was also amazed at how quickly she'd accepted Candice as her daughter! Although once that little girl had her mind set on something, nothing seemed to get in her way until she got what she wanted. And it touched Cammy's heart that Candice wanted to call her 'mom'. She knew she was lucky, blessed that Babee and Jazzy had been right! She had great children; they'd forgiven her. Now if only Caleb could.

It'd taken her too long to dress. There wasn't much to the dress, but it took Jazzy and Kim forever to fix her hair just the way they wanted it. Once *they* were satisfied, they'd gone upstairs, dressed, and headed out. Jeremiah had picked up Kimberly, and Candice was riding down with her Aunt Faye and her husband, Kevin. Cammy wondered how those husbands had reacted to the dresses that their wives had brought home. She'd had to admit that they'd all looked stunning in the dresses they'd chosen.

And now she was on her way to Smitty's café with her brother. Everyone else was probably already there. Smitty had been a little late getting her because he'd gone to the café before picking her up, and she understood. After all, he hadn't even opened his café to the public yet, but he'd never been able to deny either of her kids anything they wanted. She'd not heard from Caleb since the morning he'd found out about Kimberly. How could she face him tonight with so many people around? This was really a big mistake. And she needed a scarf or something to cover her chest!

Smitty parked and opened the door for her. She just sat there.

"Thanks for letting the girls have this get together here, Smitty."

"Shoot, sis, there's nothing to thank me for. After all, this is for Kim. I'm looking forward to it, also. If I'm lucky, there'll be at least one single lady here who's not related to me. Now come on, girl. You might as well get this over with. I'm your big brother, remember. I'm here to protect you if necessary. And there's always Frank. It's going to be all right. Come on. They'll eat up all of Babee's food if you don't hurry!"

Cammy just sat there.

"Hell, girl! I know you're not afraid of a few Wellingtons! We're got Collins blood in us; we know no fear! Now come on. I'm hungry!"

Reluctantly, Cammy eased out of the car. "Smitty, I can't do this! Let's just leave. Nobody will miss me; this is for Kimberly anyway."

"Oh, no! You don't get away that easy. You and Caleb both have got to face the music. Listen to the noise and laughter. And smell that food. It seems like a good party to me. Come on; you'll enjoy yourself. By the way, that's some kind of dress you have on. Red suits you. You'll have Caleb sweating bullets when he sees you in that! He won't be able to stay mad long!"

Smitty opened the door of the café for her. "Don't worry," her brother whispered. "I got your back."

"What I need right now is something to cover my chest! I can't believe that Kim insisted I wear this dress!"

253

"Don't look now, but it looks like one person in here appreciates the view! By the way, who's the sexy sister in the black dress?"

"That's Caleb's sister, Velma."

"Single?"

"I think so, but Smitty, you wouldn't!"

"Watch me," he whispered as he swaggered over to the buffet table where Velma was standing.

Caleb was sitting at the bar. Cammy could feel his eyes on her as she stood there by the door, but she wouldn't look directly at him. Suddenly she was surrounded by her kids – Kim, Frank, Janice, and Candice. It was only then that she looked over Janice's shoulder straight into Caleb's face. He looked as if he wanted to explode.

Well, Cammy thought, *if that's the way he wanted to behave, she'd make sure she'd have a good time. Let him be bitter all by himself.*

And, for her, having a good time proved to be easy! Heather had taken over the planning of the party from the girls, and she'd done a fabulous job! The music was great. Sweet and slow! And everyone danced, even Cammy. And those dresses! Sexy! Sensual! And it was obvious that the husbands really enjoyed the way their wives looked. Everyone was having a good time except for Caleb. All he'd done all evening was sit at that bar and frown at her.

It was embarrassing after a while. She couldn't stop glancing his way, and he couldn't stop frowning at her.

"Frank, have you spoken with Caleb tonight? Has someone said something to him that has him upset?"

Frank glanced over at Caleb and then looked down at his mom. He laughed and shook his head. "No, Mom. He's just suffering like the rest of us men."

"Suffering? Why?"

Frank laughed again. "Why? Look at how all of you are dressed! You see Janice over there? I told her there was no way she was wearing that dress tonight. She asked me if I wanted to sleep in the guest room. I thought I'd have to pull Jeremiah's head out of Kim's chest; he looked like he was too close for *my* comfort. She told me to mind my own 'damn' business! Have you seen Aunt Amelia? She's sixty-nine, and Uncle Wyatt can't take his eyes off of her! See them slow dancing? Smitty asked them if they needed a bed! We men are just in a daze; we can't figure out what's going on with all of you. But then, I don't think any of us are really complaining. But see, *we're* all talking to our significant other; the two of you are not. Look around you, Mom. Oh, and frustration can put that look on a man's face. I know; I've had it a couple of times tonight myself. I can't wait to get home!"

Cammy *did* look around. "*Sexual Healing*" was playing softly and the couples on the floor were really into each other. Romance was in the air! Goodness! Cammy wondered where Delphine and Babee had picked up moves like that! White girls didn't move like that! Smitty was whispering in Velma's ear, and she was giggling like a school girl! Jeremiah and Kim? No, they were just friends, but boy were they close.

Since she wasn't dancing and Caleb was still scowling at her, Cammy decided to help by clearing some of the dishes from the tables. Frank, Milton,

Jr., and several of the other men, walked over to the bar.

"Sir," Frank said to Caleb. "Just want you to know that you've been set up by your daughters. They'll be over here in a minute to give you your instructions. Let me suggest that if you want any peace in your life, you'll just go along."

"Yea, man," added Wyatt. "I could almost feel sorry for you, but if it wasn't for your mess up, my Amelia wouldn't be looking so damned foxy. So thanks for screwing up."

"Shit, Sug, you let her walk around all night when you could have had her in your arms. Something's wrong with your head. Glad we've got more smarts. But just listen to your girls. You could get lucky yet. Sorry, Frank. Know that's your mom and all." This advice was given by David. "Oh! Oh! Here they come. We'll be leaving now. Good luck!"

And they all walked away as Kimberly and Candice gathered around their dad. Frank stayed.

"Look, we don't have long while Mom's helping with the clean up," Kim whispered. "Dad, everyone's leaving, and you have to take Mom home."

"You don't want me alone with your mom," Caleb growled.

"Well, actually, sir, we do!" Frank added.

"What's going on with the three of you? Trust me. It'd be better if one of you took Cam home."

Candice stepped in. "We're wasting time. We're all leaving. Everyone. And you're taking Mom home. And if you're smart, you'll give her this." And

256

Candice reached into her purse and handed Caleb a ring box. He recognized it immediately.

"Where did you get this from? I threw it away years ago."

"Well, Mommy saved it. She must have known you would need it someday. Don't mess it up, Dad. We, the three of us, want a real family at last. Please do this right."

Caleb looked at Frank. "Yes, sir, the three of us. But if it's not what you want, don't hurt her anymore. She's suffered enough. It's time for her to be happy."

"Thanks, Frank. Let's hope it's what she wants too. But your mom can be stubborn. What makes you think she's going to *let* me take her home?"

"We've got it all planned. Look."

Caleb saw Babee and Cam talking to the waiter who had helped out for the evening. Then Cammy went into the kitchen with him. As soon as the door closed, Babee held up five fingers, and bam! The place started emptying. Everyone had been waiting on that signal. With whispered 'Good luck'. 'Take care of business.' 'We love you', everyone quickly exited the room.

When Cammy came out of the kitchen, Caleb was standing by the door, and everyone else was gone.

"Oh, no! Smitty didn't leave me did he?"

"Fraid so, Cam. I'm your ride home tonight."

"No!" She stepped close to him and punched him in his chest with her finger. "You've been frowning at me all night. You didn't even speak to me. You haven't called me. No way am I going anywhere with you. I'll just call Kim or Frank to come back and get me."

"Hell, I didn't ask for this job! Go ahead and call; see where it gets you. Nowhere but in my car! So come on and let's get this over with. I don't know what I was thinking to agree to this! Here! Take my coat so you can cover that little strap of material you call a dress!"

"How dare you. Everyone *loved* my dress!"

"I bet!" he muttered.

"What exactly does that mean, Caleb?"

"Just put on the jacket, Cam," Caleb said through his teeth. "Before I do something that I'll regret."

Cammy didn't like the sound of that, so she put his coat around her shoulders and marched through the door and out to his mustang.

The drive to Peaceful Sands was taken in total silence. Cammy kept glancing over at Caleb, but his eyes seemed to be fixed on the road, and his teeth were clinched.

As soon as the car came to a complete stop in front of the house, Cammy reached for the door.

"Don't do that," Caleb said. "Don't open that door. I brought you home, and I'll open the car door and the house door for you."

She turned to him so fast his jacket fell from her shoulders. Caleb took one look at her, closed his eyes, and laid his head on the steering wheel.

"Don't do me any favors, Caleb Wellington! I know how to open doors, and I know how to forget you! Look at you! Do you hate me so much you can't even look at me?"

Instead of looking at her, Caleb kept his eyes closed and leaned his head back on the seat. Softly he said, "I'm trying to control myself, Cam. Do you want me to do what I really want to do? Like toss you over into the back seat and bang the hell out of you! Is that what you want because that's what that dress makes me want to do. So I'm fighting for control here. And this is what we're going to do. I'm going to open the car door, we're going to walk to the front door, I'm going to open that door for you, and then you're going inside and wait for me. Got it?"

"And I should do all of this because…..?"

He finally opened his eyes and turned to her. "Because I have to talk to you."

"Oh, hell! Hell *no*! I should listen to something you have to say, but you wouldn't listen to me?!! You wouldn't even let me tell you how much I love you! How much I've always loved you! That I never stopped loving you! But you wouldn't listen to me; you wouldn't let me tell you that. You wouldn't let me explain about Kim and how sorry I am that I didn't tell you about her. And now you want to talk! So hell *no*, Caleb! I don't want to hear anything you have to say now or ever!"

Caleb closed his eyes and counted to ten. Aloud. Then inhaled deeply.

"I was wrong, Cam. I *should* have listened to you. But I'm glad I didn't. I know that you still love me. You wouldn't have let me make love to you if you didn't. I know you that well. But I was afraid. I didn't want anything to come between us again. I still don't. Just work with me here. Just let me get myself at least under enough control to have an intelligent

259

conversation without something," and then he looked pointedly at her dress, "getting in the way. Okay?"

Without waiting for an answer, Caleb got out, opened her door and helped her out, and then held her hand tightly as they walked to her front door. They stood facing each other as if they were preparing for battle.

"Give me the key, Cam."

"As if I can't open my own door! Who does he think has opened it all of these years?" she mumbled as she handed him the key. Caleb just smiled a little as he unlocked the door and opened it for Cammy to enter.

"And don't lock it, Cam."

"I won't!" she snapped as she slammed the door in his face. Caleb laughed.

He walked over to the top of the steps and leaned against the column. He breathed in and out slowly several times. He turned his face into the chilly late February breeze. He'd missed this during those years in the North – the nice warm days and chilly nights of North Florida. It brought back the memories of early mornings when he'd left this same house after he'd spent a passionate night in Cam's arms. He'd never left through the front door though; he'd always parked in back.

Now he had another chance. He thought of Maggie and how brief her life had been. He hoped that he had made her happy; she certainly had given him a peace that he thought he'd never have. He wondered if Maggie had known that she would die so young. Had she had a heart condition that she hadn't shared with him? Is that why she'd written that letter to Candice? Is that why she'd gotten that ring out of the garbage? He'd never really know, but he thanked her now. He thanked her for the years of their love and for the chance to have love again - with Cam.

Please let me do this right he prayed as he opened the door and walked into the house. Cam was huddled in the corner of the sofa wrapped in a throw. She'd taken the time to build a small fire in the fireplace.

Indicating the throw, she said, "I know how much you hate the dress."

He gave a slight smile as he took a sit at the other end of the sofa. "I don't hate the dress; it distracts me. All I can think about when I see you in it is getting you out of it. So thanks. Right this minute I don't need the distraction."

"So what is it you need, Caleb? I can't change the past; I can't change my mistake. I shouldn't have lied to you. I should have told you the truth twenty-six years ago. I've taken away so much from you and Kim! I'm sorry." Tears rolled down her face.

"Cam, don't cry! Please! Listen! The past is just that – past! I loved you then and I love you now. That hasn't changed! I've been such a fool! I've held on to that lie about you and Ralph all of this time. Stupid! We both made mistakes! But our children have certainly taught me a lesson in these last few days. Looking back won't change a thing. Kimberly's an adult who has decided that at this late date in her life, she'll let me be her dad. That's a real blessing, Cam. Frank loves to do a lot of the things I like to do like fishing and messing around with cars. He doesn't hate me, so that's a start. And Candice is truly amazing! If she hadn't jumped in there with all of *her* plans for our future, who knows where we'd be right now. I love you, Cam! And it's not just the lust I feel for you whenever I see you. And believe me, I feel it every time I see you. But if I never could get *it* up again, I'll still love you and want to hold you and want to find ways to give you pleasure. My love, Cam, is all about *you*."

    He looked around for his jacket. He saw it lying on the back of the sofa. Caleb reached into the pocket and pulled out the ring box. He leaned over and took Cam's hand in his.

    "Cam, will you marry me?"

    "Oh! Caleb!" Cam's hand shook. "Oh! Caleb!"

    He leaned back and opened the box. The large pear shaped diamond ring sparkled. He took it out of the box and reached for Cam's hand again.

    "That's not an answer, Cam. If you can't forgive me for being such a fool, I'll understand. But I'll never stop loving you. I never did. I bought you this ring twenty-six years ago, so the style is probably out of date. I don't know. If it's the ring you don't like, we'll get another one. I'll buy you whatever you want. I just want you to marry me. Let me take care of you, love you for the rest of our lives."

    "Oh yes, Sug, I'll marry you! And I love the ring!"

    As he slid the ring onto her finger, he leaned over and kissed her softly on her lips. "Sug?" he whispered against her lips.

    She smiled as she let the throw slide slowly from her shoulders. And she was naked underneath.

    "Oh, sweetheart, you're making my arthritis act up!" he moaned as he pressed her back into the sofa.

"That's not funny, Caleb!"

"The hell it isn't!" he laughed as he started them on their climb to fulfillment.

He stopped only once.

"Cam," he moaned. "Will we ever make it to the bedroom?"

She gave him a shaky laugh. "We'll start looking at sofas tomorrow, Sug. Maybe two so we'll have a spare!"

They laughed as they trembled together, and Cammy knew she had finally found her 'love song' kind of love; the kind that lasts forever!

Epilogue

  The wedding was held at the little white church in Two Plantations. Because of its size, only family attended the ceremony, but every Collins from the North had descended on Two Plantations and the church was overflowing with gads of Wellingtons on one side and just as many Collins on the other.
  It was absolutely beautiful! The bride wore a strapless ivory satin and lace gown with her now signature sweetheart neckline, and the groom wore a black tux with tails. The bride's party had consisted of her daughters Kimberly, Candice, and Janice, her sister, Jazzy, and her best friend, Babee. The groom's party included his brother, Milton, the bride's son, Frank along with the bride's brother, Smitty, and family friend, Danny and his son, Jeremiah.
  The church had been beautifully decorated with red and white roses, and Cammy had carried a bouquet of candy apple red roses. Heather had organized everything. Thankfully, the warm weather had continued, and the reception was held on the beautiful lawns surrounding Peaceful Sands. Babee had insisted on baking the wedding cake, but Heather had handled everything else. The girl really had a talent for planning events! If she could produce something so grand with such short notice, Cammy knew there was a future career blossoming for her!
  The entire town had been invited to the reception, and as Cammy stood in Caleb's arms, from their view from the porch, they could see the amusing story of their wedding pass from one group to

another. It was easy to tell, of course. As the word spread, people would look over at them, smile, laugh, shake their heads, and then laugh some more. And, of course, it was all Caleb's fault even though he continued to try to put the blame on her or at least on her dress.

Caleb had draped his jacket over her shoulders, and at the moment he had eased one hand inside the jacket and was slowly fondling her breast.

"Caleb, stop. You are *so* fresh! Haven't you given our families and this town enough to talk about? You have to know *they* know what you're doing!" Her breath caught on the last word as he lightly pinched her nipple. With her body tingling, she closed her eyes and leaned her head back on his chest.

He laughed softly in her ear. "It wasn't my fault that you wore this dress. I'm an ol' player, remember? You knew when you decided to wear the dress what it would do to me."

Cammy caught his wrist. "Stop it! And I thought you had more control. A sixty-four year old man should be able to get through a fifteen minute ceremony without ...without staring at my breasts as if you were just waiting for them to pop out!"

"Not true, Cam. I only looked once or twice. It still amazes me how they could just stay there like that. I was just checking, you know, to make sure there were no malfunctions or anything."

Cammy laughed. "You lie and you know it! Minister Robinson had to clear her throat at least twice during our vows just to get you to look up and refocus. She had to repeat most of your vows because you weren't paying attention."

"Wasn't I supposed to look at my bride? I mean, you were beautiful standing there in front of me. What did I do wrong?" He'd slipped his wrist out of her hold and was again fondling her. "Call me Sug and I'll stop!"

"Stop anyway." She stepped down hard on his foot." Haven't you noticed that no one's come to talk to us since you started being so frisky and in front of our children, too!"

"Okay, okay! I wouldn't want to take away their innocence," he laughed as he reluctantly removed his hand and wrapped his arm around her waist.

"Are you mad, I mean, about the vows?" He blew softly in her ear.

"Oh, no. How could I be mad?" She smiled over her shoulder at him. "It just was too funny when the minister finally said, 'Look into her *eyes*, Caleb, her *eyes* so you can concentrate, and I forbid you to look down again.' That was really funny!"

"Yea, and the entire church thought it was funny too. Even the minister had to wait a minute before she could continue. But it was worth it! I'll be the blunt of the joke anytime you wear a dress like this!"

He bit her neck. Just a nip, but her body trembled in his arms.

"How long are they going to stay around here anyway? How long do we have to stand here before we begin our honeymoon?"

"We're not going on a honeymoon right now, remember? You'll become our police chief soon, much too soon to leave town. And we have all the time in the world to honeymoon as long as we have each other. Oh, Caleb, I'm so happy! I finally have you back in my life - my love song, my forever love. And look at our children. Aren't we blessed? And look at how our two families have blended!"

"Hummm. Maybe too much! I have no idea what's going on with Velma and Smitty."

"And you shouldn't. They're adults and remember. Smitty didn't interfere with us."

"Guess you're right. Well, what is going on between your drab manager at Rachel's Haven and the artist? He can't really be attracted to her can he?"

"Drab you say," laughed Cammy as she snuggled even closer into Caleb's arms. "I have a lot to tell you about Rachel's Haven since you *are* the new police chief. You're in for a lot of other surprises as well."

"This little town has already given me too many surprises, but I guess I'm up for more. Tell me. What do you think of our interracial couple?"

"Delphine and Tim? I really like them. Don't you?"

"Not that couple, Cam. Look. Take off your blinders and look over at the punch table."

"No one's there but Kimberly and Jeremiah." She stopped and stared. "Come on, Caleb, they're friend, aren't they? I mean, she's known him forever and there's never been any...... Well, I have noticed lately.......Do you really think so?"

"I think we'll just have to wait and see. But I wouldn't be surprised if the two of them don't become the Beaufort and Sadie Mae of their generation. You don't have a problem with that, do you?"

"Oh, not at all! After all, spring did come early this year. And Candice keeps telling us that we old folks mess up things; we're too emotional. So I'm staying out of any of that. And speaking of our youngest, she seems the only one alone. You know what I mean, no guy or anything. She's happy isn't she?"

Caleb laughed. "Hell! She's like the cat that ate the canary. She takes full credit for getting us back together. I believe she's going to change her career and become a romance writer! She says she's waiting for 'mister right', but she keeps talking about her box Maggie gave her and some unfinished business. We haven't had a chance to talk about whatever that business is in detail. As you know, all of us have been a little busy. Oh! Oh! Here they all come now. Don't move, Cam. I can't hug my girls with this, well, you know what!"

"It'd serve you right for how you've behaved today. But I won't do that to you *Sug*." And she smiled as she felt his erection press further into her back.

Their children stopped at the bottom of the steps. "We've just come to say how much we love you both and that we'll wait for you to call before we visit," said Kimberly.

"But don't wait too, too long," Candice added. "I want to see the rest of the gifts. Oh, by the way, I think this is *sooo* romantic. Just like in the movies! So we're leaving now and don't forget to call! Soon!"

As they turned to walk away, Frank turned back to Cammy and Caleb. "I'm so happy for you, Mom. We all are." Then he looked at Caleb. "And, uh, Dad, once you've settled into your job, maybe we can go fishing sometime."

Caleb froze. He cleared his throat. "Sure, son. I've been looking forward to doing that for a long time."

He squeezed Cammy as he tried to hold back tears.

"Those are some amazing kids we have," he choked out.

"I think so, too. Now, if you'll release me, I think I'll go in; it's been a long day."

"I'm coming, too!"

"Give me about five minutes alone. I have a little 'thank you' prayer that I have to send up."

"I'll give you four," he replied as he watched her walk away. Then he turned his face to the sky. *"Thank you, God,"* he whispered, *"and thank you Maggie."*

Then he waved to the last remaining guests and went inside. As he stepped inside, he could hear Otis Redding playing softly. Yea, it was their song. It *had* been too long, but thank God it hadn't been too late. In his excitement, he stumbled over Cammy's shoes. He kicked them out of the way as he followed a trail of pantyhose, wedding dress, and thongs until he got to the bedroom door.

"Hallelujah!" he grinned as he opened the door. "A bed at last!"

269

Irene Gilliam still lives in the city where she was born – Tallahassee, Florida. She earned her Bachelor of Arts degree in English and Master of Education degree from Florida A & M University.

Irene retired as a community college English professor after working for over thirty-six years as an educator. She loves spending time with her two grandchildren, Kristopher and Kennedy, her daughter, 'Mickey' and husband, and her sister and brothers. She enjoys writing, traveling, and reading, particularly reading romance novels. Although she has been writing poems and stories most of her life, *Never too Late for Love* is her first published work.